W9-BTK-442

ImagineIF Libraries
Kalispell, Montana

LISTEN to the MOON

michael morpurgo

LISTEN *to the* MOON

FEIWEL AND FRIENDS

NEW YORK

A FEIWEL AND FRIENDS BOOK
An Imprint of Macmillan

LISTEN TO THE MOON. Copyright © 2015 by Michael Morpurgo. All rights reserved.
Printed in the United States of America by R. R. Donnelley & Sons Company,
Harrisonburg, Virginia. For information, address Feiwel and Friends, 175 Fifth Avenue,
New York, N.Y. 10010.

Feiwel and Friends books may be purchased for business or promotional use.
For information on bulk purchases, please contact the Macmillan Corporate and Premium
Sales Department at (800) 221-7945 x5442 or by e-mail at specialmarkets@macmillan.com.

Library of Congress Cataloging-in-Publication Data Available

ISBN: 978-1-250-04204-0 (hardcover) / 978-1-250-07861-2 (ebook)

Book design by Anna Booth

Feiwel and Friends logo designed by Filomena Tuosto

First Edition: 2015

10 9 8 7 6 5 4 3 2 1

mackids.com

LISTEN *to the* MOON

To Begin

We all come from somewhere. But in a way, I come from nowhere. Let me explain. My grandma simply came up out of the
sea a long time ago, like a mermaid, except that she had two legs
instead of a fishtail. She seemed to be about twelve years old at
the time, but no one could tell; and that was because there was
no clue as to who she was, nor where she came from. She was
half-starved, mad with fever, and could speak only one word:
"Lucy."

This is her story, as it was told to me, by those who knew her
best, by my grandpa, by other relations and friends, and most
important, by my grandmother herself. Over the years I have
pieced it all together as well as I could, using only the evidence
of those who saw it with their own eyes, those who were there.

I want to thank the Isles of Scilly Museum for their help, for
access to school logbooks and other sources, and I'd especially
like to thank the family of the late Dr. Crow of St. Mary's, for allowing

me to quote extensively from his journal. My family, and many others also, too numerous to mention—on the Scilly islands, in New York, and elsewhere—have helped me greatly and patiently in my research.

You could say this story has been a lifelong fascination for me, an obsession almost. I have certainly been working on it, on and off, for most of my life. I simply could not get it out of my head which, in a way, I suppose, is not surprising. It is my grandma's story—much of it told, as you will discover, in her own words, as she dictated it to me. So, in that sense, it is my story too, my family's story.

Grandma made us who we are—with a little help from Grandpa, it should be said. I am who I am because of her, because of him. I have done what I've done, been who I've been, lived where I've lived, done what I've done, written what I've written, because of them. So I have written it for them, and also because it happens to be the most unlikely and unbelievable story I have ever heard.

Chapter One

Be good fish, be nice fish

It was mackerel they were after that day, because it was Friday. Mary always liked to cook mackerel for their supper on Fridays, but Alfie and Jim, his father, both knew she wouldn't do it, and they wouldn't have it, unless they brought her back enough mackerel to make a proper meal for all four of them. Jim and Alfie had prodigious appetites, which his mother loved both to grumble about and to satisfy. "I swear the two of you got hollow legs," Mary would say in open admiration as she watched them wolfing down their mackerel yet again—three of them each she liked to put on their plates, if the catch had been good enough.

There was Uncle Billy to feed too. He lived in the boat shed on Green Bay on his own, because he liked it that way. It was just across the field from Veronica Farmhouse, where they lived, a stone's throw away. Mary would bring him his supper every evening, but, unlike Alfie, he would, as like as not, complain if it was mackerel again. "I like crab," he'd say. But then if Mary brought him crab, it was, "Where's my mackerel?" He could be contrary, could Uncle Billy. But then Uncle Billy was contrary in many ways. He was different from other people, different from anyone. As Mary often said, that was what made him special.

The fish were hard to find that morning. It helped keep spirits up in the boat to talk about supper, to think about it, about how Mary would cook the mackerel for them that evening: dipped in egg, rolled in oats, then seasoned with salt and pepper. She fried it always in butter. The smell of it would be wafting through the farmhouse and they'd be sitting down at the kitchen table ready and waiting, mouths watering, savoring the sound and smell of the fish sizzling in the pan.

"Course, after she finds out what you and me have gone and done, Alfie," Jim said, straining hard at the oars, "we could be on bread and water for a week. She will not be a happy woman, son, not happy at all. She'll have my guts for garters, yours too."

"We should go in closer to St. Helen's, Father," Alfie said, his mind on the mackerel, not his mother's retribution. "There's fish there almost always, just off the beach. Caught half a dozen last time we were there, didn't we?"

"Don't like going near the place," Jim said. "Never have. But maybe you're right, maybe we should give it a go. Wish the wind would get up, and we could do a bit of sailing. All this rowing's half killing me. Here, Alfie. Your turn." They changed places.

As Alfie took up the oars he found himself thinking of supper again, of the sound and the smell of frying mackerel, and then of how hard it was to remember smells and describe them, how sounds and sights were much easier to recall somehow. Once the mackerel was on the plate in front of them, they always had to wait until grace was said. Father and he were inclined to say grace rather too hurriedly for his mother's liking. She took her time over it. For her, grace was a meant prayer, and different each mealtime, not simply a ritual to be rushed through. She would have liked a proper and respectful pause after the Amen, but Alfie and his father would be at their mackerel at once, like gannets. There would be strong sweet tea and freshly baked bread to go with it, and bread-and-butter pudding, if they were lucky. It was always the feast of the week.

It was already late afternoon and they had precious little to show for nearly an entire day's fishing. Now that Jim wasn't rowing, the wind was already chilling him to the bone. He pulled his collar up against it. It was cold for May, more like March, Jim thought. He looked at his son bending rhythmically, easily, to the oars, and envied him his strength and suppleness, but at the same time took a father's pride in it too. He had been that young once, that strong.

He looked down at his hands, scarred, calloused, and cracked as they were now, ingrained with years of fishing and years of farming his potatoes and his flowers. He baited the line again, his fingers working instinctively, automatically. He was thankful he could not feel them. They were numb to the cold and salt of seawater, numb to the wind. Some of those old cracks in his finger joints had opened up again and would otherwise be paining him dreadfully by now. His feet too were numb, and his face. It was good to be numb, he thought, and just as well. He was wondering why it was that his ears hurt, why they too hadn't gone numb? He wished they would.

Jim smiled inside himself as he remembered how the day had begun, at breakfast. It had been Alfie's idea in the first place. He didn't want to go to school. He wanted to come fishing instead. He'd tried this on before, often, and rarely with any success. It didn't stop him trying again. "Tell Mother you need me," Alfie had said, "that you can't do without me. She'll listen to you. I won't be no trouble, Father. Promise." Jim knew he wouldn't be any trouble. The boy sailed a boat well, rowed strongly, knew the waters, fished with a will, and with that wholehearted enthusiasm and confidence born of youth, always so sure he would catch something. The fish seemed to like him too. It was noticeable that Jim often did better when Alfie was in the boat. With the fishing as disappointing as it had been recently in the waters around Scilly, Jim would go out fishing these days more in hope than expectation. Catches had been poor for all the fishermen in recent times, not just him. Anyway, Alfie would be company out there, good company. So he agreed to do what he could to persuade Mary to let Alfie miss school for a day, and come fishing with him.

But all pleading, all reasoning, proved to be quite useless, as Jim had warned Alfie it might be. Mary was adamant that Alfie had to go to school, that he'd missed far too much school already, that he was always trying to find ways of not going to school. Any excuse would do: working out on the farm, or going fishing with his father. Enough was enough. When Mary insisted with that certain tone in her voice, Jim knew there was very little point in arguing, that she was immovable. He persisted only because he wanted Alfie to know he really wanted him out there in the boat with him, and to demonstrate his solidarity. When Alfie saw the argument wasn't going his way, he joined in, trying anything he could think of that might change her mind.

"What does one day off school matter, Mother, one day?" "We always catch more fish when there's the two of us." "And anyway, out in an open boat it's always safer with two, I heard you say so." "And I hate Beastly Beagley at school. Everyone knows he can't teach for toffee. He's a waste of space, and school's nothing but a waste of time." "You let me stay home, Mother, and after I've been fishing with Father, I'll come back and clean out the henhouse for you, and fetch back a cartload of seaweed to fertilize the lower field, whatever you want."

"What I want, Alfie, is for you to go to school," Mary said firmly. It was quite futile. She wasn't going to give in. There was nothing more to be said, nothing more to be done. So Alfie had trudged off reluctantly to school with Mary's words ringing in his ears. "There's more to life than boats and fishing, Alfie! Never heard of a fish teaching anyone to read or write! And your writing ain't nothing to write home about neither, if you ask me!"

When he'd gone she'd turned to Jim. "I'll need six good mackerel for tea, Jimbo, don't forget," she said. "And wrap up warm. Spring it may be, but there was a keen wind out there when I went out to feed the hens. That boy of yours forgot to do it again."

"He's always my boy when he forgets," said Jim, shrugging on his coat and stepping into his boots.

"Where else do you think he gets it from?" she replied, buttoning up Jim's coat. She gave him his peck on the cheek and patted his shoulders as she always did, as he always liked her to do. "And by the way, Jimbo, I promised Uncle Billy a crab for tomorrow—you know how much he loves his crab. Nice one, mind. Not too big. Not too small. He don't like a crab all chewy and tough. He's very particular. Don't forget."

"I won't forget," Jim muttered under his breath as he went out the door. "Nothing's good enough for big brother Billy, eh? You spoil that old pirate rotten, that's the truth of it."

"No more'n I spoil you, Jim Wheatcroft," she retorted.

"Anyway," Jim went on, "I'd have thought old and tough and chewy would have suited an old pirate like Long John Silver just perfect."

When it came to Uncle Billy, it was always this kind of good-natured banter between them. They had sometimes to share the humorous side of it, because the harsh truth of so much that had happened to Uncle Billy in his life was often too painful to deal with.

"Jim Wheatcroft!" she called after him. "That's my big brother you're talking about, and don't you forget it. He ain't neither old nor chewy, just in a world of his own. He's not like the rest of us, and that's fine by me."

"Whatever you say, Marymoo, whatever you say," he replied, and with a cheery flourish of his cap, went off down the field toward Green Bay, mimicking Uncle Billy's favorite ditty just loud enough for her to hear: "Yo ho ho and a bottle of rum! Yo ho ho and a bottle of rum!"

"Jim Wheatcroft, I heard that!" In response, Jim gave her another wave of his cap. "And you take care out there, Jimbo, you hear!" she shouted after him.

As he went down to the boat, Jim was marveling at Mary's endless patience and constant devotion to her brother, but at the same time he felt more than a little vexed, as he always did, at how oblivious Uncle Billy seemed to be to all Mary had done for him, and was doing for him every day of her life. He could hear him now, singing away out on his boat in Green Bay, "the good ship *Hispaniola,*" as Uncle Billy called it.

It hadn't been a "good ship" at all, not to start with, just the remnants, the rotting hulk, of an old Cornish lugger, abandoned long ago on the beach on Green Bay. It was five years now since Mary had brought him home from the hospital and installed him in the boat shed. She had made a home for him up in the sail loft, and he'd been out there on Green Bay just about every day since, whatever the weather, restoring that old lugger. It was she who had told him about the old lugger in the hospital, and as soon as she got him home encouraged him to get back to boatbuilding, which he'd loved so much as a young man. She was convinced that he needed above all, she'd told Jim, to keep busy, use his hands, be the craftsman he once was again.

Everyone, including Jim, had thought it was an impossible task, that out there in all weathers the lugger had deteriorated too much, was too far gone, and that anyway "Silly Billy," as they called him all over the island, couldn't possibly do it. Only Mary insisted he could. And soon enough everyone could see that she had been right. When it came to boatbuilding, Silly Billy—whatever you thought of him—knew well enough what he was doing. Day by day over the years, the old lugger in Green Bay was becoming young again, and sleek and beautiful.

She lay there at anchor as Jim walked to the fishing boat that morning, resplendent in green paint, *Hispaniola* painted black on her side. She may not yet have been finished, but the fine and elegant lines of her hull were evident now to anyone walking along Green Bay. And now with the mainmast up, which Uncle Billy had raised only a few weeks before, she was looking almost complete. With no help from anyone—Uncle Billy liked to be on his own, work on his own—he had brought her back to life. Uncle Billy may have been odd—that was the general view: a bit "mazed in the head," they usually called him—but with the work he had done on that old lugger over the years, plain now for everyone to see, he had gained the respect of the whole island. He was still "Silly Billy," though, because they all knew where he'd been, where he'd come from, because of how he was.

Walking across the sand on Green Bay, Jim could see Uncle Billy up on deck. He was running the black and white Skull and Crossbones flag up the mast, as he had done every morning since the mast had gone up. He had the Long John Silver hat on that Mary had made for him, and he was singing. Uncle Billy had his ups and downs, his good days and his bad days. This morning he had the hat on and he was singing, so this must be a good day, which, Jim knew, would make life much easier for Mary. He could be a cantankerous old goat when he was in one of his black moods. And for some reason Jim had never understood, when he was like that, he was always nastier to Mary than anyone. Yet she was the one who had saved him, brought him home, and the person he loved most in the world.

It was because Jim was so busy admiring the *Hispaniola,* so preoccupied thinking about Uncle Billy, that he had not noticed until now that Alfie was out there, clambering about on *Penguin,* the family's fishing boat, making her ready. He was untying her from the buoy, then rowing her in toward him over the shallows. "What d'you think you're up to, Alfie?" Jim protested, looking over his shoulder nervously. "If your mother sees you . . ."

"I know, Father, she'll have my guts for garters—whatever that means," Alfie said, with a smile and a shrug. "I missed the school-boat. Real shame. You were there, you saw it go without me. Right, Father?"

Jim was unable to conceal his delight. "You are a very wicked boy, Alfie Wheatcroft," he said, climbing into the boat. "Don't know where you get it from. We'd better come back with plenty of good fish then, hadn't we? Or my life, and yours, won't be worth living."

Out at sea, an hour or so later, they were fishing off Foreman's Rock. It had been a hard row for Alfie against the current all the way along Pentle Bay, and Jim could see he needed a rest. He took the oars from him and rowed over to check his lobster pots. Between them, they hauled up three good-sized crabs from the pots off Foreman's Rock—so, a crab for Uncle Billy, and two to sell—and there was a nice squid in one of the pots, which would do nicely for bait. And Alfie managed to catch a couple of pollock as well. "Good for fishcakes," Jim grumbled, "and not much else. Your mother don't like pollock. We can't come home with nothing but pollock. We got to find some mackerel."

"St. Helen's," Alfie said, reaching for the oars, and starting to row again. "They'll be there, dozens of them, Father, waiting for us, you'll see."

It was a flat calm now, hardly a ripple on the sea, and the tide took them quickly toward St. Helen's. Wary of rocks, they came in with great care, Alfie rowing gently toward the shore, toward the only sandy beach on the island. Jim dropped anchor. This was where they had caught their mackerel only a few weeks before, a dozen or more, and big fish too, all of them inside a few minutes. Maybe they'd get lucky again.

Both of them knew they would have to get lucky. Mackerel were like that. You could be out fishing all day right above them, and the line would come up empty every time. Or they'd be down there begging to be caught, it seemed, and then they'd jump right onto your hooks and come up shining and silver and wriggling on the line. Jim remembered how delighted Mary had been with them before, when they came home with their great catch and showed her, how she'd given them both the best of hugs, and told them there weren't two other fishermen in the world like them.

Jim dropped his line into the sea. "Come on, fish," he said. "Have a little nibble, have a little bite. Be good fish, be nice fish, and then Marymoo will give us more hugs, and tonight we'll have the best supper of our lives. Come on, fish. What are you waiting for? I'm not going away till I get you, lots of you."

"They're down there," said Alfie, peering into the water on the other side of the boat. "I can see them. Bet I catch one before you do, Father."

It was a long while later. Neither had caught a fish, nor even felt a suggestion of a bite. Both were silent, deep in concentration. Alfie was sitting there hunched over the line, gazing intently down into the clear blue-green of the sea below, the fronds of weeds waving mockingly up at him. That was when he first heard it. The sound seemed at once strange to him, out of place somehow, not right. Alfie looked up from his fishing. It came from the island, a hundred yards or so away, from somewhere near the shore, a soft cry, a whimpering. A seal pup perhaps. But it was more human than that.

Chapter Two

A place of lost souls

"You hear that, Father?" he said.

"Just gulls, Alfie," Jim replied. And sure enough, there was a young seagull on the beach, scurrying along after its mother, neck outstretched, mewing, begging to be fed. But Alfie realized soon enough that wasn't at all the sound that he had heard. He knew gulls better than any other bird, but he had never before heard a young gull cry like that. The crying he had heard was different, not like a bird at all, not like a seal pup either. It sounded almost human. It was true that gulls were known to be good mimics, not as good as crows, but good enough. Alfie was perplexed, and distracted now entirely from his fishing. The two gulls, mother and fledgling, lifted off the beach and flew away, the young bird still pestering to be fed, leaving the beach deserted behind them, but not silent. There it was again, the same sound.

"Not gulls, Father. Can't be," he said. "Something else. Listen!"

It came from somewhere beyond the shoreline altogether, from the direction of the old Pest House, or from the great rock in the middle of the island. Alfie was quite sure by now that no gull, however clever a mimic, could possibly cry like that. And then it came to him. A child! A child cries like that! Neither does a gull cough, and Alfie could hear quite clearly now the sound of coughing.

"There's someone there, Father!" he whispered. "On the island."

"I hear it," Jim said. "I hear it all right, but it don't seem hardly possible. Can't see no one there, nothing but gulls. There's hundreds of them, and all watching us. Like I told you, Alfie, I don't like this place, never did." He paused to listen again. "Can't hear nothing now. Ears playing tricks on us, that's what it was. Got to be. Can't be no one there anyway. I didn't see no boat anchored offshore as we came in, and there's no-where else you can land on St. Helen's except right here on this beach. This is an uninhabited island, deserted. No one's lived here for years, for centuries."

As Jim scanned the island for any sign of life—footprints on the sand, the telltale smoke of a fire perhaps—all those stories about St. Helen's came back to him. He remembered landing there before, a few times. He had walked the length and breadth of it. It was no more than half a mile from end to end, a few hundred yards across the middle, an island of bracken and brambles and heather, a shoreline of great gray boulders and pebbles, with that one spit of steep shelving sand, and the great rock he remembered so well rearing up behind the Pest House. The Pest House itself had long since fallen into ruin, roof and windows gaping, walls crumbling. But the chimney was still standing.

He had gone there first as a small boy, with his father, collecting driftwood for the fire, piling it up on the beach to bring home, or scouring the beach for cowrie shells—"guinea money," as they called it. He'd climbed the rock once with his father, dared himself then to climb it again on his own and got to the top, but had been scolded for it by his father, and told never to do it again without him.

Jim had never really liked the place, even as a small boy, had never felt at ease there. St. Helen's had seemed to him even then an abandoned place, a place of lost souls, of ghosts. There was something dark and sad about the island, and he'd thought that long before he'd ever been told the stories. Over the years he had learned about its grim history bit by bit, how once long ago it had been a holy island, where monks, seeking solitary, contemplative lives, had lived out their years. The ruins of their chapel were still there. And there was, he knew, a holy well just beyond the Pest House—his mother had told him that much. He'd gone looking for it once with her in among the bracken and the brambles, but they had never found it.

But it was the story of the Pest House itself, why it had been built, and how it had been used, that had always troubled him most—so much so that he had never told Alfie about it. There are some stories, he thought, too terrible to pass on. In years gone by, in the days of the great sailing ships, St. Helen's had once been a quarantine island. To prevent the spread of disease, any sailor or passenger on board who had fallen sick, with yellow fever or typhoid or some other infectious illness, was put off on St. Helen's, to recover if they could, but much more likely to live out their last wretched days in the Pest House. The sick and dying had simply been left there in isolation, abandoned, and with little hope of survival. All his life Jim had been horrified at the thought of it. Ever since he'd been told about the Pest House, he had thought of St. Helen's as a shameful place, an island of suffering and death, to be avoided if at all possible.

Quite definitely now, and there could no longer be any doubt about it, Jim was hearing the sound of a child crying. Alfie was sure of it too. Neither said a word. The same unspoken thought occurred to both of them then. They had heard tales of ghosts living on St. Helen's—everyone had. Scilly was full of ghost stories. There were the ghosts on Samson Island, the ghost of King Arthur out on the Eastern Islands, and everywhere, all over the islands, there were stories of the ghosts of stranded sailors, pirates, drowned sailors. Stories, they told themselves, just stories.

Coughing interrupted the whimpering. This was no ghost. There was someone there on the island, a child, a child wailing, whimpering, and still coughing too. It was a cry for help they could not ignore. As they hauled in their lines, in a great hurry now, Alfie found there were three mackerel dangling on his hooks. He hadn't even felt they were there. But the fish didn't matter anymore. Jim pulled up the anchor, and Alfie rowed hard for the shore. A few strong pulls and they felt the boat beaching. They leaped over the side into the shallows and hauled the boat up higher onto the sand.

Standing on the beach, they listened once again for the sound of the child. For some reason they found themselves talking in whispers. All they could hear was the sea lapping softly behind them and the piping of a pair of oystercatchers that were flying off low and fast, their wingtips skimming the sea.

"Can't hear nothing, can you?" Jim said. "Can't see nothing either." He was beginning to wonder now if he had imagined the whole thing, if his hearing had deceived him. But the real truth, and Jim knew it too, was that he did not want to venture any further. At that moment he was all for getting the boat back into the water and rowing home. But Alfie was already running up the beach toward the dunes. Jim thought of calling him back, but he didn't want to shout. He couldn't let him go on alone.

He took off his jacket and laid it over his catch in the bottom of the boat to hide it from any sharp-eyed marauding gulls, and then, reluctantly, followed where Alfie had gone, up over the dunes, toward the Pest House.

A chill came over Alfie as he stood on top of the dunes, looking up at the Pest House, and he knew it wasn't only the cold. Gulls, hundreds of them, the island's silent sentinels, were watching him from rocks everywhere, from the walls of the Pest House, from the chimney, from the sky above. After a while Jim was at his side, breathless.

Alfie called out, "Anyone here?" There came no answer. "Who's there?" Nothing. A pair of gulls dived on them then, screeching and wheeling away, first one then another. The rest glared at them darkly. The message was unmistakable. You are not welcome here. Get off our island. "There's no one here, Alfie," Jim whispered. "Let's go home."

"But we heard someone, Father," Alfie said. "I know we did."

Becoming more fearful now with every passing moment, it was Jim who called out this time. His whole instinct was to turn away, get to the boat fast and go from this place at once. But at the same time he needed to persuade himself that there was no child on the island, that Alfie was wrong, that they must have been imagining the whole thing. They both called out now, echoing one another.

Closer and quite unmistakable now came the same whimpering as before, but more muffled now, stifled. There could be no doubt about it. It was the voice of a child, a child who was terrified, and it was coming from inside the Pest House.

Jim's first thought was that it had to be some local child who had gone out fishing maybe and had some sort of accident, lost an oar maybe, or fallen overboard. It wasn't so long ago, after all, that he had fished a young lad out of the water after the boy had got into trouble out in a boat in Tresco Channel. He'd tripped and gone overboard, and was being swept out to sea by the current. This one had been washed up on St. Helen's—there was no other explanation he could think of. But if any child had been missing, then surely he'd have heard about it. The alarm would have been raised all over the islands. Everyone would have been out looking. He couldn't understand it.

Alfie had already gone on ahead of him up the track toward the Pest House, calling out to whoever was in there, softly, as reassuringly as he could. "Hello. S'only me. Alfie, Alfie Wheatcroft. I got my father with me. You all right, are you?" There was no reply. Both of them stopped outside the doorway, uncertain now as to what to say or do.

"We're from Bryher," Jim went on. "You know us, don't you? I'm Alfie's father. What you doing over here? Tipped yourself out of a boat, did you? Easily done. Easily done. You must be half frozen. We'll have you out of here in a jiffy, get you back home, cup of nice warm tea, tatty cake, and a hot bath. That'll shiver the cold out of you, won't it?"

As Alfie stepped tentatively through the doorway into the ruins of the Pest House, the whimpering stopped. There was no sign of anyone inside, nothing but bracken and brambles. At the far end of the building, in under the chimney, there was a fireplace, covered in dried bracken, a thick carpet of it, almost as if someone had been making a bed. A sudden bird flew up out of a niche in the wall, an explosion of fluttering that set Alfie's heart pounding. He pushed his way through the thick undergrowth that had long since made the ruins their own, brambles tearing at his shirt and trousers as he passed. Jim held back at the doorway. "No one here, Alfie," he whispered. "You can see there isn't." Alfie was pointing into the corner of the fireplace, and waving his hand at his father to be quiet.

"Don't you worry none," Alfie said, treading softly as he went, and slowly. "We'll have you out of here and home before you know it. We got our boat. Won't hurt you none, promise. S'all right, honest. You can come out now."

He had seen a face, a bone-white face peering through the bracken, a child, a girl, hollow-cheeked, and with dark lank hair down to her shoulders. She was cowering there in the corner of the building, her fist in her mouth, her eyes staring up at him, wide with terror. She had a gray blanket around her. Her face was tearstained, and she was shaking uncontrollably.

Alfie crouched down where he was, keeping his distance—he did not want to alarm her. He did not recognize her. If she had been from the islands, he would have known her for certain—he knew all the children on Scilly, everyone did, whichever island they came from. "Hello?" he said. "You got a name then, have you?" She shrunk from him, coughing again now, and shivering under her blanket. "I'm Alfie. You needn't be afeard of me, girl." She was staring at Jim now, breathing hard. "That's Father. He won't hurt you any more'n I will. You hungry, are you? You bin here long? You got a terrible cough on you. Where'd you come from then? How'd you get here, girl?" She said nothing, simply crouched there, frozen in her fear, her eyes darting wildly from Jim to Alfie, from Alfie to Jim. Alfie reached out slowly and touched her blanket. "It's wet through," he said.

Her bare feet were covered in sand and mud, and what little he could see of her dress was nothing but tatters and rags. There were empty limpet shells scattered all about her feet, and a few broken eggshells, gulls' eggs they were. "We got mackerel for tea back home," he went on. "Mother does it beautiful, rolled in egg and oats, and we got bread-and-butter pudding for afters too. You'll like it. We got our boat down on the beach. You want to come with us?" He inched his way toward her, holding out his hand. "Can you walk, girl?"

She sprang up then like a frightened fawn, leaped past him

and was stumbling through the bracken toward the doorway. She must have tripped because she suddenly disappeared into the undergrowth. Jim found her moments later lying facedown, unconscious. He turned her over. She was bleeding profusely from her forehead. He leaned over her. There were scratches and cuts all over her legs. One ankle was swollen and bruised. She wasn't breathing. Alfie was there on his knees beside her.

"Is she dead, Father?" he breathed. "Is she dead?" Jim felt her neck. He could feel no pulse. With panic rising in his chest, he remembered then how Alfie had once fallen down onto rocks when he was little, how he'd run all the way home with Alfie in his arms, quite sure he must be dead. He remembered then how calm Mary had been, how she had taken charge at once, laid Alfie out on the kitchen table, put her ear to his mouth and felt his breath on her skin. He did the same now, put his ear to the girl's mouth, felt the warm breath, and knew there was life in her yet. All he had to do was get her home fast. Mary would know what to do with her.

"You get to the boat, Alfie," he said. "Fast. I'll bring her."

He picked her up and ran out of the Pest House, along the path to the dunes. She was light and limp and damp in his arms. He could feel she was little more than skin and bones. By the time he got there Alfie had the boat in the water. He was standing there in the shallows, holding it. "You get in, son," Jim said. "You look after her. I'll row." They wrapped her in Jim's coat and laid her down with her head on Alfie's lap. "Hold her close," Jim told him. "We got to keep her warm as best we can." He pushed off then, leaping into the boat and gathering the oars almost in one movement.

Jim rowed like a man possessed out into the swell of the open ocean past the lighthouse on White Island, and at long last into the calm of Tresco Channel. Every few moments as he rowed, he'd glance down at the girl as she lay there in Alfie's arms, her head bleeding, her eyes closed. Alfie could feel no life in her. Jim could see no life in her. She was sleeping as if she would never wake. Alfie talked to her all the time, he hardly stopped. Holding her tight to him as the boat reared and rolled through the waves, he kept calling to her, willing her to wake up and open her eyes, telling her it wouldn't be long now, that she'd be all right. And sometimes Jim would join in too, whenever he could find the breath to do so, begging her to live, pleading with her, yelling at her even. "Wake up, girl! For Chrissake, wake up! Don't you dare go and die on me, you hear. Don't you dare!"

Chapter Three

Just like a mermaid

All the while, as Jim pulled for dear life, straining his every sinew with every stroke, the girl lay there, lifeless, in the boat, her head cradled on Alfie's lap, as pale as death. He didn't want to keep asking Alfie how she was, if she was still alive, because he could tell how anxious and upset Alfie already was. Jim longed to stop rowing, just for a moment, to see for himself if she was still breathing, but he knew he had to keep going, to get the girl back to Bryher, and to Mary, as fast as he could. Mary would know what to do, he told himself. Mary would save her.

Never had it taken so long to row up Tresco Channel, Alfie thought. He was quite sure by now that the girl must be dead, so much so that he could hardly bring himself to look at her. Close to tears all the time, he did not trust himself to speak. He kept catching his father's eyes, then looking away fast. He could not tell him how cold she was in his arms, how still, that she was gone.

Wind and current and exhaustion were slowing Jim all the way. As he rowed into Green Bay he was yelling for help with what little breath he had left. Dozens of islanders were hurrying along the beach, Mary among them, along with a gaggle of excited children, back from school by now, running along behind. Only Peg, the island's workhorse, seemed unconcerned at their arrival, intent as she was on browsing the dunes.

As Jim brought the boat in to the shore, everyone came wading out through the shallows to meet them, to haul the boat in. Before Jim had time even to ship his oars, Mary had taken the girl from Alfie's arms and was carrying her up the beach. Alfie stayed to help his father out of the boat. He seemed unsteady on his feet, so Alfie held on to his arms for a few moments. Stumbling out of the water, he fell on his hands and knees on the wet sand, all his strength spent, his chest heaving to catch his breath. His head was spinning, his shoulders on fire. There was no part of him that was not aching.

Farther up the beach Mary had laid the girl down on dry sand and was kneeling over her. She was calling to them. "Who is she, Jimbo?" Mary was asking him. "Who is she? Where'd you find her?" All Jim could do was shake his head. He couldn't speak a word. A crowd was gathering by now, pushing and shoving to get a closer look, all of them full of questions. Mary waved everyone back. "Give her some air, for goodness' sake. Child needs to breathe. She's half dead, can't you see? Get back! And someone send to St. Mary's for Dr. Crow. Quick about it now! We'll get her home, warm her up in front of the stove." She touched the girl's face with the back of her hand, felt her neck. "She's shivering somethin' terrible. She's got a fever on her. We'll use the cart. Someone fetch Peg, hitch her up and hurry up about it."

Jim and Alfie found a way through the crowd. Just at that moment the girl's eyes opened. She looked up in bewilderment at all the faces staring down at her. She was trying to sit up, trying to say something. Mary bent closer. "What is it, dear? What is it?"

It was only a whisper, and very few heard it. But Mary did, Alfie did. "Lucy," said the girl. Then as Mary laid her down again, her eyes closed and she lost consciousness again.

They rushed her home to Veronica Farm in the cart, with Alfie leading Peg and Mary riding in the back, holding the girl in her arms. Half the island was following along behind, it seemed, in spite of Mary telling them again and again that there was nothing they could do, and they should all go home. No one did. "Can you hurry that horse on, Alfie?" she said.

"She won't go no faster, Mother," Alfie told her. "You know Peg."

"And I know you too, Alfie Wheatcroft," she went on, with

29

a certain tone in her voice. "Had a nice day at school, did you?" Alfie didn't know what to say, so he said nothing. For a while neither of them spoke. "Father tells me it was you that found her," Mary began.

"S'pose," Alfie replied.

Mary went on: "Well then, when all's said and done, I reckon it was a good thing you were there. Say no more about it, shall we? Now trot that horse on, whether she likes it or no."

"Yes, Mother," Alfie replied, both relieved and contrite.

An hour or so after everyone reached the farmhouse, Jim and Alfie with all the men and boys were still gathered in the garden outside, waiting for news, while as many of the women as could were crowded into the farmhouse kitchen—much to Mary's irritation, which she did not trouble to hide. They were full of loud advice, which Mary was doing her best to ignore. She simply busied herself getting the child into some dry clothes, rubbing her down, and making her as warm and comfortable as she could in front of the stove. Out in the garden, with Alfie at his side, Jim had recovered enough by now and was busy answering everyone's questions about how he and Alfie had discovered the girl on St. Helen's. They all wanted to know more, but there was little to tell, and once he had told it, there was nothing more to say. He could only repeat it. But still the questions came.

Dr. Crow finally arrived from St. Mary's, took one look at the crowd of people gathered outside the house, and at once took control. Standing at the farmhouse door, pipe in hand as usual, he declared: "This is not a circus, and I'm not a clown. I'm the doctor and I've come to see a patient. Now be off with the lot of you, else I'll get ugly."

Unkempt and bedraggled as he always was, a vestige of cabbage left lingering in his beard after his lunch—he wasn't nicknamed Dr. Scarecrow for nothing—Dr. Crow was much loved and respected throughout the islands. There was hardly anyone who hadn't had good cause to be grateful to Dr. Crow at some time or another. For years he had been wise counselor and kindly comforter to the islanders. He only had to come into a house for everyone to feel at once reassured. But he was also a little feared No one argued with Dr. Crow. Most of the men walked off with hardly a murmur, and the women in the kitchen might have grumbled about it as they left, but they all went in the end. "Here, hold my pipe, lad," he said to Alfie as he came into the house, "but don't you go puffing on it, you hear me. Now where's the patient?"

Lucy was sitting in Jim's chair by the stove, swathed in blankets, wide-eyed with alarm, and shivering violently. "She's called Lucy, Doctor," Mary told him. "That's all we know about her, all she said, just her name. I can't seem to get her warm,

Doctor. Tried everything. Can't stop her shivering." The doctor bent down at once, lifted the girl's feet, and put them right up against the stove. "In my experience, Mrs. Wheatcroft, we get warm from the feet up," he said. "We'll soon have her right. Nasty ankle she's got. Sprained, by the look of it."

"I tried to give her some hot milk and honey," Mary went on, "but she wouldn't take none."

"You did well to try, but it's water she needs most, I think, lots of water," the doctor said, taking his stethoscope out of his bag and then folding the blankets down from around her neck a little to examine her. The girl at once pulled the blankets up to her chin again and broke into a sudden fit of coughing that wracked her whole body.

"Easy, girl," the doctor said. "Lucy, isn't it? No one's going to hurt you." He reached out, more slowly this time, and felt her forehead. He took her wrist and felt her pulse. "Well, she's got a burning fever on her, that's for sure," he said, "and that's not good. I wouldn't be surprised if some of these cuts on her legs are infected. They've been there some time, by the look of them." He turned to Jim then. "It was you that found her, Mr. Wheatcroft, so they tell me. And on St. Helen's, wasn't it? Horrible place."

"Alfie and me, Doctor," Jim replied.

"What was she doing over there?" the doctor went on. "All on her own, was she, when you found her? That right?"

"Think so," Jim replied. "We didn't see no one else. But to be honest, we didn't have much time to look. Never gave it a thought, not then. I thought about it after though, that she might not have been alone, I mean. So I sent Cousin Dave off in his boat and told him to have a good look around the island, just to be sure. He'll be back soon. He shouldn't be long now, I reckon."

"Out fishing, were you, Mr. Wheatcroft?"

"Mackerel," said Jim.

"She's a good enough size for mackerel," the doctor went on, smiling for just a moment, "that's for sure. Catch of the year, I'd say. But it's a very good thing you found her when you did. This is a very poorly girl, Mrs. Wheatcroft, dehydrated, feverish. It doesn't look to me as if she's eaten properly in days, weeks maybe. Half-starved, she is."

He was feeling the girl's neck with both hands, lifting her chin and then peering into her throat. He leaned her forward, tapped her on the back, then put the stethoscope to her chest and listened for a while to her breathing. "A lot of congestion in her lungs, which is not what I like to hear," he declared. "Weak as a kitten. And that cough of hers is down on her chest, where it shouldn't be. It's pneumonia I'm worried about most. You keep her warm, just like you are, Mrs. Wheatcroft. Keep those cuts and scratches clean. Warm vegetable broth, hot Bovril, maybe some bread. Not too much at first, mind.

A little food and often, that's the best way. Sweet tea is always good too, if she'll take it. And, as I said, plenty of water. She's got to drink. We have to get that fever down, and quickly. I don't like this shivering, not one bit. We get rid of the shivering, the cough'll go soon enough too." He leaned closer to her now. "You be a good girl now, Lucy, eat and drink all you can. You've got a second name, have you, girl?" Lucy stared up at him, silently, vacantly. "Not much to say for yourself, eh? Where'd you come from, Lucy? Everyone comes from somewhere."

"She don't seem to speak much, Doctor—just her name," said Mary.

"Came up out of the sea, I heard," the doctor went on, lifting her eyelids one by one. "Like a mermaid, eh? Well I never." He reached out and lifted up the bottom of the blanket, uncovering her knees. He crossed her legs, and then tapped her knees, one after the other. He seemed satisfied. "Don't you worry, Mrs. Wheatcroft, once she's better she'll speak soon enough, and we'll all know more. She's in deep shock, in my opinion. But I'm here to tell you that I am quite sure she can't be a mermaid—because she's got legs. Scratched, they might be, but she's got two of them. Look!" They all smiled at that. "That's better. We have to be cheerful around her, you know. It'll make her feel better, cheerfulness always does. But now comes the question: Who's going to look after her? And what about when she gets better? So far as we can tell, it's not as if she belongs to anyone, does she?"

Mary did not hesitate. "We will, of course," she said. "Won't we, Jimbo? All right with you, Alfie?"

Alfie didn't say anything. He was hardly listening. He could not take his eyes off her. He was so relieved she was alive. He was wondering now who this strange little girl was, how she got herself onto St. Helen's in the first place, and how she had managed to survive over there all on her own.

"She's got to belong to someone, Mary," said Jim. "Every child's got a mother or father somewhere. They'll be missing her."

"But who is she?" Alfie asked.

"She's called Lucy," said Mary, "and that's all we need to know for the moment. As I see it, God has brought her to us, up out of the ocean, sent you and Father over to St. Helen's to find her. So we look after her for as long as she needs us. She'll be one of us, for as long as she has to be, till her mother or father comes to fetch her home. Meanwhile this is her home. You'll have a sister for a while, Alfie, and your father and me, we'll have a daughter. Always wanted one of them, didn't we, Jimbo? Never quite managed it till now, did we? We'll nurse her back to health, Doctor, you'll see, feed her up, put some color in her cheeks." She brushed away the hair from the girl's forehead. "And then we'll see. You'll be all right with us, dear. Never fear."

The doctor left soon afterward, saying he'd be back in a week or so to see how Lucy was getting along, telling Mary very firmly that if the fever got worse, he was to be sent for at once. He took his pipe back off Alfie before he left. "Horrible habit, my lad," he said. "Don't you never smoke, hear me? Bad for your health. Nasty habit. Else you'll have the doctor calling round all the time, and you don't want that, do you?"

He hadn't been gone more than an hour or two before they had their next visitor. Big Dave Bishop, Cousin Dave, was at the door, and knocking loudly. "Jim! You in there, Jim?" He didn't wait to be asked in. He burst in, filling the room with his bulk, his voice loud with excitement. He was cradling an untidy-looking bundle in both arms. "I been over there, Jim, to St. Helen's, just like you told me," he said. "No one else there, not so far as I could see. I went all over. Lots of oystercatchers, and gulls, and a seal or two on the rocks. Didn't find no one else. But I did find this." It was a blanket, a gray, sodden-looking blanket. And then he unfolded it. "There was this too, Jim. Just lying there in the corner of the Pest House, it was. S'one of they teddy bears, isn't it? Hers, isn't it? Got to be."

Mary took it from him. Like the blanket, it too was bedraggled and wet through, with a soiled pink ribbon around its neck, and one eye was missing. It was smiling, Alfie noticed.

Suddenly Lucy was sitting upright and reaching out for it.

"Yours, is it, Lucy dear?" she said. The girl grabbed it from her, clutching it fiercely to herself, as if she'd never let it go.

"Hers all right then," Jim said. "No doubt about that."

"And there's something else an' all," Cousin Dave said. "This here blanket, it's got some funny foreign-like writing on it, like it's a name sewed on, or something." He held it up to show them. "I don't do reading, Jim. What's it say?"

Jim spelled the name out loud, then tried to pronounce it. "Wil . . . helm. Wilhelm. That's the Kaiser's name, in't it? I'm sure it is. Sounds like William. Kaiser Bill, he's called that, isn't he?"

"The Kaiser!" said Cousin Dave. "Then it's German, isn't it? Got to be. And if it's German, then that's where that girl comes from then, isn't it? Stands to reason, don't it? She's one of them. She's a lousy Hun. Could be the Kaiser's ruddy daughter."

"Don't talk soft, Cousin David," Mary said, pulling the blanket away from him. "And I don't care who she is, whether she comes from Timbuktu. We're all God's children, wherever we come from, whatever we're called, whichever language we speak. And don't you never forget it."

She walked right up to him then, and looking him right in the eye, she spoke very softly. "You listen to me, Cousin Dave. I don't want you never saying anything about the name on this blanket. You hear me? Not a word. You know what it's like

37

these days, with all this tittle-tattle about German spies, and all that. Nothing but poisonous nonsense. This gets around, and people will start talking. Not a word. We keep it in the family, right? You promise, promise me faithfully now."

Cousin Dave looked away, first at Jim, then at Alfie, hoping for some help. He was clearly nervous. He didn't seem to know quite where to look, nor what to say. Mary reached up and took his face firmly in her hands, forcing him to look at her. "Promise me? Faithfully?" she said again.

It took Cousin Dave a while to reply. "All right, Aunty Mary," he said at last. "I shan't say nothing about it. Promise. Cross my heart and hope to die."

But Jim didn't trust him. Everyone knew that after a drink or two David Bishop would say almost anything. "We won't say a word, will we, Cousin Dave?" said Jim, and with just enough menace in his tone that Cousin Dave would understand that he really meant it. "You went over to St. Helen's and you found the teddy bear, and you found the blanket, just an ordinary gray blanket. That's all you say, like your Aunty Mary said. And you don't want to upset your Aunty Mary, do you? 'Cos if she's upset, then I'm upset. And I get ugly when I'm upset, don't I? And you don't want that, right?"

"S'pose," Cousin Dave replied, shamefaced.

All this time Alfie had been staring at Lucy. "I never saw anyone who was German before," he said. "No wonder she

38

don't say nothing. She can't speak English. And she can't understand a word we say, can she? Not if she's German, she can't."

As he was speaking, Lucy looked up at him, and held his eyes just for a moment. But it was long enough for Alfie to know for certain that she had understood something, maybe not every word he had said, but something.

Chapter Four

Lucy Lost

Lucy's mysterious appearance from out of nowhere had been the talk of the islands for weeks now, eclipsing even the news of the war from over in France and Belgium, which had been the main anxiety and preoccupation of just about everyone in the islands since the outbreak of war nearly a year before—every islander except Uncle Billy, that is, who lived his life in another world altogether, seemingly quite oblivious to the real world around him.

All the news they read in the newspapers, or picked up from any passing sailors coming into port at St. Mary's, dashed once again their hopes of an early peace, and confirmed their worst fears. To begin with, the papers had been full of patriotic fervor and cheery optimism, the headlines rallying cries to the nation. But in recent months, much of that had vanished, as they read yet again more news of the losses, of "heroic stands," and "bravely fought" battles in Belgium, or "strategic" retreats in

France. Armies that were going backward and losing men by the thousands were clearly not winning—as some newspapers were still trying to insist—and most people knew it by now. None of the boys was going to be home by Christmastime, as everyone had hoped, that was for sure. The islanders were doing their best to put a brave face on it. They tried all they could to keep the home fires burning with hope, but nothing any longer could hide the truth behind the daily reports of ever-mounting casualties, those dreadful long lists in the papers of the killed, the wounded, and the missing in action. And in recent months there had been four drowned sailors from Royal Navy ships washed up on the shores of Scilly, every one of them a stark reminder that the war at sea was not going well either.

These were islands accustomed enough to tragedy. "Lost at sea" had always been a common enough cause of sudden disappearance and death, as was witnessed on monuments in churches all over the islands. But when the news came in that the islands had suffered their first losses of the war—two young lads whom everyone knew, Martin Dowd and Henry Hibbert—a pall of grief settled over everyone. Both had rowed in the St. Mary's gig, and both had been killed near Mons on the same day. They were Scillonians. They were family. The war had truly come home.

But it was what had happened shortly afterward to young Jack Brody that was the most difficult to bear, particularly for the people of Bryher. He was known throughout the islands as a cheeky, cheery sort of a fellow, a bit of a show-off, the life and soul of any get-together, always boisterous and full of fun. He had joined up at sixteen—underage—the first to volunteer from the islands, full of his usual bravado and banter, bragging how once he got out to France, he'd sort out Fritz soon enough. A couple of years older than Alfie, Jack had been his hero all the way through school, always in and out of trouble, champion of the school at boxing, and the best footballer in the whole school without any question. He was everything Alfie admired, everything he wanted to grow up to be.

But now, only six months after going off to war, he was back home again. From time to time Alfie would see him around the island, sometimes being pushed in his wheelchair along the path by his mother, sometimes limping along on crutches, a couple of medals pinned to his jacket, his left leg missing. Jack could still put a brave face on it. He'd wave wildly at anyone and everyone he saw. Miraculously, despite his destroyed mind and mangled body, the heart of him still seemed to be there. Whenever he saw Alfie, he'd call out to him, but he didn't know anymore who Alfie was. Alfie dreaded meeting him. His speech would be garbled, his head rolling uncontrollably, his mouth slack and dribbling, one eye dull and blinded. But it was the tucked-up trouser leg that Alfie could not bear to look at.

Alfie hated himself for doing it, but once or twice he had

even hidden himself behind some escallonia hedge when he'd seen him coming, just to avoid having to meet him. Sometimes, though, there was no way out, and he'd have to force himself to go over and say hello to him, to confront again the leg that wasn't there, the livid scar across his forehead where the shrapnel had gone in, and where, as his mother told him every time they met, it was still lodged deep in his brain. "How are you today, Jack?" he'd say. And Jack would try to tell him, but the words came out as scrambled as his mind. He would keep on trying, desperate to communicate. Humiliated, frustrated, and angry, Jack would often have to turn away to hide his tears, and then there seemed nothing else to do but to leave him. It shamed Alfie every time he did it.

So during that summer, for Alfie, as for so many, the finding of "Lucy Lost" —as she was now known all over the islands— had been a welcome distraction. She took everyone's mind off poor Jack Brody, and the loss of Martin and Henry. The overwhelming shadow of the war itself receded. Lucy Lost gave them all something else, something new, to talk about. Speculation was rife. Imagination ran riot. Rumors were everywhere— plausible, or implausible, it made no difference. Stories and theories abounded, anything that might possibly explain how Lucy Lost had turned up alone and abandoned on St. Helen's, with nothing but an old gray blanket and a raggedy teddy bear with one eye and a gentle smile.

How had she got there? How long had she been there? And who on earth was she anyway? Everyone wanted to know more about her and, if possible, catch a glimpse of her. A few of the most inquisitive had even gone so far as to take a trip over to St. Helen's to scour the Pest House and the island for any telltale clues. They had found nothing. All anyone knew for sure was that her name was Lucy, that this was the only word this strange little girl had ever uttered, and that Big Dave Bishop had discovered the teddy bear and the blanket in the Pest House—both presumably hers. Big Dave had talked a lot about his discovery—but true to his word, had made no mention of the name embroidered on it. There was so little to go on. But what the islanders didn't know about Lucy Lost, they more than made up for by invention.

The stories became more and more fantastical. It was said that Lucy was deaf and dumb, and so she had to be "a bit mazed in the head," like Uncle Billy. Just as he was "Silly Billy" to some, so she was "Loony Lucy." Some thought her mother must have died in childbirth, that she had been marooned on St. Helen's, deliberately abandoned there by a cruel father who had tired of providing for her. There was another favorite story going round too, that she was the child of one of those unfortunates who had been quarantined in the Pest House on the island centuries before, that she had perished there long ago, and ever since had wandered the island, a lost soul, a ghost child. Or maybe, it was said, Lucy Lost had fallen overboard from some ship in the Atlantic and had been saved from drowning by a passing whale and carried safely to shore. It could happen, some argued. Hadn't Jonah himself been saved just like that in the Bible? And hadn't the Reverend Morrison only recently preached a sermon about Jonah in Bryher church, telling everyone that these stories from the Bible weren't just stories, that they were the truth, the word of God himself, God's truth?

Then, most fantastical of all perhaps, and certainly the most popular theory of all, there was the mermaid yarn at school— Alfie had heard it often enough in the school yard. Lucy Lost was really a mermaid, and not just any mermaid, but the famous Mermaid of Zennor, who had swum over to the Scilly Isles from the Cornish coast many years ago, who had come up out of the sea onto St. Helen's and sat on the shore there and sung sweet songs to passing sailors and fishermen to tempt them onto the rocks, combing her hair languorously as mermaids do. But she had grown legs—mermaids can do that, some said, like tadpoles. Doesn't a tadpole grow legs out of a wiggly tail every spring? All right, so they might not sing songs or comb their hair, but they grow legs, don't they? All these stories were so unlikely as to be ridiculous, laughable, and quite simply impossible. It didn't matter. They were all fascinating and entertaining, which is probably why the mystery of Lucy Lost remained the talk of the islands for weeks and months that summer.

Most of the islanders did realize, of course, when they really thought about it, that there had to be some more rational, sensible explanation as to why and how Lucy Lost had been marooned on St. Helen's, how someone so young could have survived. They all knew that if anyone had any idea of the truth of all this, then it would very likely come from Jim Wheatcroft or Alfie, who had found her in the first place, or from Mary Wheatcroft, who was looking after her at Veronica Farm on Bryher. Surely they would know. Maybe they did know. They were certainly being overly secretive about her and protective, as they always had been about Silly Billy, ever since Mary had brought him back from the hospital. They all knew better than to ask questions about Silly Billy—he was family, after all—that Mary would snap their heads off if they dared. But Lucy Lost, they thought, wasn't family. She was simply a mystery, which was why wherever any of the family went, they were liable to be badgered by endless questions and opinions from anyone they met.

Mary was able, for the most part, to keep herself to herself, to avoid too much of this intrusion into their lives, staying inside the farmhouse and around the farm as much as possible. But she did have to leave Lucy alone in the house, and venture off the farm at least twice a day to visit Uncle Billy to bring him his food, and tidy up around him as best she could. She'd find him in the boathouse, in the sail loft above, or more often these days out on Green Bay itself, on the *Hispaniola,* but always working away.

She'd been bringing him his food, seeing to his washing, cleaning around him, looking after him, for five years or more now. She'd done this every day without fail, ever since she'd brought him home from the hospital in Bodmin, from the County Asylum, or the "madhouse," as everyone called it. It was on her way to and from Green Bay to see to Uncle Billy that more often than not she'd meet one or two of her neighbors on the beach. Some, she knew, had been deliberately loitering there with the intent to ambush her, and that whoever it was would sooner or later begin to ply her with questions about Lucy Lost. It hadn't escaped her notice that before the coming of Lucy Lost she had hardly ever met anyone on her way to or from Uncle Billy. She fended them all off. "She's fine," she'd say, "getting better all the time. Fine."

But Lucy wasn't fine. Her cough may not have been as rasping, nor as repetitive and frequent as before, but at nighttimes in particular it still plagued her. And sometimes they could hear her moaning to herself—Alfie said it was more like a tune she was humming. But moaning or humming, it was a sound filled with sadness. Mary would lie awake listening to her, worrying. Night by night, lack of sleep was bringing her to the edge of exhaustion. She gave short shrift to anyone who turned up at the door "just visiting," but quite obviously trying to catch a glimpse of Lucy. Her frosty reception seemed in the end to be enough to deter even the most persistent of snoopers.

It fell to Jim much more often to confront the endless inquisitiveness about Lucy Lost. Like it or not, he had to mend his nets and his crab pots down on Green Bay, where all the fishermen on the island always gathered together to do the same thing when the weather was right. He had to see to his potatoes and his flowers in the fields. He had to fetch seaweed from the beaches for fertilizer, and to gather driftwood there for winter fires. Wherever he went, whatever he was doing, there were always people coming and going, friends, relations, and they all pestered him about Lucy Lost at every possible opportunity.

If Jim was honest with himself, he had at first quite enjoyed the limelight. He had been there with Alfie when Lucy Lost was first discovered. They had brought her home. All the attention and admiration had not been unwelcome, at first. But after a week or two he was already tiring of it. There were so many questions, usually the same ones, and the same old quips and jokes bellowed out across the fields, or over the water from passing fishing boats.

"Caught any more mermaids today, have you, Jim?" He tried to laugh them off, to remain good-humored about it all, but he was finding that harder by the day. And he was becoming ever more concerned about Mary. She was looking tired out these days, and not her usual spirited self at all. He'd tried to suggest, gently, that she might be taking on too much with Lucy Lost, that surely she had enough to do caring for Uncle Billy, that maybe they should think again about Lucy, and find someone else to look after her. But she wouldn't hear of it.

Alfie too, as time passed, was being given more and more of a hard time over Lucy Lost. Every day at school he found himself being quizzed, by teachers and children alike, and teased too.

"How old is she, Alfie?"

"What's she look like?"

"Your mermaid, Alf, has she got scales on her instead of skin? Has she got a fish face? Green all over, Alfie, is she?"

Zebediah Bishop, Cousin David's son, who took after his father and was always the laddish loudmouth of the school, had always known better than most how to rile Alfie. "Is your mermaid pretty then, Alfie boy? Is she your girlfriend, eh? You done kissing with her yet? What's it like kissing a mermaid? Slippery, I shouldn't wonder!" Alfie did try his utmost to ignore him, but that was easier said than done.

One morning as they were lining up in the school yard on Tresco to go into school, Zeb started up again. He was holding his nose and making faces. "Cor," he said, "there's something round 'ere that stinks something awful, like fish. Could be a mermaid, I reckon. They stink just the same as fish, that's what I heard."

Alfie had had enough. He went for him, which was how they ended up rolling around on the ground, arms and legs flailing, kicking and punching each other, till Mr. Beagley, "Beastly Beagley," the headmaster, came out, hauled them to their feet by their collars, and dragged them inside. The two of them ended up in detention for that all through afternoon playtime. They had to write out a hundred times "Words are wise, fists are foolish."

They were not supposed to talk in detention—you got the ruler if Mr. Beagley caught you—but Zeb talked. He leaned over and whispered to Alfie: "My dad says your mermaid's got a little teddy bear. Ain't that sweet? Alfie's got a girlfriend who's got a little teddy bear, and who's so dumb she don't even speak. She don't even know who she is, do she? Doolally, mad, off her ruddy rocker, like your daft old uncle, like Silly Billy, that's what I heard. He should've stayed in the madhouse where he belonged, that's what my ma says. And that's where your little girlfriend should go, and take her teddy bear with her. Not all there in the head, is she? And I heard something else too, a little secret my dad told me, about her blanket, the one my dad found on that island. I know all about it, don't I? She's German, she a Fritzy, your smelly girlfriend, isn't she?"

Alfie was on his feet, grabbing Zeb and pinning him against the wall, shouting in his face, nose to nose. "Your dad promised he wouldn't tell. He promised. If you say anything about

that blanket, then it'll make your dad a big fat liar, and I'll—"
Alfie never finished because that was the moment when
Mr. Beagley came storming in and pulled them apart. He gave
each of them six of the best with the edge of the ruler, on their
knuckles this time. There was nothing in the world that hurt
more than that. Neither Alfie nor Zeb could stop themselves
from crying. They were stood in the corner all through last les-
son after that. Alfie stared sullenly at the knots in the wood
paneling in front of his face, trying to forget the shooting pain
in his knuckles, fighting to hold back the tears. The two dark
knots looked back at him, a pair of deep, brown eyes.

Lucy has eyes like that, he thought, *eyes that look into you,*
unblinking, eyes that told you nothing. Empty eyes.

Chapter Five

Just an idea

Standing there in the corner, Alfie forced himself to go on thinking of Lucy—anything to take his mind off the agony of his knuckles. He decided he was in two minds about her. He liked having her there in the house. He hadn't been sure about it at first, mostly because his mother seemed to have become so preoccupied with Lucy that she seemed to have less time for him or for anyone else. Alfie had seen her before like this. It was how she'd been with Uncle Billy, during her long search for him, then her determined campaign, with Dr. Crow's help, to get him out of the asylum in Bodmin and bring him home so she could look after him. He had understood then why she had to do it, as he understood now that it was the right and proper thing to do to take Lucy Lost in. He was doing his best to persuade himself not to mind too much.

But he did mind, and he knew his father did too, though nothing had been said. He remembered then what his father always said to him whenever he needed cheering up: "Always look on the bright side, Alfie." It wasn't easy, but as he stood there in the corner feeling miserable, his knuckles paining him, he tried to do it.

At least, he thought, he had a companion in the house now, a sort of sister, however strange, however silent. And he did like going upstairs to see her. He'd even read to her sometimes if his mother asked him to, and he'd never read aloud to anyone before. He hadn't ever liked reading aloud at school, in case he made mistakes—Mr. Beagley didn't like mistakes—but with Lucy Lost, he'd just read the story and listen to it himself as he was doing it. And he liked taking milk and tatty cake upstairs to her for her tea when he came home from school, liked being left in the house to look after her when his mother went down to Green Bay to see to Uncle Billy. But he was more and more troubled by her silence, by the vacant stare she would give him. He longed for her simply to say something to him, anything. He had tried to talk to her, to ask her questions, to get her to talk. But she would lie there looking blankly up at the ceiling. Asking questions wasn't working, because she never replied. And talking to her didn't work, because either she didn't understand or she wasn't listening. She simply didn't react or respond in any way.

Despite all this, he did look forward to being with her, and he couldn't work out why. It was, he thought, a bit like going to see Uncle Billy down on Green Bay. With Uncle Billy, Alfie would chatter away happily for hours, and all he'd get in reply was a grunt or two, yet he always knew Uncle Billy liked him to be there, even if he was deep in one of his black moods. He was sad when he was like that. He could see that Lucy was sad like he was, that she needed company just as Uncle Billy did. That was enough for Alfie. He liked being company for her, and silent and strange as she was, the truth was that, even so, he liked her company too.

Alfie's knuckles were still tingling. He tried not to think about them and turned his mind instead to Uncle Billy. Alfie knew, as everyone in the family did, that the only way to get Uncle Billy out of one of his "grumps," as they called them, was to talk to him, and go on talking to him. Sometimes it worked, sometimes it didn't. You had to be patient. Uncle Billy could stay in one of his grumps for days sometimes, and if he was really bad, he'd even stop working on the *Hispaniola* and just sit there in his sail loft in the boathouse, staring into space, saying nothing, eating nothing that anyone would bring him. But sooner or later, he'd come out of it, and then there would be days and weeks when he'd be Long John Silver again, working happily on the boat all day, wearing his pirate hat, talking and singing away to himself.

Whenever Alfie visited on days like this, Uncle Billy would often prattle on and on as he worked on the *Hispaniola,* about

Treasure Island, quoting long passages from the book. It never ceased to amaze Alfie how Uncle Billy could do that. He knew the book by heart from cover to cover, and would talk of the characters in it as if they were real people. About Jim Hawkins, he'd often say: "A good lad and a lot like you, young Alfie." He'd talk the same way of mad Ben Gunn, or of Captain Flint, the parrot, and, of course, of "the good ship *Hispaniola.*"

Whenever he spoke of *Treasure Island,* Alfie knew it wasn't just a story to him, but a real and true happening, a story he had lived, was still living whenever he spoke of it or told it. Sometimes he'd even call Alfie "Jim lad," and Alfie realized then that, for Uncle Billy, that wasn't just a slip of the tongue, that there were moments when to Uncle Billy, Alfie really was Jim Hawkins. And he himself was Long John Silver, building his boat, a new *Hispaniola,* which one day, he said, when it was finished, he'd sail away to Treasure Island again. On those days, he'd be busy from dawn to dusk, sawing or planing or hammering away on the *Hispaniola,* singing out his pirate's song at the top of his voice. "Fifteen men on a dead man's chest, yo ho ho and a bottle of rum!"

Alfie stood, face in the corner, humming Uncle Billy's Yo Ho Ho song softly to himself, under his breath, so that Mr. Beagley could not hear. It was a song of defiance as well as a song of comfort. To hum, to move, would provoke a whack on the head from Mr. Beagley. Lucy's eyes, the twin knots in the wood paneling, stared back at him. Talking, he was thinking, had never worked with Lucy as it could sometimes with Uncle Billy. She stayed locked away inside herself, no matter what he said, no matter how long he stayed with her, and to him there seemed very little prospect that this would ever change. Alfie flexed his knuckles. They were still stiff with pain. He would go on talking to her, keep trying. If it worked sometimes with Uncle Billy, then it could work with Lucy. "Always look on the bright side," he whispered to himself, louder than he had intended.

"Silence!" roared Mr. Beagley.

Alfie steeled himself for the whack on the head. It came sure enough, and it hurt, but not like his knuckles hurt.

———◆———

There were times in the weeks that followed when Alfie felt he was talking to Lucy only because someone had to say something, to fill the silence between them. He knew he was talking to himself, but he would tell her anyway, tell her all the news. He'd tell her what had gone on at school that day, who Mr. Beagley had picked on in particular, who had had the cane, who had had the ruler, who had been stood in the corner, or about the peregrine falcon he'd seen hovering over Watch Hill, or the sleeping seal he'd seen basking on the rocks off Rushy Bay. He tried his best to make his day interesting for her, and funny too when he could, however tedious and ordinary the day had been. And some were.

Alfie may have had plenty of practice at this with Uncle Billy, but with Lucy it was different. He had no idea who he was talking to. He knew Uncle Billy, all about who he was, his whole sad story, how Uncle Billy was his mother's twin brother. He'd been born and brought up with her on Bryher, but at fifteen years old, after an argument with his father, he'd run away to sea, without ever telling her. For years his mother never knew where he had gone, nor what had happened to him.

She had found out how, twenty or so years later, and a master shipbuilder in Penzance by now, his wife had died in childbirth, his baby too, how grief and guilt had driven Billy mad, how he'd gone off wandering the wild moors of Cornwall, and had ended up in the County Asylum in Bodmin, how Alfie's mother had asked after him, searched for him for years, and finally tracked him down in the asylum, and with Dr. Crow's help, had brought him home. He had one thing only with him, his mother told him, a copy of *Treasure Island*. All through his time in the asylum he had read and read it. Talking to Uncle Billy, Alfie always had this whole story in his head. They knew one another, trusted one another.

But he didn't know Lucy like he knew his Uncle Billy. He was talking to a face, someone from nowhere. He wanted to get to know her. He longed for her to talk back, to tell him about herself, who she was and where she had come from. So on he'd go, day after day, telling her his stories: about the porpoises he'd seen swimming out in the Tresco Channel, about Uncle Billy and how he was getting on with his work on the *Hispaniola,* what fish his father had caught, about another merchantman sunk out in the Western Approaches by a German submarine, how there'd been no survivors.

Whatever he told her, though, however he told it, no matter how animated, inventive, and expansive he became in the telling, her face remained quite expressionless. But what was so frustrating and disconcerting for Alfie was that he was sure that from time to time she was in fact listening, that she was understanding something of what he was telling her. He had the feeling too—and this always encouraged him to go on—that she liked him to be there with her, liked listening to his stories. Even so, she simply would not or could not show it, would not or could not respond.

Then, out of nowhere, there came a quite unexpected breakthrough. It happened on the afternoon after yet another fight with Zeb at school. He found Dr. Crow in the house when he got back, talking earnestly with his mother and father around the kitchen table. Alfie sensed he was interrupting something the moment he walked in. When his mother asked him to take Lucy up her milk and cake, and sit with her for a while, he knew there were things they'd prefer to talk about without him there. He didn't mind anyway. He wanted to see Lucy. He had plenty he wanted to tell her.

He found her sitting up in bed, looking out the window and humming softly to herself. It wasn't the first time she had been humming when he walked in. It was always the same tune—he had noticed that. She looked a little brighter than usual, still unsmiling, but it occurred to Alfie that she had sat up in bed because she had heard him coming, that she might even have been looking forward to it. He could see she had noticed his split lip, and had a sudden hope that she might ask him about it. She didn't, but she did stare at it. And better still, she did reach out and touch it.

Alfie could hear the doctor talking downstairs with his mother and father. He was tempted to try to listen to what they were saying, but the words were a mumble, too indistinct to hear properly. And besides, he had things he needed to tell Lucy. Lucy ate her cake slowly—she always ate slowly—nibbling at it, while Alfie gave her a blow-by-blow account of his fight with Zebediah Bishop, and of the punishment he'd been given too, showed her his bruised knuckles, told her all about Beastly Beagley and his ruler, showed how he held your arm in a vise-like grip and hit you on the knuckles with the edge of the ruler so hard you couldn't move your fingers afterward at all. He told her how Zeb had again threatened to tell everyone about

Lucy's blanket with "Wilhelm" on it, but how he wouldn't dare because he knew about Zeb and his cronies robbing the money box in the church, and how he had threatened he would tell the Reverend Morrison if Zeb ever mentioned a word about the name on the blanket.

It was at that moment that Lucy responded for the first time to anything he had ever said to her. She looked up at him for a moment, and then lifted a corner of the blanket to show him. The word came out slowly, and only with great concentration and effort. "W . . . Wil . . . helm," she said softly, and said no more.

But she had spoken! Lucy had spoken! It was indistinct, but it was a spoken word, a recognizable word, definitely a word.

Alfie had to tell someone, anyone, at once. He ran downstairs and burst into the kitchen. "Lucy spoke!" he said. "She said something. She did! I'm sure she did."

"You see, Doctor? Did you hear that? She is getting better, she is!" Mary said, and she reached out to grasp Alfie's hands. "That's wonderful, wonderful, Alfie, what did she say?"

"Wilhelm" was on the tip of his tongue. Then he thought again. No, he thought, no one must know, not even the doctor. He had so nearly blurted it out. Trying to gather his thoughts, he said, "I'm . . . I'm not sure. Couldn't really tell, but it was a word, promise, a real word. It was!"

The doctor smiled up at him, prodding the tobacco deep

into his pipe with his thumb. "It doesn't matter what it was," he said. "She was trying to speak, that is what is important. You have done well, Alfie, very well indeed. But in spite of this—and it is good news, Alfie, very good news—as I have been telling your mother and father, I do still have grave concerns about Lucy's future. I have examined her again this afternoon, and I have to say there is a great deal I do not properly understand. I should have expected her to have recovered much more quickly by now than she has. Her health and strength are much restored—her ankle is now as good as the other one—thanks in large part to how well your mother has cared for her. But it is not only Lucy's inability to speak properly that worries me, it is also her reluctance to get up out of bed. And this is not just physical. There is something else wrong here, something in her mind."

"In her mind?" Alfie asked. "What do you mean, in her mind?"

The doctor sighed. He lit up his pipe and sat back. "Listen," he went on. "This is how I see it. Only a few weeks ago—what is it now, eight or nine weeks, is it, Mr. Wheatcroft?—you found that poor child half dead from cold and starvation on St. Helen's. A couple more days out there on her own, and I'm telling you she would not have survived. You found her just in time. And you've all done wonders with her, brought her back from the dead. She's eating better now, that terrible cough of

61

hers is all but gone, and she's stronger now every time I see her. She is in no danger anymore. She will survive, of that I have no doubt—in her body, at any rate. But as for her mind, as I say, there I do have some concerns. It is a good sign that she spoke, Alfie, very good. But all the same, I do worry for her sanity. And I do have to say that, in this regard, I have seen very little improvement up till now."

He paused, puffing long on his pipe before beginning again. "To me she seems lost, lost deep inside herself, as lost as she was on that island. The child has clearly been traumatized, in shock, you understand. How this has happened or why, we do not know, for she cannot tell us. She can hear—I have done tests and established that. But for one reason or another, she cannot or will not speak. What is it? Two words in nearly two months now—that is hardly speaking. Maybe she has always been like this from birth, we simply do not know. I do know, however, that the mind is as fragile as the body, and that sadly, we know far less about it. But what I do know is this, and am quite sure of this—I have observed this often among the wounded sailors and soldiers I have treated—that the body can help cure the mind. Body and mind work best together. The first step, and I am convinced of this, is to persuade her to get out of her bed. We have to get her moving, to take an interest in life again. It is the only way."

"I told you, I've tried. She won't be moved, Doctor," said

Mary. "I've tried everything I know. She just lies there. I don't know what else I can do."

"Believe me, I understand, Mrs. Wheatcroft, I do," the doctor went on. "No one could have done more. But that's my point. I'm afraid that sooner or later, if she does not improve, she may need more . . . well, let us call it, specialized help. And that she can only get in a hospital on the mainland."

Mary started to her feet, tears in her eyes. "You mean the madhouse, don't you, Doctor? That's what you're talking about, isn't it! Like the asylum in Bodmin, where Billy was. Over my dead body! I have been to that place. We were there together, Doctor. Or have you forgotten? It is a hell on earth, you know it is. I won't let that happen, not again. I saw what they did to Billy in that place. For goodness' sake, Doctor, you helped me get Billy out of there. You know how they live, how they are treated. They don't live, poor souls, they just exist. It's a prison, Doctor, not a hospital. They just lock them away and throw away the key. There's no care in the place, no hope. No, until her mother or father come for her, she is ours to care for. You hear me, Doctor? I'll not let her into one of those dreadful places in a million years. We shall make her well in body and mind, you'll see. And God will help us. Didn't Lucy just speak to Alfie? Isn't that a good sign?"

"Indeed it is, but I just want you to face the possibility, Mrs. Wheatcroft, that's all," said Dr. Crow.

"It is not going to happen, Doctor," Mary whispered fiercely through her tears.

"None of us want it to happen," the doctor went on. "All I can tell you is, that if we're to have any hope of healing her mind, then you have to get her up and walking, somehow. She must be strong enough by now to walk. You have to try to get her outside."

"I've tried, Doctor," Mary told him, despairingly. "Do you think I haven't tried?"

The doctor turned to Alfie. "What about you, Alfie? You got her to speak just now. Take her round the island, take her out in the boat, maybe over to Samson to see the cottages, or down to Rushy Bay to see the seals. We've got to get her to take an interest in life, to get her out of herself. And Mrs. Wheatcroft, you go on doing just what you've been doing, talk to her, read to her, care for her, but try to bring her downstairs more, get her helping in the kitchen, out on the farm."

"She seems so damaged, so fragile," Mary said. "I can't force her, can I? How can I make her do what she doesn't want to do?"

"Marymoo," said Jim, reaching out and taking her hand in his. "Let's do what the doctor says. Let Alfie try to take her out a bit. He's more her age. She might go with him. You can't do it all by yourself, Marymoo."

"She's got to learn to live again, Mrs. Wheatcroft," the

doctor said, getting to his feet. "Even then we can't be sure she'll get well. But it's her best hope. It's my best advice, that's all. Get her up, get her moving, whether she wants to or not."

He stopped at the door as he was leaving. "This is just an idea," he said. "Music. Maybe music would help. I've got one of those wonderful gramophone contraptions back at home on St. Mary's, and some records to go with it. I'll bring them over next time I come. Easy enough to operate, you just wind it up, put the needle on, and out comes the music. Magic. Extraordinary invention. Everyone should have one. No one would need a doctor then, put me right out of a job, but I shouldn't mind. Very healing stuff, music."

———◆———

All that week Alfie tried, and his mother tried, but no amount of gentle persuasion or cajoling could induce Lucy to get out of bed. Then the next time Dr. Crow came calling, a week or so later, he brought his gramophone with him as he had promised. As soon as he arrived he wound it up and put a record on. Miraculously, piano music filled the room, filled the whole house. Jim, Mary, Alfie, and the doctor, all of them simply stood there, watching the record going round and round, listening in wonder, utterly lost in the music.

"It's Chopin," said the doctor after a while, conducting the music with his pipe.

The stair door opened behind them. Lucy was standing there in bare feet. She was swathed in her blanket, her teddy bear in her hand. She drifted across the room toward them, toward the gramophone. For long moments she simply stared down at it.

"Piano," she whispered, and then again, "Piano."

Chapter Six

We are on our way, Papa

I remember I was playing Papa's favorite piece on the piano when Old Mac brought the letter in. Old Mac was Papa's uncle and had always lived with us in the house, along with Aunty Ducka, who had been my nanny and nurse. She had looked after me all my life, taught me to sew, to make bread, and to say my prayers at night. She had looked after Mama too before me, when Mama was little. I called her "Ducka" apparently because she was the one who pushed me in the pram down to the lake in Central Park to feed the ducks every day. So Ducka I called her, and Aunty Ducka she became to everyone else too after that. And Old Mac had taught me how to fly kites in the park, and skim stones, and look after the horses and saddles. The two of them looked after just about everything else as well, house, stables, garden, our every need. Life could not have gone on without them.

I hated my daily piano practice, especially scales, but Mama had ways of persuading me every time.

Threats: "You will not be allowed to go out riding unless you practice first."

Bribery: "Play well enough, Merry, and you can go for a ride afterwards."

Or blackmail. Since Papa had left for the war, it was Papa she had often used to blackmail me into doing my daily piano practice: "Your Papa will be very disappointed in you, Merry, if you have not learnt your pieces by the time he comes home. Remember, Merry, you promised him you'd practice your scales every day."

The trouble was that it was true, I had promised him. But I still did not like Mama reminding me of it, and I most certainly did not like her sitting there watching me either, which was why I was sulking that morning as I played my scales, with as little application as possible and with no enthusiasm whatsoever, just so she would know how I felt.

The routine was always the same with Mama. She'd stay in the sitting room with me until I had played my scales three times without hesitation or mistake. Only then would she let me play what I wanted to play. I rarely played the pieces that my music teacher, Miss Phelps, had told me to. First of all, I didn't like her, as she was always so unsmiling and severe. She frowned all the time, and had very thin lips, and several long brown whiskers growing out of the two moles on her chin. And the pieces she told me to practice were either too difficult for me to play or I didn't like them—one or the other, usually both— which was why, as soon as I'd done my scales to Mama's satisfaction that morning, I decided not to play my practice pieces at all, and instead, began playing my favorite Mozart piece, "Andante Grazioso."

Papa loved it. I loved it too, because I thought it was the most beautiful tune I had ever heard, because I could play it well, and because Papa loved it as much as I did. He would stand behind me sometimes and hum along as I played. He always called it Merry's tune, which was why I was reminded of him every time I played it. I could almost feel he was there with us in the room that morning, his hand resting on my shoulder, even though I knew he was far away at the war.

I missed him so much: running down the path to him when he came home from work, leaping at him, making him catch me and hold me, his deep voice in the house, sitting on his lap and listening to the gramophone with him, our games of chess together by the fire in the evenings, his footstep on the stairs coming up to say goodnight to me, reading *The Ugly Duckling* to me in bed. I only had to play our tune, his tune, to feel he was back home and with me again.

As I played, I forgot my sulking, forgot Mama was there, and lost myself entirely in the tune, and in thoughts of Papa.

I was aware of Old Mac coming in with a letter for Mama, and leaving moments afterward, and paid little attention as Mama read it. But then she started up suddenly out of her chair, hand to her mouth, choking back her tears. At once I dreaded the worst.

"What, Mama?" I cried, rushing over to her. "What is it?"

"It's from your Papa," she said, recovering a little by now. "It's all right, he'll be all right. He's been wounded. He's in a hospital, in England, somewhere in the country, he says."

"Is he bad? Will he die, Mama? He won't die, will he?"

"He says we're not to worry, that he'll be up and about in no time." She was reading fast, turning the page, but saying nothing.

"What's he say, Mama? Can I read it? Please?" I asked. But she was hardly hearing me.

"It's to you as well," she replied, handing me the letter at last. As I was reading I could hear his voice in every word.

My dearest Martha, my dearest Merry,

Since I last wrote, I am afraid things have not gone too well with the regiment or with me. We were putting up a good enough fight, holding the Germans back around Mons as best we could, but there always seemed to be too many of them and too few of us, and the worst of it was they always had more men, and more horses and guns too. Big guns. There was nothing for it. We had to pull back. No army likes to retreat, but we did so in good enough order, and I know the men are still determined and in good heart, despite all the reverses and all the terrible losses we have suffered. They will stand now and hold their ground, I am sure of it.

Unfortunately though, I am no longer with them. I have been luckier than many, far too many. We have lost so many fine and brave young men, no more than boys some of them. A few weeks ago I was wounded in my shoulder, shrapnel it was, that broke my bone. They took me out of the battle, and after a couple of days in a field hospital in France, they have shipped me back to England, to a rather grand old mansion like many you see on Long Island, but grander still, which they have transformed into a military hospital for Canadian officers. It is not too far from London, and is called Bearwood House. Isn't that a strange and extraordinary coincidence? I am lying in a hospital in England that goes by the very same name as our cottage in Maine. In so many ways this place reminds me of our holidays in Maine. I look out of my window and see great trees, and at night I can often see the moon riding high through the dark clouds. I sing to the moon and I listen to the moon, as I promised. I hope you do too, Merry.

We have a park where we sit when it is sunny—which is

not very often, I have to say—and a lake with ducks that cruise about as if they own the place, very much as they do on our lake in Central Park. So, eyes open or eyes closed, I can imagine myself back at home in New York or in Maine. There are many Canadian officers here, so I am amongst friends. I must count myself a very fortunate fellow.

I am comfortable enough now, and well cared for, although I find I cannot use my left arm at all. How lucky I am that it was not my right shoulder. I can at least write to you. They tell me that, in time, when the wound is healed and my bone is mended, I shall make a full recovery. So with a bit of luck I shall be back at the Front with the men in a month or two. But for the moment, it is good to be out of it for a while. It is quiet here, and peaceful, so very peaceful. I wonder if there is anything in the world more beautiful than peace.

I long to see you both again, and think of you often, of your dear faces, of Old Mac and Aunty Ducka, our home in New York, of the trees and ducks in the park, and the rocks we climbed, and the rides we had there on Bess and Bunty, and the little black squirrels—they are all gray here in England—of the cottage in Maine and the seashore, the fishing and the sailing we did together there, all the old familiar things. How happy we were before all this. But I have to be over here, you know that.

Merry, keep practicing the piano, and not just the

Mozart piece even though, as you know, I love it the best. Groom Bess and Bunty well each morning and pick out their hooves before you go riding. And remember to tighten Bunty's girth properly, you know how he blows himself out just to fool you. I like to think of you riding out with Mama in the park—you both look so very fine on horseback. I can see you now walking by the lake, and stopping by our favorite statue of Hans Christian Andersen. Do you remember, Merry? I remember that was where I first read you The Ugly Duckling, and there would be ducks all around our feet sometimes, and listening too when they weren't quacking.

Dearest Martha, dearest Merry, do not worry about me. All will be well. Be sure, we shall in time win this war, and then I shall be home, and we shall be together again.

Ever, with my fondest love to you both, and to Old Mac and Aunty Ducka too. You are all dearer to me than you will ever know.

Papa

"Oh, Merry?" said Mama, tearful again now. "Why did I listen to him? I told him when he went to England that we should go with him, to be near him. But oh no, he wouldn't hear of it. He can be so obstinate sometimes, your Papa. 'You have to stay home in New York, where it is safe,' he said. 'The war is being fought at sea too, you know,' he said. 'It is far too dangerous for you to cross the Atlantic. There are enemy submarines out there, warships. And after all, Merry has to go to school, and she has to do her piano lessons. When all's said and done,' he said, 'it's best you stay in New York, and stay safe.' Oh, why did I listen to him, Merry? Why?"

I remember only too well the arguments before Papa went. There had been so many of them, so much begging and pleading, first that he should not go at all, but then if he really had to, that he should at least take us with him. But he was determined to go, and equally determined that we should stay. Mama and I went down to the docks that day to see him off together. I may not have wanted him to go, but in my heart of hearts I was so proud that he was, so proud to see him looking grand and smart and neat in his uniform. Even his moustache looked neater. And he stood taller in it somehow too. I remember how he had held me to him on the dockside that last time, remember the words he whispered in my ear.

"And be good to Mama, Merry. Don't be a nincompoop with her." I loved it when he called me a nincompoop, or a ninny. It's what he always said when he was trying to tick me off, but he always said it with a smile. I loved being ticked off by Papa, loved being called a nincompoop, or a ninny, loved the sound of it, loved the smile that went with it. "Whenever I see the moon, Merry," he went on, "I will think of you and sing our Mozart tune. You do the same, so that whenever we look up at the moon, wherever we are, we shall listen to the moon, and hear one another and think of one another. Promise me." I promised, and I kept that promise too.

How often afterward did I look up at the moon and hum our tune, how often did I listen to the moon and think of him.

The day when the letter came, I crouched down in front of Mama and took her hands in mine. "Silly old school, silly old piano lessons," I told her. "You were right all along, Mama. We shall go. They have schools in England, haven't they? And they've got piano teachers over there too, and probably a lot less whiskery than Miss Phelps. Let's go, Mama. We have to go. We can't just leave Papa alone in the hospital. Didn't he say how much he wants to see us? It's his way of telling us to come, I know it is."

"Do you think so, Merry? Do you really think so? What about the house, and the horses? I mean, who'll look after everything?"

"The same people who look after everything all the time, Mama," I told her. "When we go up to the cottage in the summer, doesn't Old Mac see to the garden and the horses, Mama? He loves the garden, and he loves Bunty and Bess to bits, you know he does. And they love him too. And while we're up in the cottage in Maine, having a fine time sailing and fishing and picnicking and all, doesn't Aunty Ducka keep everything in the house just fine? We have to go, Mama. Papa wants us. He needs us."

"You're right, Merry," said Mama, holding out her arms to me and hugging me close. "It's decided then. We shall go to England and see your Papa as soon as possible."

We sat down that evening and wrote a letter back to Papa, writing alternate sentences as we often did in our letters to him. It ended with me writing in capital letters. "WE ARE ON OUR WAY, DEAREST PAPA."

<hr/>

It took several weeks to arrange passage across the Atlantic. At school, when it became known I would be leaving soon, and going to England, most of my friends and teachers seemed more put out than sad, most of the teachers warning me how unwise and reckless it was to go anywhere near Europe these days, "with that terrible war going on over there." They'd been the same when they heard Papa had joined up and gone to France the year before. "Surely he doesn't need to go," said my teacher, Miss Winters, who seemed more upset than anyone by it. "I mean, after all, Merry, I thought he was Canadian, not British. So there's no call for him to go. This war is a quarrel between the British and the Germans. What has Canada got to do with it, for goodness' sake? I don't understand it."

I tried to explain Papa's decision to join up as he had explained it to me: that all his old school friends, and college friends, from Toronto, in Canada, were going, that although he had lived and worked for some time in America, he was Canadian through and through, and proud of it. He belonged now with his friends, he told me, with the boys he grew up with. If they were fighting, he should be too. He had to go. He had no choice.

Miss Winters had always been most vociferous in her opinions, something I had always admired in her, and she was again now when I told her I would be leaving school and going over to England. "Well, I've got to say what's in my heart, Merry. I think it's just a crying shame, I really do, you going off and leaving us all of a sudden like this, and you doing so well in your lessons. Your reading and your writing too are coming on so well, and they have never been easy for you, I know. You going like this, it's a crying shame! Don't get me wrong, Merry, I know why you and your Mama think you've got to do what you've got to do, we all do; and believe me, we're mighty sorry your Papa got wounded over there. But truth be told—and there are times you have to tell the truth as you see it, as you feel it—I don't think your Papa should have gone over there to fight in the first place. I mean what does all this fighting, all this killing and wounding, ever achieve? It's no way for civilized folk to sort out right from wrong. Never was, never will be. I can tell you one thing for certain sure, Merry, we aren't going to send our American boys over there to France to fight in that war, not if I have anything to do with it, that's for certain sure."

For certain sure was one of Miss Winters's favorite expressions. "I want you to promise me one thing, Merry," she went on. "Once your Papa's all well again, you'll come right back here to New York with him, where you belong, and finish your education with me. You hear me now?"

She was near to tears by the time she'd finished. I always liked Miss Winters a whole lot. All my life I'd had difficulties with reading and writing. Every other teacher I'd had, sooner or later, lost patience with me, because I couldn't read properly what was up on the blackboard or in schoolbooks like the others could, because I would take forever to write my letters and words, and even then they weren't right. All this only made things worse. Everything would go haywire in my head, letters and words would jump over one another, jumble together, and I would panic. I was often accused of not paying attention, of being lazy and stupid.

Miss Winters, though, had always explained things carefully, helped me through my difficulties, and given me time to think, to work things out. She was full of encouragement. "Your writing and reading may not be the best, Merry," she told me once, "but you play the piano wonderfully well, and you draw like an artist, like a true artist." She had a way of making me feel good about myself, about my drawings and paintings in particular. And she was the only teacher in the school who really meant what she said, who wasn't afraid to show her true feelings. We'd often hear her voice tremble and break with emotion, especially when she was reading Longfellow's poems. She loved those poems so much, which was why, I guess, we did too, most of us. Compared to her, the rest of my teachers were all so stiff and proper and buttoned up. Goodbyes with them were all very formal. Miss Winters, though, hugged me tight and long, reluctant to let me go. "God bless, Merry," she whispered in my ear. "You take care, you hear me."

Of all my friends, I knew it was only Pippa I'd really miss, Pippa Mallory. She had been my best friend since the very first day at school five years before, probably to the exclusion of any other close friendship. She was the only one who had never once teased me about my reading and writing, who had not, at one time or another, made me feel stupid. We had been almost constant companions, always in the same class at school, sitting beside one another whenever we could, walking home together, skipping through the leaves, stomping through the snow, feeding the ducks on the lake in the park, going riding, going out boating. She'd come with us to Maine most summers. The hardest thing I had to do before I left was to break the news to Pippa that I was leaving, that I had to go to England to see Papa in the hospital, and so I wouldn't be coming back for a while, not till the war was over. She hardly left my side after I told her. She never spoke about my leaving. Unlike everyone else, she was the only one who never tried to persuade me I shouldn't be going, who just seemed to understand that I had to go, and left it at that.

On the last day she never even said goodbye. When the time came, she couldn't bring herself to speak and neither could I. We stood there by the school gates, two best friends so used to telling one another our deepest secrets, revealing our highest hopes, confiding in each other our most terrible fears, and now we couldn't even find the words to say goodbye. We stood in awkward silence for some moments. In the end she handed me an envelope, then turned from me quickly and ran off.

I opened the letter. It read:

Dearest Merry,
Come back, please come back. Write me.
I love you.

Your best friend for life,
Pippa

I called after her: "I will come back, Pippa! I promise! I will!" But she was gone. I don't think she even heard me.

Chapter Seven

New York, May 1915

Time will tell

I walked the long way home that last day, as downcast as I'd ever felt. It wasn't so much that I loved school particularly. I didn't. I was simply used to it. It was my world, a part of me, and I did fear deep down that I might not be coming back, that I might never see Pippa or Miss Winters ever again. I remember it seemed to me to be like a parting of the ways, from one life to another, from the known to the unknown. As I walked, I was filled with an aching sadness, but I didn't cry, which I found strange, because I cried easily. I think perhaps I must have been too sad for tears. Wandering through the streets, with the traffic and people all around me, I was feeling utterly alone and apart. It was as if I had gone already, that I didn't belong here anymore. No one noticed me. I was invisible, a stranger in my own city, already gone, already a ghost.

At home, Mama and Old Mac and Aunty Ducka were still busy packing. It was all they seemed to have been doing for weeks. But now, many of the trunks and cases were there in the front hall. We really were going. We had our last supper together—Mama, Old Mac and Aunty Ducka, and me, where we always had it, at the long, shining table in the dining room, polished religiously every day by Aunty Ducka. In the center of the table stood the two silver pheasants glittering in the candlelight, and the four silver candlesticks, all of which Aunty Ducka kept polished too, and which she always lit for supper. Papa's place was laid too, as usual. Mama wanted it that way, she said, so it should be ready for him on the day he returned.

We hardly spoke. Aunty Ducka kept sniffing and dabbing at her nose and her eyes with her napkin, which I could see irritated Mama. Old Mac cleared his throat from time to time, just to break the silence, I think. Unlike the rest of us, he did try to make some conversation. "I hear she's a fine ship, Martha," he said, "just about the biggest there is, I reckon, and fast too. Someone told me she holds the Blue Ribbon—that's the prize awarded for the fastest ship across the Atlantic. Four red funnels, with black tips. I've seen her. She's very smart, quite magnificent. Huge. Massive. Not another ship like her. And comfortable too, luxurious, by all accounts."

Mama was too preoccupied to be listening. She kept worrying about what they might have forgotten to pack. She wasn't eating either. "Ducka, are you sure you put in my gray coat with the frogging? I told you, I'll need it in the autumn. And my peacock dressing gown, I must have that with me. And what about the photograph album? We've forgotten the photograph album, I know we have!"

"It's in, Martha," Aunty Ducka told her. "I wrapped it up and put it in myself. It's in the smaller trunk. I promise you, Martha, everything is in. And I put your peacock dressing gown right at the top, with your slippers, so they would be the first thing you see when you open the trunk. You mustn't worry so."

"Are you quite sure, Ducka? You are liable to forget things these days, you know."

"Quite sure, Martha," Aunty Ducka replied. She was used to Mama's anxiety, and her petulance too, and was endlessly patient with her. But I could see Aunty Ducka wasn't coping at all well with the thought of us leaving the next morning, which was why she left the dining room in tears some moments later.

"What's the matter with Ducka?" Mama said, quite unaware, as she often seemed to be, of Aunty Ducka's feelings. Aunty Ducka adored Mama, and did everything for her, and always had done, but Mama hardly ever seemed to notice her. She was inclined to take both Uncle Mac and Aunty Ducka for granted. She wasn't ever unkind to them, not as such, and certainly not intentionally, she couldn't be. Mama wasn't like that. But she was thoughtless, even a little offhand sometimes, and I could tell it hurt them when she was, Aunty Ducka particularly.

I went out after Aunty Ducka and found her sitting at the bottom of the stairs, her head in her hands. I sat down beside her. "You're not to worry so, Ducka," I told her. "We'll be back before you know it, all of us will be, Mama, me. Papa too. You can't get rid of us that easily." She broke down sobbing then, and leaned her head on my shoulder. It was a strange moment. I thought of how often I had been upset and crying, feeling wretched and miserable about this or that, and how I had come to sit down on these very same stairs, and of the number of times Ducka had come and sat beside me, putting her arms around me and hugging me till the tears stopped. Now here I was, doing the same for her.

"You will be a good girl, Merry, won't you?" she said through her sniffling. "Don't you go being any trouble to your Mama. And keep your feet dry. I heard tell it rains almost all the time over there in England, in that London place. Don't you go getting yourself all wet through and catching a chill, will you now?"

"I won't, Ducka," I told her. "I won't, I promise."

A few days later, and in circumstances I could never possibly have foreseen or imagined in my wildest nightmares, I would be thinking of those last moments alone with Aunty Ducka on the staircase, and how I was failing to keep that promise, like so many others I'd made to her over the years, and how, at least in this case, it wasn't my fault. There are times when it is impossible to keep promises we make.

When we came back into the dining room some minutes later, I saw that Old Mac was reading aloud from a newspaper. He stopped at once when he saw us come in. He was clearly in the middle of reading something he did not want me to hear. But I did catch the end of what Mama was saying. "It'll be all right, Mac, it's silly rumor, tittle-tattle, that's all. We are sailing tomorrow morning, and that's that, whatever the papers say. We have to. We must. It'll be fine."

"What is it, Mama?" I asked.

"Nothing, dear," she said, with a dismissive wave of her hand, "nothing that need concern you, or me, for that matter. Now Ducka, let's get this child into bed. We have an early start in the morning."

I didn't sleep much that night. The moon rode through the treetops outside my window. I sung my Mozart tune, my "Andante Grazioso," humming it again and again. I listened. Papa was there. I could hear him singing too.

Old Mac had been right. The ship wasn't just big, it was gigantic, twice the size at least of the ship Papa had sailed on, and ten times more magnificent too. She towered over the quayside, dwarfing the docks and every other ship around. She was the grandest, most majestic ship I had ever seen. Even the cranes seemed to be bowing down to her, overawed in her presence.

◆•◦•◆

Old Mac and Aunty Ducka found porters for us and escorted Mama and me up the gangplank onto the ship. Inside, the ship was as splendid as it was huge, more how I had always imagined a palace to be than a ship. Everyone on deck seemed to be rushing about in a high state of excitement, going somewhere, but not quite sure where. They were, I remember thinking, rather like excited chickens. There was shouting and laughing and crying all around me, a cacophony of human confusion.

The sailors, the porters, the maids were all in uniform. I never saw so many smart salutes or bobbed curtsies in all my life, a smiling "Welcome on board, Miss" with every one. There were chandeliers and mirrors everywhere, gold paint, carpeted staircases, polished wood and gleaming brass handrails.

Without Old Mac and Aunty Ducka there to help us along, I think we should have been lost entirely, and never found our cabin at all. We kept losing sight of our porters and our luggage in the melee of passengers that crammed the corridors, corridors that seemed to go on forever. The porters were always rushing on ahead, and Old Mac had to keep calling them back. Aunty Ducka was holding my hand very firmly all the time, as she always had done when we crossed roads in New

York; and she was doing it now partly so that I didn't get lost, or left behind or knocked over, but also, I am sure, because she knew the time for parting would be soon, and she didn't want it to come, didn't want to let go of me. That was certainly why I clung to her hand just as tightly.

Somehow, we kept our porters in sight and eventually caught up with them. After they showed us into our cabin, we found we still had an hour or two to go before we were due to sail. Once inside, and with the door closed, it was a lot calmer and quieter. But none of us seemed to know quite what to say. Even Old Mac was lost for words. Aunty Ducka and Mama busied themselves unpacking our trunks and our cases, and filling the closet and bureau, while Old Mac sat in a chair clearing his throat and reading the newspaper, looking rather too often at his fob watch. I simply wanted this parting to be done with, for the crying to happen, which I knew it would. I could feel it welling up inside me. I wanted it to be over, for them to be gone. Aunty Ducka was laying out Mama's peacock dressing gown on the end of her bed, putting out her slippers. That was the moment she could not contain her tears any longer. I went to sit beside her, and put my head on her shoulder. She patted my hand. She had kind workaday hands, familiar hands.

The cabin was much larger than I had expected, and as palatial as the rest of the ship. We had our own porthole, and my bed was right underneath it, so I could kneel on it and look out.

I could see the dockside below was crowded with passengers still boarding, some soldiers in uniform among them, Canadian soldiers, Old Mac told me. And it was true; some had uniforms just like Papa's. There were, as well, several families with children coming on board; some of the children looked about twelve or so, about my age, and that cheered me. Passengers in their hundreds were crowding the rails, waving and laughing, and many of them crying too. I could hear a band playing somewhere, the big drum thumping. I could feel the engines throbbing. It would not be long now. Aunty Ducka was kneeling beside me on the bed, looking out of the porthole, her arm around me. "I so wish I was coming with you, Merry," she said.

"Me too, Ducka," I told her. "Me too."

I was aware then that Old Mac was talking in urgent whispers to Mama behind me. I turned to look. The two of them were in a huddle together by the cabin door. I listened hard because I could tell from the confidential way they were speaking that they did not want me to overhear. He was showing her the same newspaper he'd been reading. "It's in this paper too," he was saying. "I'm telling you. I don't like it, Martha, that's all I'm saying. They wouldn't say it unless they meant it. Why should they?"

"Stop it, Mac," Mama whispered. "Merry will hear. I told you before. I don't listen to tittle-tattle. And that's what it is, just rumor. No, it's worse, it's propaganda. Yes, that's what it is, German propaganda, German threats. You cannot believe everything you read in the newspapers. Anyway, I don't care, even if it is true. I have to get to England, I have to be with him, that's all there is to it, Mac. England is where this ship is sailing, and we're sailing with it. You said it yourself, there's no ship afloat that will get us there faster than this one."

That was when the ship's siren sounded, and moments later someone came knocking loudly, insistently, on the cabin door. "Pardon me," came a voice. "All ashore! All ashore now, if you please! If you're not sailing with the ship. All visitors ashore!" The four of us looked at each other, and then found ourselves clinging to one another. I never in my life before had seen Old Mac cry. He did then. We all did, Mama too. Aunty Ducka held her and kissed her, and for just a moment I saw my mother become a little girl again in her arms, a child in need of comfort.

We were up on deck a while later, leaning over the rails, as the ship prepared to leave. I was waving down, shouting my last goodbyes at Uncle Mac and Aunty Ducka again and again, until my arm ached, until my throat was sore with crying. Then, all of a sudden, I noticed there was an excited kerfuffle down below on the dockside, and I heard gales of laughter and cheering from the crowd both down on the quay and around us up on deck. It was a moment or two before I saw what the kerfuffle was all about. It was a young family, a father carrying two tearful children and a mother with a babe in arms. They were struggling to find a way through the crowd on the quayside, arriving flustered, breathless and full of apologies, at the very last moment at the foot of the gangplank, just as it was about to be hauled away. To raucous cheers and applause from all around they were helped through the crowd, and up the gangplank.

But then came a strange change of mood. There was quite suddenly no more cheering, but instead a murmur and a hush passed through the crowd, like a chill wind, like an ill wind. It seemed to me like a universal shudder of fear, which became an unnatural silence. I could not understand the reason for it at all, until I glimpsed what so many seemed already to have noticed. As the family were almost up the gangplank and into the ship, the porters helping them with their luggage, a black cat was dashing down past them. Just at the very last moment, even as the gangplank was being withdrawn, he leaped out over the gap onto the dockside and disappeared into the crowd. There was laughter then, but nervous laughter. The band struck up again, but the mood of celebration was broken. Gulls circled the ship, crying, screaming. I looked up at Mama. She tried to smile at me, to reassure me, but she could not.

As the ship's siren sounded, and she edged slowly away from the dockside, the deck throbbing under our feet, I was still waving. But neither Uncle Mac nor Aunty Ducka was waving back anymore. Aunty Ducka could hardly bear to look at us. She kept turning away and burying her head in Old Mac's shoulder. Uncle Mac, though, was looking. He never took his eyes off us, not for a moment. It was as if he knew he was looking at us for the last time, and I found myself thinking just the same about him, about them, about New York and everyone I had known there. Under my breath I said goodbye to Pippa, to Miss Winters. The cheering and waving, ship to shore, shore to ship, had resumed by now, but it was halfhearted, sporadic. We stayed there until we were so far away that Uncle Mac and Aunty Ducka were lost in the crowd, and we couldn't make them out anymore.

Mama wanted to go down to the cabin at once, but I insisted on staying on deck. "Please, Mama, just until we pass the Statue of Liberty." So we stayed. I could not get over how much smaller Liberty seemed as we sailed by her in our great ship. Some of the other passengers were waving her goodbye, as if she too were family they were leaving behind. So I did too. But Mama didn't. She had turned away, and was glancing down at the folded newspaper in her hand. I could see she was worried. "You and Uncle Mac," I said. "You were talking about something, something in that newspaper. You were, weren't you? Back at home you were doing the same, and down in the cabin just now too. What was it, Mama?"

"I told you, Merry. Nothing," she replied firmly, angrily almost. "Nothing at all. Everything is fine, just fine. Come along, Merry. Let's go down to the cabin. It's cold up here. I'm shivering."

I realized then that I was too. I took one last look at the Statue of Liberty, at the skyline of New York, then turned away and went below.

As I lay in our cabin that night, I wasn't thinking about Uncle Mac or Aunty Ducka, or Pippa, or even Papa lying wounded in a hospital in England, as I knew I should have been. All I could think of was that black cat running down the gangplank and leaping out over the water onto the quayside. A black cat leaving the ship like that had to mean something, I was sure of it. But I couldn't work out whether it meant good luck or bad luck. *Time will tell,* I thought, *time will tell.*

Chapter Eight

A beacon of hope

They had all hoped that Dr. Crow's instincts were right, that music might somehow restore Lucy's sunken spirits and lift her out of herself, that it might even unlock her memory, and her voice too. But Jim was, from the start, deeply skeptical about the whole thing—he wasn't too fond either of the music that all too often wafted through the house these days. He could see, though, that for Mary, any hope was better than none, that she was pinning so much on Lucy's recovery, that this strange, silent child from nowhere had come to mean the world to her. So Jim did his best to keep his doubts to himself, and put up, mostly uncomplaining, with the sound of music that, day in, day out, filled the house, that greeted him every time he came home.

After a while, though, even Jim had to acknowledge that there were some signs that Dr. Crow's faith in the restorative powers of music had not been entirely misplaced. Lucy did come downstairs sometimes, only very rarely, but this was a change, an improvement. They never heard her coming, no creak on the stairs, no lifting of a latch. She would simply be there, a sudden silent presence in the kitchen. They'd turn and see her standing there—still as a ghost, Alfie thought sometimes—an apparition at the bottom of the stairs, always wrapped in her blanket, and holding her teddy bear. She would not be looking at them, but rather at the gramophone, listening intently to the music, seemingly almost hypnotized by the record going round and round. Realizing it had to be the music that was at last getting Lucy up and about, Mary or Alfie—even Jim sometimes, if Mary reminded him—would wind up the gramophone whenever they passed it by, or whenever they heard the music slowing down, trying always to keep the gramophone playing as constantly as possible.

Despite all this, Lucy still spent most of her days lying upstairs in bed, propped up on her pillows, living inside her silence, staring out the window or more often up at the ceiling. But from time to time Mary did discover her out of her bed, more often at nighttimes, and when no music was playing too. They would hear her humming away in her room—and they were all sure by now it was humming, not moaning. Several times now, when Mary had looked in on Lucy as they came up to bed, she had found her out of bed and standing by the window, gazing up at the moon and humming that tune again, softly, sadly, and not just to herself, Mary thought, but to the moon. She seemed fascinated by the moon.

As time went by, they did notice that Lucy seemed more and more to time her appearances downstairs—and they were becoming ever more frequent now—to coincide with meals. As she listened to the music she would stand there by the gramophone, still keeping her distance from them, but watching them eat. Every time she came down, Mary would make a great fuss of her, hugging her fondly and taking her hand, trying all she could to encourage her to come to the table to be one of them.

"You're family now, Lucy dear," she would say. "You, Uncle Billy, Alfie, Jim, me—we're all your family now." She would tell her about Uncle Billy, how he was one of the family too, and how once she was up and about a bit more, she would take her down to the boathouse to meet him, and to see the *Hispaniola*. "Billy's done wonders with that boat, Lucy. It's beautiful, beautiful. You wait till you see it."

But Lucy would not sit with them, however often Mary encouraged her to. It was Alfie's idea to put a chair for her against the wall beside the gramophone. It quickly became her place. She would always sit there, and eat her food there too. She seemed to eat much better with them down in the kitchen than upstairs alone in her bedroom. She was eating properly now, not picking at it as she had before.

One evening, before Lucy came downstairs, Alfie decided to try something. He moved her chair from the wall by the gramophone over to the kitchen table. When she saw it there, she hesitated for long moments, her brow furrowed, clearly unsure of herself. They all thought she was going to turn around at once, and go back upstairs, but to their great joy and surprise, she walked slowly across the kitchen and came to sit down with them at the table.

As they sat there with her, they all realized that they had just witnessed a moment of supreme importance. Not a word had been said, not a look passed between them, but they all felt a surge of sudden hope. They all felt that a corner had been turned, and that this might really be a promise of better things to come.

The next day Alfie showed her how to wind the gramophone up herself, to blow the dust off the needle, how to wipe the record with a damp cloth before you put it on, how to lower the needle on gently to make it play, everything in fact that Dr. Crow had taught them a few weeks before, all of which had become almost second nature to them by now. Alfie had tried to teach her once or twice before, but she had shown little interest in learning how to operate it. Now, quite suddenly, she was not only attentive but clearly impatient to get on and do it for herself. And when she did, it was soon obvious to Alfie that he needn't have bothered to teach her at all. She seemed to know how it had to be done perfectly well already. She managed it with consummate ease, an ease born of familiarity. Alfie was sure she had done it before.

From that day on Lucy always put the records on for herself—no one else had to bother anymore. She took complete charge of the gramophone, made it her own. Dressed now in the clothes Mary had made for her, she'd be downstairs, all day and every day, playing the gramophone. As soon as a record was finished, she'd play it again or put on another one. She'd never let it wind down either.

She may not have been communicating with them any more than she had before, but she was there, living among them. Sometimes she would even help Mary with her bread-making. Lucy seemed in particular to love kneading the dough. But mostly, she would sit there for hour after hour, swathed in her blanket, one foot tucked under herself, rocking back and forth, her teddy bear sitting smiling beside the gramophone. Sometimes Lucy would be humming along to the music. Humming seemed to bring Lucy great comfort, even if the tunes were sometimes sad. For her they all seemed to be like lullabies. She seemed to know many of them already—either that or she was picking them up very fast. It was the humming—and the bread-making too—that gave the whole family even more cause to be optimistic now about her recovery. After all, if she could hum, then surely one day she must speak, and not just a word or two, but properly.

One day soon, Alfie kept reassuring his mother, Lucy would speak her memories, would know who she was again, and tell them at last how she came to be there. What a story she would have to tell.

Dr. Crow always brought along a new record every time he came to visit, but Lucy did not like all of them. Anything too loud she would not play. It was above all piano music she liked to listen to, and one particular record by Mozart best of all. She played the doctor's record of Mozart's "Andante Grazioso" piano sonata over and over again. She began and ended every day playing only that piece on the gramophone, often with tears in her eyes as she listened, as she hummed. She clearly adored it. And in time the whole family came to love it too, even if Jim still found the constant music hard to bear sometimes. But he too came to love "Lucy's tune," as they called it.

"She sings it beautiful, don't she?" he told Mary one evening, after both Lucy and Alfie had gone up to bed. "She sings it like an angel."

"That is because Lucy is from heaven," Mary told him. "Like all children. I never believed anything before as much as I believe this, Jimbo: that child is a gift to us from heaven, just as Alfie was. I told you before. It weren't just luck that it was Alfie and you who found her on St. Helen's and brought her home. It were meant to be."

But despite everything, all the progress, all the hope, it was obvious to Jim and Alfie that from time to time Mary was near to despair. The weeks and the months had gone by, and still Lucy would not speak to any of them, or could not. So it was impossible to know what she understood and what she did not. All questions went unanswered, and were scarcely ever acknowledged even with a look. She avoided eye contact almost entirely, except just occasionally with Alfie; and even then, if their eyes ever met, she would always look away quickly.

Every time the doctor came over to Bryher, Mary and the doctor discussed Lucy's condition, in depth and at length: what might be the cause, or causes, of Lucy's unwillingness, or inability, to communicate, and what might be done about it. Dr. Crow had become both fascinated and disturbed by this strange and unfathomable child at the Wheatcrofts' house, and kept a meticulous record of every visit in his journal.

***

From Dr. Crow's journal, 28th July 1915

Just returned this evening from Bryher, having called on four patients, including Jack Brody and Lucy Lost. Rather fatigued. Mrs. Cartright has made me fish pie again. I can never abide it, but dare not tell her so. Eleven years she has been with me now as Housekeeper, and for eleven years I have been hinting to her that fish pie is not to my taste. Nothing I say makes any difference. She is an admirable woman, and a great help to me in the house, looks after me, and the patients, most diligently. But her fish pie … her fish pie is execrable.

Lucy Lost in the Wheatcroft household is an enigma to me, a sheer bewilderment, but a wonder too. Physically, there can be no doubt that she is much improved. The cough that has troubled her for so long, ever since she was discovered on St. Helen's, has all but left her. Her chest is clear, her temperature normal. Her ankle is quite mended. But she has put on very little weight. She is, in my opinion, still far too thin and frail. But Mrs. Wheatcroft is caring for her wonderfully well, of that I have no doubt.

Mary Wheatcroft is a woman who knows her own mind. I know how long and hard she fought to bring her poor brother Billy home out of the asylum a few years ago. I was with her in her fight, witnessed her fierce courage and determination throughout it all. She was like a tigress. And she has cared for him, day in, day out, every day since. She's a marvel. And now, not content with that, she has taken on Lucy Lost, and with the same fierce determination too. She mothers the child as if she were her own. I might even say, though not to her of course, that she over-mothers her, such is her overwhelming affection for the girl.

Indeed, the whole family seems to have welcomed her wholeheartedly into their midst. None of them seems in the least perturbed by Lucy's strange ways of being. Jim Wheatcroft does confide in me that the music she plays almost constantly on my gramophone does make him want to scream sometimes. And he often scolds me—as indeed he did today, tongue in cheek, I hope—for bringing what he sometimes refers to as "that ruddy machine" into the house in the first place.

But they know, and I know now, that the music she listens to has awoken something in her, some distant memory, it is to be hoped, and has without doubt given her an interest in life again. She is finding herself through the music—I am convinced of it. She is clearly a great deal happier inside herself, although it is true that she still never smiles—something, I know, that greatly upsets Mrs. Wheatcroft. I suspect that deep down this is because she has little to smile about. But at least the child now seems to be quite at ease in the house with her new family around her.

I can see she likes to wear the clothes Mrs. Wheatcroft has made for her. She likes to make bread, and to have her hair brushed for her in front of the fire. She still does not speak of course, but she does hum to the music. I believe she finds a real and deep joy in music, as I do. I do not think I am being fanciful, but sometimes I believe I can see the light of understanding in her eyes as she listens to the gramophone, in particular when she plays the last record I brought to her, the Mozart piano piece. I have forgotten the name of it, but it is beautiful, supremely beautiful, and she loves it.

There is still no telling of course where she came from, nor who she might be. The only words she has been heard to speak: "Lucy" and "piano." She has not repeated any of them, I am told. She does not seem to me even to want to speak, so she does not try. Observing her, I have the feeling that there is within her a deep sadness that inhibits both her speech and her memory. The music has helped lift the sadness a little, but only a little. (Quite why she appears to be so obsessed with piano music in particular, I cannot imagine. Sadly, she now has all the piano records I possess.)

She does, I have noted, especially like to be with young Alfie. Mrs. Wheatcroft confirmed this impression. This morning, Mrs. Wheatcroft tells me, before Alfie went off to school, Lucy followed him outside to feed the hens with him. Whilst Mrs. Wheatcroft is delighted by this, she did confess to me that it vexed her that Lucy seemed to go out so willingly with Alfie—and without being asked too—when she herself has so often tried unsuccessfully to persuade Lucy to accompany her out onto the farm, to go to see Uncle Billy down in his boatshed, or on the 'Hispaniola,' to go shrimping, or on walks around the island.

(I saw Uncle Billy working away on his beloved boat as I came away from the house, and he waved to me cheerily, and he was singing. He is clearly in good heart. His moods will return of course, they always do, but he has been well for a good while now—or as well as a seriously delusional depressive, for that is what he is, will ever be. I am sure this is entirely due to Mrs. Wheatcroft's diligent care and attention.)

This morning was, I am told, the very first time Lucy Lost has ventured outside since she was found, and must be, it is to be hoped, a sign of significant progress. I did emphasize again to Mrs. Wheatcroft how important I felt it was now to encourage Lucy to go outside rather more, to make a habit of it if possible. I told her that walking will make her stronger, and improve her appetite, that the natural world about her will make her happier, which it does, of course, with all of us—this I firmly believe to be true. Mrs. Wheatcroft told me again that she is reluctant to oblige her to do anything, that Lucy only turns away from her if ever she tries. But she has assured me she will try to encourage her as best she can. More fresh air, more walking, more chicken-feeding, that's the best medicine for her, I told her.

After I left the house, I met Alfie down on the quayside on his way back from school, and I took the opportunity to commend his efforts on Lucy's behalf, and to tell him also how important it is that he should continue to take Lucy out and about whenever he possibly can. He has promised he will try. He is a fine boy. They are indeed a fine family, but I do have some sympathy for Jim. Mrs. Wheatcroft is a marvelous woman, strong and handsome too, but formidable, determined, outspoken, ferociously so at times—in some ways, not unlike Mrs. Cartright. Neither of them are women to cross, I should say. Such women make me glad I am a bachelor, and confirm in my mind my determination that I should always remain so.

But then again I have to acknowledge a sneaking envy of Jim. Formidable though his wife may be, she is nonetheless a very personable and pleasant woman, and I should imagine therefore the best of companions. A man like Jim Wheatcroft deserves such a woman. I think there is no one on these islands better thought of than he, though many of his fellow fishermen tell me that he is far better at growing potatoes and flowers than catching fish. But then fishermen are inclined, I have discovered, to be somewhat critical of one another's prowess, even un-kind sometimes.

As I crossed back to St. Mary's this evening under gathering storm clouds, my thoughts turned to poor young Jack Brody, whose leg—what is left of it—still will not heal, still pains him night and day, and always will, I fear, despite anything I can do. He cannot speak in words that make any sense. I see in his eyes that he only wishes to be out of it, that every mo-ment of every day is an agony for him, that it shames him to be like this, that he'd make an end of himself if he could. He is scarcely more than a boy. His sad plight brought to mind all the thousands of dreadfully wounded young men living out such lives all over the country, and the thousands more there will be of them before this terrible war is over.

I stood at the prow of the boat and breathed in deep, hoping the salt sea air might clear the heaviness in my heart. But there was no comfort there. As I looked out over the surging gray sea, all I could think of was our brave ships far away over the horizon, and the German submarines lurking beneath the surface, and the terrible losses they have inflicted upon us. The thought of all those poor drowned boys, of their grieving mothers, and the thought of Jack Brody, condemned to wretchedness and pain for the rest of his life, saddened my heart more than I can say. Lucy Lost is a beacon of hope to me, as she is to so many on these islands.

----------◆◆◆◆----------

Lucy would often stand in the kitchen these days gazing out the window, particularly when she was waiting for Alfie to come home from school. She would linger by the door, longing, it seemed to Mary, to go out, but never quite daring to do so on her own. No matter how much Mary encouraged her, she never ventured farther than the front door step, unless it was with Alfie. Seeing to the hens with Alfie, picking up the eggs and feeding them, morning and evening, had now become the highlight of every day for her.

First thing in the morning she would listen to her Mozart piece on the gramophone, then go out with Alfie to open up the hens, and last thing at night she'd help him shut them up. Even before he was ready, she'd be waiting there by the back door as Alfie put on his cap. "Coming, Lucy?" he'd say, shaking the bucket of corn. He could see that she was full of anxiety every time she stepped outside, but that even so she still wanted to do it. She'd follow him out, moving like a frightened fawn, looking around her nervously, staying close to his side, holding on to his elbow sometimes, all the way across the garden to the henhouse. Alfie tried all he could to persuade her to carry the bucket of corn for him perhaps, or to open the henhouse door, but she would stand back, watching him, nervously chewing her knuckle, and always clutching her teddy bear, always swathed in her blanket. Both teddy bear and blanket went with her everywhere.

It was many days before Alfie managed to get her to come up close to the henhouse when he opened it up, to throw a handful of corn to the hens, or to collect the eggs or fetch the water for them. He could see that throwing the corn for them made her particularly fearful. The hens would come running toward her and cluck around her feet, and when they did she'd always cling on tighter to Alfie's arm, or hide behind him. It was collecting the eggs she really took to, just so long as the hens were far enough away and busy feeding. Each egg seemed like a wonder to her as she picked it up. She'd hold it to her cheek and feel the warmth.

Afterward, at breakfast, Mary would get her to choose her own egg, and soon Lucy was boiling it herself, buttering her bread and slicing it, then dipping her "soldiers" in. Every egg was a treat for her, and that was just the start of it. There were still no smiles, no words; but Mary minded less now, because Lucy's appetite was becoming almost as voracious as Alfie's. And within a week or two, all that earlier nervousness over the feeding of the hens had vanished. She had made everything to do with the hens her responsibility—just as long as Alfie came with her.

Meanwhile Alfie was beginning to feel a fondness for her that he had never felt with anyone before. She could not speak, yet he felt they were somehow in tune with one another, easy together, trusting. There came an evening when this silent friendship was sealed in a most unexpected way. Lucy was sitting by the kitchen window, looking out at the darkening sky. She was humming quietly to the music on the gramophone, when she suddenly got up, came over to him, and took him by the hand. Mary and Jim were as astonished as Alfie was. She was insistent, pulling him to his feet. He went out with her into the moonlit garden. They could hear the sea lapping listlessly on Green Bay. They could see the glow of the lamp in the window of Uncle Billy's sail loft. There wasn't a breath of wind. They could hear singing.

"That's Uncle Billy, Lucy," Alfie said, "I told you about him and his singing, didn't I? Mother said he was in a grump today when she took him his lunch. Better now, by the sounds of it. Only sings when he's happy. I'll take you down to meet him one day, shall I? I've told him all about you. Only if you feel like it, of course."

But Lucy wasn't listening. She was tapping him on the shoulder urgently, then pointing up at the moon. Alfie looked. It was full, and seemed close, as close as he had ever seen it, so close he could see quite clearly the mountains on its surface. Alfie felt her hand creep into his. He knew somehow that he mustn't speak, that she wanted him to join her in her silence, and simply listen. It was, he thought, as if they were sharing the same secret, a secret they shared only with the moon, a secret that couldn't be spoken.

They stood there for long moments, listening to the sea. Then she began to hum, that same tune, her favorite tune. Alfie hummed it with her, because he felt she wanted him to. When it was over, they stood there listening for a while longer, listening to the moon now, it seemed to Alfie, as much as to the breathing of the ocean. Alfie found himself thinking of those moments for days afterward. He could make no sense of what had happened, only that he was sure it had been as precious a time for her as it had been for him, a time he would never forget.

———◆———

It was while she and Alfie were opening up the hens one foggy morning a week or so later, just before Alfie went off to school, that she happened to look up and see the horse. Peg came wandering out of the fog through the field toward the house, grazing as she went, tugging at the grass, swishing her raggedy tail. When the horse lay down and rolled and rolled, loving every moment of it, and snorting and farting as she did so, Lucy looked up at Alfie, and smiled. It was the first time Alfie had ever seen her smile.

"So you like horses, do you?" he said. "I'm telling you, you got to watch out for that Peg, Lucy. She's got a real nasty streak in her, she has. She does her work all right, but she don't like people one bit. Bites your bum whenever she can, likes to have a good kick at you too. And whatever you do, Lucy, don't you never try to get on her and ride her."

Lucy seemed transfixed by the horse, and was clearly not

listening to a word he was saying. "I hope to goodness you understand what I'm saying, Lucy. I been talking to you for a long while now. What is it? Three months? And I still don't know for sure if you've understood a single word. I think you have, but I'm still not sure. You don't have to speak to me, not ever, not if you don't want to. Just nod if you understand me, right?"

She nodded then, without turning round. She could not take her eyes off the horse. "That's good then," Alfie went on, as surprised as he was excited. "I'll go on doing all the talking then, shall I? And you can do all the listening, and the nodding. That suit you? And you'll talk when you're good and ready, is that it?"

She nodded again.

Alfie went off to school with a spring in his step and a song in his heart that day. Lucy had smiled! Lucy had nodded! Lucy had understood, definitely understood.

Long after Alfie had gone to school she was still out there in the garden, still gazing at Peg. Jim came out later, and found her there on his way down to the boat. He called Mary outside to look. He spoke quietly so that Lucy wouldn't hear. "Mary-moo," he said. "I reckon that's the first time she's stayed a while outside the house, on her own, without Alfie."

"Then why don't she speak to us, Jimbo?" Mary said. "She's got so much to say, I know she has. Why don't she let it out?

There's so much she could be telling us, so much we don't know about her."

"And a fair bit we do," Jim told her. "We certainly know she likes music, right enough, don't we? Not much doubt about that, is there? She hums her tunes. That ruddy gramophone is on all the time, isn't it? That's something, surely to goodness. And look at her. She likes horses too, even Peg, and no one likes Peg. She'll come round. We got to give her time, Marymoo. I mean, look how she's come on. She's up and about all the time now. She even eats like a ruddy horse these days, and she loves feeding the hens. And she's taken quite a shine to young Alfie, if you ask me. He's done wonders with her, Marymoo, wonders. And so have you, so have you."

"You think so, Jim?" Mary said, turning to him, and becoming tearful. "You really think so?"

"You heard what Alfie told us before he went off to school," Jim went on. "When she saw Peg, she smiled at him, didn't she? That's the first smile! And he's dead sure now that she understands a whole lot more than we ever thought she did. Honest to God, I never thought that girl understood a word anyone said. For God's sakes, did you ever think she would smile? Well, she has. So cheer up, girl."

"That's twice now you've taken the Lord's name in vain this morning, Jim Wheatcroft," Mary said, suddenly herself again, and quite recovered. "You should wash your mouth out with soapy water." She pushed him away from her playfully. "Go fishing, do something useful, why don't you? And don't go too far out in this fog. I don't like the look of it at all."

"Oh, stop your worrying, Marymoo, it'll lift," Jim told her. "Bit of sea mist, that's all it is."

Chapter Nine

Whiteout

It was later that morning when Jim was out fishing in the fog off the back of Samson, and while Alfie was still at school, that Lucy went missing. Mary had gone out for a few minutes to dig some potatoes for supper. She had left Lucy sitting by the gramophone listening to her music as usual, but when she got back she was gone, and there was no music. The record was still going round and round on the gramophone, the needle clicking away rhythmically, ominously, in the silence of the house. A terrible fear came over her. Lucy would never have left it like that, not if she was at home. She ran upstairs to Lucy's bedroom, calling for her all the time, but knowing already in her heart of hearts that she had gone. Downstairs again, she saw Lucy's blanket, folded neatly on Jim's fireside chair, her teddy bear lying on it, arm outstretched. Wherever she went, in or out of the house, she had always taken them with her. Mary had never known her to be parted from either of them before, not for a moment.

Beside herself now with worry, Mary ran out of the house and stood there, calling for her, shouting for her. She could not imagine where she might have gone, and so could not begin to think where to start looking. The island was small enough, no more than a couple of miles end to end, but she could be anywhere. Small though it was, Lucy would be utterly lost out there, especially in this fog. After all, she had never been farther than the henhouse at the bottom of the garden. Wherever she had wandered off to, she would have no idea how to get back again. There were the towering cliffs, hundreds of feet high, at Hell Bay. If she were to get too close to the edge of the cliff path . . . It didn't bear thinking about.

And then Mary remembered it was low water, the tide turning. If Lucy wandered too far out onto the sandbanks, she could easily be trapped by the incoming tide. It had happened only the year before to little Daisy Fellows. The water was already up around her neck when they found her, and she couldn't swim. They'd only just got to her in time.

There was old Mr. Jenkins's mad dog that he never had tied up. He'd attacked children before. And the bull was in with the cows in the field below Watch Hill, and everyone knew he had a nasty streak in him. Lucy could be anywhere. Anything could have happened to her.

Panic was rising in Mary, erupting. She could not control it. She found she was not shouting for Lucy anymore but screaming for her. And she was running. Wherever she ran—up Watch Hill and Samson Hill, into the town, around the church and the graveyard, along Popplestones Bay, out to Heathy Hill—wherever she went, whoever she met, she'd ask time and again if anyone had seen Lucy Lost, but no one had. The alarm once raised, soon almost everyone was out scouring the island for Lucy, but by now the blanket of fog had settled thick over the island. It was a whiteout. Mary couldn't see more than a few yards in front of her.

Lucy was still missing when Alfie and the other Bryher children came back from Tresco on the school-boat later that afternoon. Once they found out what had happened, all of them joined in the search with everyone else. Someone told Alfie his mother was in the church. He found her there, on her knees, praying silently. She looked up at him, her eyes full of tears. "God is good," she whispered. "He will protect her. He will, won't he, Alfie?" They held one another in the dark silence of the church, until all the tears stopped, until she was calm enough to gather herself again. "Come along, Mary," she said then. "No good weeping and wailing, and feeling sorry for yourself. Don't help no one. God helps those who help themselves. Let's go and find her, Alfie."

They searched together after that, each reassuring and en-couraging the other as best they could, both of them all the while hiding their worst fears. With the island shrouded in this whiteout of a fog, and still no sign of Lucy after long hours of searching, people were beginning to lose hope. Fog or not, everyone knew well enough that, as time passed, it was less and less likely she would be found safe and well. She wasn't just lost. Something must have happened to her. They shouted and called for her all over the island, blew whistles, even rang the church bell, but there was no sign of her, no response. The fog seemed to soak up all sound, muffling even the crying of the gulls and the piping of the oystercatchers. The light was fading fast now, the fog darkening around them, and with it came a sense of hopelessness.

Everyone was beginning to realize there was little point in calling out anymore, or even in looking for much longer. After all, Lucy Lost could not speak to answer, could she? And anyway, hadn't they searched everywhere again and again, all along the cliffs and the beaches, every field and hedgerow and garden, every barn and shed? Lucy Lost seemed to have vanished as mysteriously as she had appeared. She had come out of nowhere. She had gone back there.

There were even whisperings now—and not only among the children—that maybe the story about Lucy Lost being a ghost might be true after all. She was the ghost child of St. Helen's, a poor lost soul condemned to wander there alone till the end of time. Ghosts come and go as they please, don't they? They can be visible or invisible, materialize as and when they like, can't they? As the search became ever more desperate, this idea, however absurd it seemed to some, gained more and more credence. Some believed it absolutely. If Lucy Lost had disappeared, and there was no sign of her, no body found, then Lucy Lost had to have been a ghost all along.

Even Alfie and Mary, who of course knew her far better than anyone else there, and who knew well enough that Lucy was flesh and blood, could not get it out of their minds that there might be some truth in the story. They too were losing heart with every hour that passed. But like everyone else they went on looking through the blinding fog, searching the heather on the high moors, on Watch Hill, on Samson Hill, checking again all the cists and ancient burial sites up there where Lucy might possibly have climbed in and taken shelter, and then around the rocks in Hell Bay and Droppynose Point. Even when Mary and Alfie were on the coastal path and close to the cliff edge, with the sea no more than a stone's throw away, still they could not see the water below. They could hardly hear it either. The sound of the sea was all but swallowed by the fog, like everything else, like Lucy Lost herself.

Mary and Alfie did not speak anymore. There was no need. There was no point. They shared each other's worst fears. Alfie held his mother's hand tight, as tightly as she was holding his. Every shadowy figure that loomed up out of the fog they hoped would be Lucy, but it never was. It was someone else out searching, as they were.

"Nothing?" Mary would ask them, always hopefully, but fearing and knowing already the answer.

"Nothing" came the reply, every time.

"We keep looking then, and we keep praying," Mary would say, "looking and praying." To everyone they met, she sounded as determined as ever, but Alfie could sense now that even she was losing any last vestige of hope.

They had searched the dunes behind Rushy Bay yet again and were walking back along the beach on Green Bay when they heard Jim's voice ahead of them in the fog. "That you, Marymoo?" he said. "It is, isn't it! And Alfie too? What you doing out in this?" They could see him better now, a walking shadow looming out of the fog. "Never seen a fog like it. Fish seemed to like it though." He held up his bucket of fish and shook it. "You'll be pleased with me, Marymoo, a dozen good mackerel, and a fine sea bass. I got a nice crab for Uncle Billy too. Not bad, eh? And look who was there to greet me on the beach when I came in!"

Out of the gloom behind him came Peg, plodding over the sand, and she wasn't alone. Lucy was up there on her back. "We never knew our Lucy could ride, did we?" said Jim. "What's up? You're looking like you seen a ghost or something."

Mary couldn't say a word. She simply stood there on the beach, covering her face with her hands and sobbing. Alfie did the explaining for her. "Lucy's been missing all day, Father. The whole island's been out looking too, all of us. We thought she'd gone over a cliff or something. Where's she been?" Peg had walked right up to him now and was nuzzling his shoulder.

"She's been with Uncle Billy, haven't you, girl?" Jim said. "Billy says he were out in the fog, on his way back from doing a bit of shrimping out in the bay like he does when no one's about—he likes fog, our Billy does—and along Lucy comes riding up on Peg, and she don't seem to know where she is, he says, which is hardly surprising, and she's a bit upset. So he takes her home to the boatshed. They been eating shrimps all afternoon, he says. And working on the sails for the *Hispaniola*. She's good with a needle, he says. Then after a while he thought time was going on, and didn't quite know what to do with her, so he'd reckoned he'd bring her home, her and Peg both. And that's when I met up with them, on the beach, when I came in from fishing. They was just walking out of the fog. Give me quite a fright, they did. Uncle Billy went off home, and here she is.

"And look at her, Marymoo," he went on. "Happy as you like, I'd say. What're you crying for, Mary?" he said, putting his arm around her. "She's back, isn't she? Seems she likes horses as much as her piano music, I reckon. Knows how to ride them too. Look, she got no reins, no saddle, no nothing. Rides Peg with her knees. She knows her horses all right, rides like she's been doing it all her life. And you know what Peg's like. She don't allow it. She don't allow no one to ride her, do she? She's a pullin' horse, a cart horse, not a ridin' horse. I've tried getting on her once or twice in my time, so's young Alfie, so have lots of folk, and every one of us has ended up on our bottoms in a hedge or a ditch or in a patch of nettles. She can't stand anyone sitting on her, can she? But look at her now. Who'd have thought it, Marymoo, eh! Lucy riding Peg easy as pie."

Laughing, he reached up, and lifted Peg's forelock. "See that? That's Peg smiling! You ever seen that before. And look, so's our Lucy! You got a nice smile, Lucy. Lights up your whole face. You should do it more often. Maybe you should go riding more often. Here, Alfie," he said, handing the fish bucket to Alfie, "you're younger'n me, you can carry the fish. Come along, Marymoo," he went on, taking her arm. "Home. Took forever coming back in. Had to feel my way down the channel. Soupy old fog, could hardly see beyond the nose on me face. Lucky I got a good map of everything in my head. Should have, shouldn't I, after all these years. Need my supper, Marymoo, I'm famished. I could eat a ruddy horse—oh, beggin' your pardon, Peg."

When it got around that Uncle Billy had taken Lucy in and looked after her all day, there were a few mutterings about Silly Billy, and how he should've told Mary, told someone, told anyone where she was and saved the whole island a lot of trouble.

But most didn't care about that. They were simply relieved that Lucy Lost had been found, that was all that mattered. She was safe and sound.

The story of Lucy's disappearance that day was, of course, the talk of the island for days, but soon enough it wasn't just Lucy that everyone was talking about, it was the horse. During those hours lost in the fog—and how long it was before Uncle Billy had found her had never been quite discovered—an extraordinary transformation had somehow come over Peg. People thought it was almost as if Lucy had put some sort of spell on her. Everyone on Bryher knew Peg, how moody and mean and stubborn she could be. A whiskery old horse, black all over with feathery hooves and a crooked nose, she was the island's communal workhorse, but one who would only work if she felt like it, and if she was fed right and treated right. She much preferred to be left alone to wander the island, grazing peaceably, a ubiquitous and benign enough presence, until she felt hard done by in any way, until someone upset her.

Peg was the plowing horse, the harvesting horse. She was the island's only cart horse too, used to haul loads of seaweed up from the beaches to fertilize the potato fields and the flower fields. There were one or two donkeys on the island, used for fetching and carrying mostly, but the islanders couldn't do without Peg. They knew it and she knew it. No one owned her, and she knew that too, or seemed to. She was her own master and her own mistress. She guarded her independence fiercely, and liked to be treated always with the greatest respect.

She made it quite plain that she didn't like people, she tolerated them, so long as they behaved as she liked them to behave. Ask too much of her, work her too long, and there would be trouble. Try to ride her or take a stick or a whip to her, take liberties of any kind, and she'd let you know soon enough who was boss. Groom her when she didn't want to be groomed, pick out her feet when she didn't feel like enduring it, and she could turn nasty. She was quite capable of giving anyone, young or old alike, a sharp nip, even an occasional sly kick. Everyone on the island knew better than to take Peg for granted.

She was, though, for the most part, as good as gold with youngsters, especially if they came with a carrot. With a carrot, the smallest child could fetch her in for work, and work her too. She hardly had to be told where to go, nor where to stop. But try to get up and ride her home after a day's work, and child or not, you were in big trouble.

No one rode Peg. Many had tried, for a dare, but it had always ended badly, in tears mostly. No one had ever ridden Peg and stayed on, but now everyone on the island knew that Lucy had. It was unheard of. Lucy Lost had stayed on Peg for hours, for the best part of a day, a day that seemed to have changed Peg out of all recognition.

After that first, and now famous, ride in the fog with Lucy,

Peg would often be seen making her way to Veronica Farm, where she'd stand outside the door in the garden, even peering in at the window, while she waited for Lucy to come out and ride her. Most mornings now, they'd be seen out riding around the island, each of them obviously enjoying it as much as the other. And it was noticeable now that whenever anyone went looking for Peg, to fetch her in for work, to put her in harness, she would not be easy to find, nor to catch, nor to be tacked up.

She'd stamp her foot and snort and shake her straggly mane, leaving no one in any doubt that she'd rather be somewhere else altogether, and everyone knew who with. As soon as the work was done, plowing or harrowing, mowing or fertilizing, as soon as they had taken the tack off her, she'd be trotting off right away, back to Veronica Farm to find Lucy. What's more, Peg had never ever been known before to break into a trot. She did now, with Lucy. They'd been seen cantering along Rushy Bay, and once even breaking into a gallop. Peg cantering! Peg galloping!

Chapter Ten

We must always live in hope

By the time Dr. Crow came over to Bryher, some weeks later on his next visit, he discovered that the horse had almost entirely supplanted his gramophone and his records in Lucy's affections. And he was not at all disappointed by this development.

———◆———

From Dr. Crow's journal, 27th August 1915

Thank the Lord for Lucy Lost and Peg. Never in all my life has there been a day of greater contrasts than today. It began badly.

I was woken at dawn by a knock at my door. It was Mrs. Merton, with an urgent message from Bryher, summoning me at once to attend young Jack Brody again. She is not a person I care for greatly, for she is a habitual busybody, and unquestionably Scilly's most pernicious gossip—and we have a few of those on these islands. However, it has to be said that on this occasion she had good enough cause to wake me. News had come from Bryher that poor Jack was delirious again and in a dreadful state. I had to come quickly, she said.

I do not ever begrudge Jack Brody a visit. Indeed, no one on these islands deserves the attention of a doctor more than he. But as a doctor I hate to have to witness the prolonged suffering of anyone. He is crippled not just by his wounds, but by his pain. The amputation of his shattered leg was done well enough, but has become infected yet again. I did what I could, cleaning and dressing the wound, showing Mrs. Brody again how to do it herself, and how important it is that her hands are clean. I worry about septicemia. Once that takes hold, there is little that can be done. With luck, the wound may heal in time, but I cannot heal the agony in his eyes. I tried to make him as comfortable as I could. But if I'm honest I know he can never be comfortable again, that the pain he lives with, in his leg and in his head too, is almost constant. He endures bravely, but knowing him as I did before, he is a truly pitiful sight. The kindest thing any loving and merciful God could do would be to let him go, and quickly too. Mrs. Brody, a widow of many years, is used to suffering, but I think the suffering of her son is almost too much to bear.

As I came away from that sad, sad house, I was called to a much happier place altogether, and no more than a few hundred yards away. It turned out on this occasion that I was in the just right place at the just right time. This was to prove a most timely and entirely joyous visit—to assist at the birth of Mrs. Willoughby's second child. If only all births were so easy. The child, a boy, she is calling Handsome—an unusual but most suitable name I think for such a beautiful child. He is large, at nearly nine pounds, and with a full head of dark hair.

I left with a spring in my step, feeling that after all, all can and will be well again in this troubled world. As I came away, nature herself seemed to confirm this. The sun was shining out of the deepest blue sky, the sea lapping lazily onto the sand, swallows skimming over the shoreline.

But then, as I came along Green Bay I happened to meet old Mr. Jenkins out mending his nets, his fearsome dog beside him. He's a gruff old so-and-so, and his dog is no better, both to be avoided if at all possible. So I thought it best to keep my distance. But when he beckoned me over, I had to go. He asked me if I'd heard the latest news. It seems another of our ships, a merchantman, had been torpedoed in the Western Approaches. No survivors had been picked up, he said. I wish now I had not stopped to speak.

I saw Uncle Billy busy on his boat as usual. He didn't see me. He sees very few people because either he does not look, or he does not wish to, or both. I think Uncle Billy may have the right idea. He speaks to no one, except his close family, and then only rarely. He keeps himself to himself, attends only to what is near and dear to him. He does not want to know about the sadnesses of the wider world. It is as if he understands, and maybe he does, that for him, and for all of us, this is the only way that can lead to sanity, and to salvation. Billy may sometimes be deluded, but in this I believe he is right, that his example is one we should all follow, or I fear this war and all its sadness will make us all mad.

I rage against the horror of this war. I can say this to no one at the present time, especially since the sinking of the Lusitania, for fear of seeming to be unpatriotic, and unsupportive of our soldiers at the Front. I love England as well as any man, but do I have to love war to love England? I know that no good can ever come of it, no matter who wins or who loses. I only want the suffering and the pain and the grieving to stop. I have seen and tended to sailor after sailor, many little more than boys, all brought ashore at St. Mary's, already drowned, some of them, some terribly burnt, some half dead with cold. All, like Jack Brody, are some mother's son, some girl's sweetheart. Not so long ago they were all newly born, like Handsome, with life and happiness ahead of them.

So, with heavy heart now I made my way across the island to see young Philip Blessed, who has been in bed for a while now with the whooping cough, one of three children on the island currently suffering from this disease. The others are almost well again, but Philip has a weak chest, and has been taking longer to recover. But I discovered Philip up and about and quite cheerful, and hardly coughing at all. Mrs. Blessed was cheerful too, and clearly much relieved that Philip was getting well again. I could tell she was eager to sit me down, give me a cup of tea, and talk. (Tea is such a dreary drink, and there are so many times in a day of visits when a doctor has to drink it.)

It was Mrs. Blessed who first told me the extraordinary story about Lucy Lost, how a couple of weeks before she had got herself lost in the fog all day, and everyone had been out looking for her, and how, not knowing where she was at all, she had been riding around on Peg—"and that horse has the very devil in her, Doctor," she said—when Silly Billy found her and took her in. It was, I have to say, a rather garbled story, and one that at first I found somewhat difficult to believe. But, sure enough, shortly after I had left the Blessed household, and was walking down past the church, I saw Lucy Lost come riding down the hillside from the top of the island. I noted at once that her whole demeanor was altered. Gone was any sign of that pinched, haunted look, the dull sunken eyes. There was color in her cheeks, and a new light in her eyes. She even waved at me in greeting, and smiled as she passed me by. I hoped, of course, that she might also speak, but she did not. She rode bareback, and in bare feet too, and was clearly at ease and at one with the horse.

The horse seemed happy too, which is remarkable enough in itself, because that animal, as Mrs. Blessed had reminded me, is well known for her sullen and morose nature. I looked on in amazement, and then called out after her that I'd be coming in to see her presently. She did not appear to hear me.

Mrs. Wheatcroft was effusive in her welcome, a much changed and altogether happier person, it seemed to me. I heard the whole story then from her too, about Lucy and the horse getting lost in the fog—I didn't like to tell her that Mrs. Blessed had told me much of it already.

"Do you know, Doctor, that is the first time Billy had ever had anyone in the boathouse in five years, 'ceptin' me and Jim and Alfie, of course. I mean, you know how surly and grouchy Billy can be with strangers. I told him about Lucy coming to live with us, all about how Jim had found her, and that, but I hadn't never introduced them. Didn't like to risk it, in case he went and upset her. And then Uncle Billy finds her out in the fog and takes her back and looks after her, and sits her down to do some sail-making with her, for goodness' sake."

We sat down over yet another cup of tea, and some of her delicious tatty cake—without question the best I have ever had on the islands. Even tea is easier to drink with Mrs. Wheatcroft's tatty cake. (Would that Mrs. Cartright made a cake like hers!) She thanked me then for all I had done, and told me how my gramophone and my records, and now the horse, had done such wonders for Lucy.

"Miraculous, Doctor," she said. "And I do mean it too. It is miraculous. My prayers have been answered. Lucy is stronger and happier every day. I never saw such a change in anyone."

She leaned toward me then, put her hand on my arm, and whispered confidentially, "Don't go saying nothing, Doctor, but I think Alfie is smitten with her, and she with him, Doctor. When she's not on that horse, she's off around the island with him. She still won't go out in the boat, and she won't go diving off the quay with him, neither—Alfie says she's fearful of water. And, do you know she's even taught Alfie how to ride that horse? He'd tried before, and been thrown off every time. Had a nasty fall last time, always swore blind he'd never try again, but somehow she got him up on her again. No bits, mind, no spurs, no whips. I been watching her teaching him. All she does, she blows gently into the horse's nose, smoothes her neck, kisses her ear. But she never says nothing—she still don't speak. Hums like a bumblebee, all the time, Alfie says; but she don't speak, Doctor, never a word, just shows him what to do. Alfie blows a bit, smoothes her neck a bit, strokes her ears, then up he gets and away he goes. Works a treat every time."

As she finished talking, Lucy came running into the house, quite breathless, as contented a child as I've ever seen. When I talked to her, she looked at me and smiled. She had never looked me in the eye before. Much encouraged by this, and by everything I had heard and seen, I spoke to her, asked her how she was. She did not reply. Instead, she turned away, went straight to the gramophone and put on a record. I confess to having felt at that moment a keen sense of disappointment at her continuing silence, which is absurd of course. Her transformation has already been quite miraculous, as Mrs. Wheatcroft had said. I should not have expected more.

But there was indeed more. She came and sat and had tea with us, and wolfed down her cake. This was a different child altogether, silent maybe, but not nervous anymore, not reticent. And when she heard Alfie come whistling up the path, she was on her feet and at the door as quick as a flash. Alfie barely had time to have his tea before she dragged him outside. From the window I saw them both riding off down through the field, Alfie riding up behind, and both laughing out loud. I think Mrs. Wheatcroft may well be right. They did indeed look quite smitten with one another.

So what has caused this girl to recover so miraculously, as she clearly has? I am a man of science. My medicine helped, I have to believe that. I hope that the music helped also, but I do have to acknowledge that it was very probably the horse that was her best medicine, that and the love of a good family. Let us hope they can between them help her find her voice and her memory, and restore her completely. I dread to think that a child like Lucy might still end up in the asylum in Bodmin, like Uncle Billy. To be different in this ignorant world is often mistaken for madness. And we all too often put away those we believe to be different. Difference frightens people, and Lucy Lost is most surely different, very different.

There is, however, some worrying news. Mrs. Wheatcroft told me today that she has arranged, albeit reluctantly, with Mr. Beagley at Tresco School, for Lucy to go to school with Alfie next term. Mr. Beagley has apparently insisted that as the child is of school age, it is his duty to see to it that she attends, as all other island children do, that there can be no exceptions. It seems he threatened to report her to the authorities if Lucy does not attend.

He is in my opinion an officious little man, far too fond of himself and of the power he is accustomed to wielding in his school. There is something of the tyrant in him that I do not like. Threatening is second nature to him. Everyone knows he does not spare the rod. In my opinion he is most certainly lacking in the sensitivity one needs to be a good teacher. I have little confidence in him. I have to hope both he and the other children will treat Lucy kindly. School can be a very unforgiving place. Children can be very unkind, even cruel, to one another, particularly to a new child, to a stranger not from the islands. And Lucy is the strangest of strangers, one that still does not speak, a different sort of child altogether, who, as everyone knows, does not seem to know who she is, nor where she comes from.

I have not spoken of my concerns to Mrs. Wheatcroft, for I do not wish to alarm her unnecessarily, but I am not at all sure that school is the right place for such a child at the moment, particularly Mr. Beagley's school. She is without doubt much improved, but she is still fragile in her mind. I can only hope that her recovery will not in any way be undermined by life at school. I have every confidence that Alfie will do all he can to look after her and protect her all he can, but I fear there is only so much he can do.

A calm crossing back to St. Mary's this evening, the sunset bloodred and lingering long. I am tired as I put down my pen, fearful for Lucy Lost, for Jack Brody, but hopeful too. I have to be. Hope, we must always live in hope.

Chapter Eleven

SCILLY ISLES, SEPTEMBER 1915

Unwilling to school

Mary and Jim left it to Alfie to break the news to Lucy about her having to go to school. It was only Alfie she seemed to listen to and understand at all. If ever they did try to speak to her these days, she'd turn to Alfie for reassurance, for some kind of explanation or interpretation. If anyone could reach her, it would be Alfie. So in the end whenever they wanted anything explained to her both Mary and Jim left it to Alfie to do the talking. And even then in answer to any questions there would only ever be a shake or nod of the head. But it was clear to all of them by now that she understood at least something of what Alfie was trying to tell her.

Alfie picked his moment to explain to her about school. Lucy was riding Peg up over Watch Hill, and he was walking along-side her, picking blackberries as he went and handing one up to her from time to time. "You got blue lips, Lucy," he told her after a while. But she wasn't listening. She was shielding her eyes against the sun while watching a bird gliding high overhead then twisting, then diving, plummeting down through the air.

"That's a peregrine falcon," Alfie told her. "They nest on White Island, in the lighthouse, you know, near St. Helen's, near where we found you. Beautiful, isn't he? They can dive at over ninety miles an hour, d'you know that?" This seemed the right moment. He reached up and touched her elbow. "Lucy, I got something to tell you. And you have to listen. It's school time again soon, next week. Holidays will be over, worst luck. You want to come with me?"

She shook her head. She was listening.

"Thing is, Lucy, Mother says you got to, else she'll be in trouble. She don't want you taken away, see? And they could too, Lucy, if you don't go to school, if they think Mother's not doing right by you, not sending you to school, not looking after you proper like she should."

She looked down at him now. He could see she was trying to concentrate, trying hard to understand.

"You been to school before, haven't you? Must've been. Be about the same here, I reckon. All schools are about the same," he went on. "My school's not so bad, honest it isn't. 'Ceptin' for Mr. Beagley, that is. Beastly Beagley. You just have to keep out of his way, that's all. You seen me go off in the boat in the morning, and come back in the afternoon, haven't you? We'll do it together, shall us? You'll be fine, promise."

She shook her head again, more vigorously this time. Then with a click of her tongue she geed up Peg, and trotted over the hill and away. Alfie called after her. "Ain't no use running away, Lucy. You got to go. We all got to go to school, Lucy. It's a rule. I'll look after you, honest I will. You'll be all right, honest." But by now she was too far away to hear. Alfie had the distinct feeling that she'd understood quite well enough, and just didn't want to hear any more.

That evening she stayed up in her room and would not come down for supper. In the end Mary took it up to her, but she just lay there curled up on her bed, face to the wall. Mary talked to her, stroked her hair, kissed her, but Lucy would not even turn to look at her, let alone eat. Alfie went upstairs later to see if he could do any better, but it was no good. When he reached out and put a hand on her shoulder, she pulled away from him and buried her head in the pillow, crying quietly. He left her then and came downstairs.

"It's no use," he said. "I've upset her bad. She ain't ready for it, Mother. We can't make her go, not unless she wants to. I don't blame her neither. I wouldn't go, 'less I had to."

"If she won't go, Marymoo, then she won't go. S'all there is to it," said Jim. "She's got a mind of her own, that one. Quite like someone else I know—her mother's daughter, if you see what I'm saying. Nothing more to be done about it. She'll come round. Maybe we just got to give her time to get used to the idea."

"And what if Mr. Beagley won't give her time?" Mary said, fighting back the tears. "You know what he's like. You want him reporting us, do you? And he would too, I'm telling you. He'd rather see her taken away and locked up in that madhouse like Uncle Billy than miss a day of school. Rules, rules, that's all he cares about."

At that moment the door from the staircase opened. Lucy was standing there looking at them stone-faced. She had a folded-up piece of paper in her hand. She walked over to Alfie and gave it to him, then turned and went out. "Never knew she could write," Jim said.

"Not writing, Father, it's a drawing," Alfie told him. "Look." The drawing, in pencil, was of a boat, a rowing boat full of children going across the channel to Tresco. Mr. Jenkins was rowing—they could tell that from his peaked cap. And the quay on New Grimsby harbor and the houses on Tresco were all quite recognizable too. There was a girl in the water, hand waving, a girl who was drowning. And right across the picture she had drawn a cross, heavily indented. "It's the school-boat," Alfie said. "It's the boat, don't you see? She's trying to tell us she don't want to go in the boat. That's what it is. It's not the school she's frightened of. It's the sea, it's the boat. I told you, didn't I? She's scared stiff of the water, won't go nowhere near it."

"Then how the devil are we supposed to get her across the channel to school?" Jim asked. "Can't hardly walk on water, can she? She ain't Jesus, is she? S'cuse me, Marymoo—slip of the tongue. And she can't hardly fly herself to Tresco. What're we going to do?"

"Somehow, we got to get her into that boat," Mary said, and turned to Alfie, reaching out to grasp his hand. "You're the only one who can do it, Alfie. You got to persuade her. You got to, else they'll come and take her away. If we give them any cause, they will. I know they will. Mr. Beagley will see to it. And then we'll lose her for good."

"It'll be all right, Mother." Alfie was trying to sound as reassuring as he could, but he wasn't sounding at all convincing, even to himself. "One way or another, I'll find a way to get her across on that boat, you'll see." Even as he spoke, Alfie had no idea at all how it could be done. Time and again he had witnessed Lucy's reluctance to go anywhere near the sea. Even riding up on Peg, she liked to keep her distance from the water's edge. He'd tried to cajole her many times to get into *Penguin* so they could go out fishing together, but so far she had always refused, point-blank. And when he ran splashing into the sea to swim, she'd never come with him. She'd never set foot in the water, no matter how calm it was, nor how warm.

--- ◆ ---

In those last days before the school term began, Alfie tried to encourage her again and again to come fishing with him in *Penguin*. But nothing he said or did could persuade her even to come near the boat. He could see it was upsetting her, so he gave up trying. Night after night, Alfie lay there wondering how he was ever going to manage to get her into the school-boat on that first morning of term. It came to him then that it wasn't so much the boat she was frightened of, it was the sea itself. So he decided to do all he could to entice her into the water.

He took her kite flying on Green Bay, running through the shallows, splashing, whooping and laughing. She didn't need any instruction. She flew his kite like an expert. She loved doing it too, but would never go anywhere near the sea. Skimming stones didn't work either. Alfie would stand knee-deep in the water, showing her how to choose the right stone, how to throw it. She knew how to do that too, and was clever at it, but every time she would stand well back from the water's edge, not even getting her feet wet. No matter what he did, nothing would induce her into going anywhere near the water.

Alfie did notice how often she appeared distracted by the boats moored out in Green Bay, most of all by the *Hispaniola*, particularly when Uncle Billy was working on it. She would stand there sometimes just gazing at it, as if she was waiting for Uncle Billy to come over and say hello. He never did. Alfie knew well enough he wouldn't come, that Uncle Billy wasn't like that. But he could see Lucy was disappointed. Once, while they were out there, they heard him breaking into his Yo Ho Ho song.

"Uncle Billy's happy today," he told her. "If we wave at him, he'll like it all right, but he won't always wave back. Uncle Billy don't do waving, not often. But we can try." Alfie waved then, and moments later, Lucy did the same. As Alfie had said, Uncle Billy didn't wave back. He didn't even acknowledge they were there.

"He's not unfriendly, you know that, Lucy, don't you?" he said. "He's just a shy sort of a person. Likes being on his own, don't like being interrupted. Didn't speak to me for two years after Mother brought him home. He's all right with me now, he's all right with all of us. But he don't say much even so, not even to Mother. Everyone else on the island is a stranger to him, and he don't much care for strangers. Mother says he don't like the way they look at him. He hears what they call him, the things they say behind his back about him, all about the madhouse he came from. There's some who think Mother should never have brought him home, but that's because they're scared of him. They got no cause to be. Uncle Billy's the kindest person I ever knew. Fetched you in from that fog, didn't he? Looked after you. Wouldn't hurt a fly. He don't like being stared at, that's all. That's why he stays in his boathouse all on his own, less he's working on the lugger, that is.

"Don't you worry none. Uncle Billy likes you all right. He wouldn't be singing else. I reckon maybe he's singing just for you. I mean, like Mother says, you're family now. But even so, if we go over there now to see him, it might upset him. And when he gets like that he gets sad, so sad he won't eat even. Mother says he don't like us to come too close, to come into his boathouse or near his boat, not unless he asks us first. And Mother knows him better'n anyone, understands him. After all, they grew up together. Twins, they are. Brother and sister."

Even as he was talking, Alfie was realizing more and more that Lucy was unusually intent on his every word. The more he told her, the more she seemed to want to hear about Uncle Billy. She was really listening. If she was that interested, Alfie thought, then it had to be because she was understanding most of what he was saying. He hoped all the time that she might even ask him a question. She looked at times as if she wanted to, but she didn't.

On the very last day of the holidays Alfie thought that he might at last have found a way to get Lucy into the water. He'd take her shrimping out in the rock pools on Green Bay, after the tide had gone out. They could have shrimps for supper, he told her, just as she'd had with Uncle Billy. Her eyes brightened. She liked the idea. As he had expected, at first she stayed on the shore and watched as Alfie waded into the rock pools up to his knees, scooping the shrimping net through the weed. He knew all the places where the shrimps liked to hide away. With the first few sweeps of his net he had caught a dozen or so, big ones too, and emptied them into his bucket. He brought them back in triumph to show her.

When he offered her his net, she took it. "It's easy," he told her, taking her hand. "C'mon, Lucy, I'll show you." He could feel her grip tighten as he led her slowly down toward the sea. But she was doing it, she was doing it, she was coming with him. They stepped in. The water was up over her ankles now, up to her knees now, and she was still walking.

Then, out of nowhere, a gull came diving down on them, squawking and screeching. Ducking down, they felt the wind of its wings as it passed overhead. Lucy screamed, broke away from him, and then ran back up the beach. She wouldn't come back in after that. She sat there on a rock, clasping her knees, watching Alfie from a distance, and glancing from time to time across the bay at the *Hispaniola*. She was looking for Uncle Billy, Alfie thought, but he was nowhere to be seen that morning. Alfie kept calling for her to come and join him, kept coming back to show her his catch, to encourage her to try again. But she wouldn't budge. It was hopeless, and Alfie knew it.

That evening he didn't like to tell his mother how badly everything had gone down on Green Bay that day. He did tell his father though, in a quiet moment. All his father said was, with a shrug: "You done all you could, Alfie. Like I said, you can't make that girl do a thing she don't want to do. She's spirited, that one, got a mind of her own. If she don't want to get on that school-boat tomorrow morning, then she won't. S'all there is to it."

Chapter Twelve

We don't do grinning here

Alfie thought Lucy might stay in bed the next morning, the first day of school, and simply not come downstairs, but surprisingly he found Lucy was already up and about before him. She had even fed the hens without him—the first time she had ever done that. Dressed in the new school clothes that Mary had made especially for her—another ruse to get her interested in going to school—Lucy sat at the kitchen table with them and ate her boiled egg and soldiers, and drank her milk. And when Alfie left for school she went along with him, her familiar silent shadow following him, Peg trailing behind them as she so often did.

They heard the raucous voices of the children all waiting for the boat down on the quay. Lucy stopped, and for some moments, stood there listening to them. She seemed reluctant to go on. Alfie felt her hand in his, and then they were walking on together, Lucy staring straight ahead, her face set. She was going to do it, Alfie thought, she was going to get in the boat. Behind them Peg was clomping along, snorting and snuffling. By the time they got to the quay the boat was already there, the children piling in, the boatman, Mr. Jenkins, trying in vain to get them to calm down and be still. No one was paying him any attention, which was quite usual.

Lucy hesitated again. And then she spoke. "No," she said, suddenly withdrawing her hand. "No," she said again.

Alfie could not believe it. "You spoke!" he said. "Just then, you spoke!" She smiled at him, then turned and walked away. Alfie thought of calling her back, of pleading with her. But he knew there was no point in trying anymore, that nothing would change her mind. As soon as he got into the boat, he had to endure all the usual ribald banter, about his "mermaid sister" who'd "lost her marbles," and was "mazed in the head," "so dumb she couldn't even talk." Some of them, Zeb being the ringleader, of course, began jeering at her as she walked away down the quay. "Miss La-di-dah not coming to school then? Too dumb for school, are we?"

Alfie ignored them for the moment, but promised himself he'd settle things with Zeb later, when Beastly Beagley wasn't around. The boat pulled away, Mr. Jenkins still bellowing at everyone to sit down and behave. The last Alfie saw of Lucy, she was walking away beside Peg along the path toward Green Bay, her hand resting on the horse's neck. She did not look back.

It took longer than usual to get across the channel that morning because of the spring tide. There was very little water between Bryher and Tresco. So all the children from Bryher were late for school that morning, which meant, and everyone knew it would happen, that Beastly would be in a foul mood. As the boat came into Old Grimsby harbor on Tresco, Alfie remembered a dream he had had during the holidays, that the school had fallen down, that Beastly Beagley had turned into a crow and flown away. It had been the most vivid of dreams. But sadly, as he very soon discovered, the school was still there. Beastly was still there, still ringing his bell in the school yard. Alfie wondered if he'd been standing there all through the summer holidays ringing his confounded bell. He smiled at the thought, and Beastly spotted it. "What you grinning about, Alfred Wheatcroft? We don't do grinning here, lad, or had you forgotten?"

"No, sir."

Once they were all lined up in the school yard, Mr. Beagley called the roll in his usual rasping manner, thumb hooked in his waistcoat pocket, glaring at each child from under his bushy, twitchy eyebrows as he read out the names. Beside him, Miss

Nightingale ticked them off in the register one by one as each of them answered.

"Lucy," Mr. Beagley intoned, "known, I am told, as Lucy Lost?" In the silence that followed, one or two of the children began to titter and giggle. "Lucy Lost? Where are you?" Mr. Beagley looked up and down the lines, frowning with menace. "Do you know where she is, Alfred Wheatcroft?" Alfie shook his head. "Well, we shall see about her, won't we? All absentees are malingerers, and I eat them for breakfast, don't I, children?"

"Yes, sir," they chorused obediently, a ritual response to any Beastly Beagley quip. Alfie didn't join in. Then Zeb put up his hand.

"P'raps she's swimming over, sir, on account of she's a mermaid. She wouldn't get in the boat, sir. She's too dumb for school anyway!" The laughter was loud and full of hilarity.

"Silence!" roared Mr. Beagley.

There was silence at once, but a silence interrupted by the sound of someone snorting with laughter, someone, Alfie thought, who was going to be in very big trouble, who was really going to get it in the neck from Mr. Beagley. Alfie looked around to see who it was who was snorting, who was in for it. But no one was snorting. No one was even smiling. Instead he heard, as by now they all had, from behind the hedgerow, the rhythmic clomping of hooves.

Moments later, and to everyone's astonishment, Peg came walking up the path toward the school gate, tossing her head and snorting as she came. She was soaking wet, as was Lucy Lost, who was riding up on her in bare feet, with no saddle, no bit, no reins, riding her with such easy rhythm that she seemed almost part of the horse itself.

Chapter Thirteen

A child of obscure and dubious origins

Thirty-five children answered the roll on this the first day of the Michaelmas Term. No absentees.

It should be noted, and indeed the vicar has been informed yet again, that the tiling above the east window has still not been repaired, and neither has the broken pane of glass in the window itself been replaced, as I have repeatedly requested. I have made it abundantly clear that if those repairs are not carried out before the onset of winter gales, the rain will drive in and will render the back of the classroom unusable. Rooks have again nested in the chimney and blocked it, as I already reported at the end of last term. Again, nothing has been done. I wish to record here that I cannot and will not be held responsible for any consequent disruption to the running of this school, and that in such circumstances, with wind and rain coming in, with the fire in the stove unable to be lit, I should have no choice but to close the school.

There is one new pupil in the school this term. She is known as Lucy Lost, and is thought to be about twelve years old, a child of obscure and dubious origins, having been found neglected and abandoned on St. Helen's some three months ago. She is being cared for by Mr. and Mrs. Wheatcroft of Veronica Farm on Bryher. She came to school late, and on horseback, having refused to take the boat from Bryher with the other children. Instead, there being a low spring tide, it seems she took it into her head to ride across the Tresco Channel. This caused great disruption at roll call, and indeed was the talk of the school all day, making teaching most difficult, so unsettled were the pupils by this event. As a result I was forced to administer punishment on several occasions during the day. For the record:

Alfred Wheatcroft. Two strokes for impudence.

Patience Menzies. Three strokes for blaspheming.

Billy Moffat and Zebediah Bishop. Two strokes each for riotous behavior, and for throwing stones in the playground.

Lucy Lost is, I fear, likely to prove a most troublesome and disruptive pupil. She is a surly child, with the wild unkempt look of a waif and stray. She will need to learn some manners, to learn to do as the other pupils do. She does not speak. It seems she cannot, or will not. I suspect the latter. She does not, or will not, write either. Since she is so woefully backward and so clearly incapable, I have seen fit to place her with the Infants in Miss Nightingale's class, until she can learn to speak and write as befits one of her age.

In addition, I should say that she has a most disagreeable character. She does not look me in the eye, which in my experience is always the sign of dishonesty or obstinacy in a child, very probably both. I have spoken to her severely about her refusal to speak when spoken to, and have forbidden her expressly from arriving at school on horseback again. I have made it perfectly clear to Alfred Wheatcroft that it is his responsibility to see that she travels to school in the boat tomorrow, as do all the other children of Bryher, that there will be serious consequences for both him and for her if he does not.

In conclusion, I have this morning instigated the custom of raising and lowering the flag each day, and the singing of the National Anthem, in order to instill proper patriotic *fervor in the pupils. I shall continue this practice until the day the war ends. until victory is achieved.*

After school Alfie and Lucy had to wait until later that afternoon, until the tide was low enough again to be able to ride Peg safely back across Tresco Channel to Bryher. Alfie had insisted they do the return journey together, and rode up front, Lucy clinging on behind. At one point, in the deepest part of the channel, it became obvious to both of them that Peg wasn't walking anymore but swimming. Alfie felt Lucy's arms tighten around him, her face pressing hard into his back. Alfie thought at first it must be out of fear, but then began, first to hope and then to believe, that it was nothing of the kind, that it was done out of gratitude, in affection for him, even out of admiration too.

He had sensed her admiration back at school that morning, when he had stood up in front of everyone and told Mr. Beagley that Lucy should not be relegated to the Infants class, that it was not right and not fair at her age. He had been punished for his impudence, two strokes of the cane on his hand. There was, he recalled, bewilderment and horror on Lucy's face as she watched—she had clearly never witnessed such a thing before. And there were tears in her eyes too, tears for him, and Alfie liked that.

If anyone was truly fearful out there in the middle of the channel, where the sea flowed much deeper and faster than he had expected, Alfie knew it was himself. "S'all right, Lucy, don't you be frightened," he told her, quite aware that if anyone needed these words of reassurance, it was himself, not Lucy. "Peg knows where to go. Just hang on. She'll get us there, you'll see."

And so she did too, to Alfie's great relief. Peg struggled through, and soon they were out of the deep water and trotting through the shallows up onto Green Bay to be greeted on the beach by dozens of waiting islanders, Mary and Jim among them. Uncle Billy was there, up on the deck of the *Hispaniola* in his pirate's hat, watching them through his telescope as they came riding in. It was a joyous and triumphant return. There was no one on Bryher, it seemed, who did not by now know the amazing story of Lucy's first day at school, how she'd ridden across, and how Alfie had been caned by Beastly Beagley for talking back, for standing up for Lucy.

But the second day at school, as it turned out, was to be even more momentous than the first. Everyone knew that once the spring tides were over there was no way Lucy would be able to ride across the channel to Tresco to school, as the water would simply be too deep in the middle, and far too dangerous. She would either have to take the boat with all the others, or stay behind. The schoolchildren, along with an increasingly impatient Mr. Jenkins, were all waiting in the boat for Lucy and Alfie to arrive. It was a boat full of excitement and debate and dispute. Would they come? Would she get in the boat? Would she chicken out? And what would Beastly do if she didn't get to school?

They all hushed at once, as they saw them coming round the corner, both riding on Peg, then dismounting on the path. They left Peg behind, and walked slowly down the quay toward the boat, Mr. Jenkins bellowing at them to hurry along, that they were late already, that "Mr. Beagley would eat them alive."

Alfie jumped in first and held out his hand to help Lucy on board. For long moments she hesitated, standing there looking first at him, then out across the channel. Everyone was wondering what would happen next, Alfie as much as anyone. "Hurry up, haven't got all day, missy," growled Mr. Jenkins. "Is you coming, or ain't you?" They all saw Lucy close her eyes, and take a deep breath, and another. Then she opened her eyes again, reached out for Alfie's hand, gripped it tight, and stepped down into the boat. Everyone clapped, and some even cheered. Lucy sat down close beside Alfie, and kept her head down and her eyes shut the whole way across.

He stood beside her in their lines in the school yard as the flag was raised, as the National Anthem was sung, and she stuck close to him again inside the school room at Assembly, as Mr. Beagley intoned the prayers from the lectern, and Miss Nightingale played the piano. They sang "What a Friend We Have in Jesus," Alfie's favorite hymn—he'd always loved the tune, it was his mother's favorite too. He was belting it out with great fervor when he became aware that beside him, Lucy wasn't singing, and he wondered why, whether she knew any hymns, whether she had ever been to church at all. Then he thought: *Of course she isn't singing. How can she sing if she can't speak?* But as he was reflecting on this, he noticed that her whole demeanor had changed. She was suddenly intense, like a cat about to pounce, her eyes wide and fixed. She seemed hardly to be breathing. She was, he saw then, staring hard at Miss Nightingale, almost as if she recognized her, as if she was a long-lost relative suddenly discovered, as if she couldn't believe her eyes. She was remembering her, remembering *something*—Alfie was sure of this, quite sure.

After the hymn was over, Miss Nightingale stood up from the piano, put the lid down gently, and went and stood, as she always did, beside Mr. Beagley for him to say the last prayer. It was as he was beginning to say the prayer, that Lucy, quite suddenly and unaccountably, left Alfie's side, and began to walk toward Miss Nightingale. Alfie reached out to try to stop her, but it was too late. No one moved without permission in Mr. Beagley's Assemblies. But Lucy was. She was moving as if in some kind of trance, gliding through the assembled children like a ghost. No one spoke. Even Mr. Beagley was stunned to silence in mid-prayer. Alfie expected him to explode in fury at any moment, but clearly dumbfounded like everyone else there, he could only stand and stare, as Lucy drifted past him, past Miss Nightingale. She was making straight for the piano.

Lucy sat down, lifted the lid, and began at once to play. She played softly, leaning over the keyboard, intent only on the sound of the music she was making; and everyone, from the smallest infant to Mr. Beagley himself, listened just as intently. Amazement at this brazen defiance of Beastly Beagley's authority gave way to wonder at how beautifully she was playing. Miss Nightingale turned to Mr. Beagley. "It's Mozart, Mr. Beagley," she whispered. "She's playing Mozart. I think I know this piece. She's playing it so well too."

Now Mr. Beagley did explode. "How dare you interrupt my Assembly!" he roared, striding across the classroom toward Lucy at the piano. "Go back to your place at once."

But lost in the music, Lucy played on. Mr. Beagley stood over her fuming for some moments before slapping her hands away and banging down the piano lid. "Piano," she said quietly and then her whole face broke into a smile. "Piano," she said again, looking up at him.

Mr. Beagley was beside himself with anger. He grabbed Lucy by the arm and jerked her to her feet. "So you do speak!" he raged. "It's just as I thought. All this playing dumb is fakery, nothing but pure fakery, a deceit, nothing but a way of drawing attention to yourself. I told Dr. Crow, I told Mrs. Wheatcroft, that I shall soon have you speaking and writing, and behaving like every other child in my school. And believe you me, I shall. I shall. Do you understand me? Do you?"

In his fury he took her by the shoulders now, and shook her. Lucy said nothing. She was crying silently, the tears running down her face. He frog-marched Lucy back to her place. Then, returning to the lectern and gathering himself, he spoke to the whole school. "Lucy Lost will now apologize to all of us for interrupting our prayers. Speak out, child, speak out. Say you are sorry. Go on, say it."

Lucy didn't speak, but brushed away her tears, and then looked up at him, full in the face.

"Dumb insolence, nothing but dumb defiant insolence," Mr. Beagley went on. "Two can play at that game, you know. You want to play dumb, then so can I, so can every child in my school. We shall send you to Coventry, all day. You know what this means? No? Well, I shall tell you. No one will speak to you from now until the end of school. That will teach you. It will be the cane—no, the ruler!—for anyone who dares to speak to Lucy Lost, do I make myself quite clear?"

Alfie had most certainly been worried at how his strange new "sister," his "mermaid sister," might be treated by everyone when she came to school. All the early indications, after her mysterious appearance on the island, after they had taken her in, had not been good. Zebediah Bishop's constant niggling and mockery, and all his cronies' endless japes and jibes and wise-cracks, had, until now, made his school life a misery. He had only expected things to get worse, now that she was actually coming to school with him. But quite unexpectedly, it did not turn out like that at all.

Instead, Lucy had been catapulted at once to huge fame and universal popularity: firstly by that dramatic arrival on horseback, and then by the playing of the piano in Assembly. These would have been quite enough on their own to make her the talk of the school, but being sent to Coventry as a punishment by Beastly Beagley turned her instantly into a folk hero. Alfie found himself suddenly popular too, by associa-tion, especially after Mr. Beagley had caught him talking to Lucy Lost in the school yard at playtime. He was punished for it there and then in front of everyone—three strokes of the dreaded ruler, edge first on the knuckles, Mr. Beagley's favorite punishment. It hurt, hurt horribly, but with every stroke Mr. Beagley administered, his tongue between his teeth, his face contorted with fury, Alfie could sense he was becoming ever more popular. And that helped a very great deal to soothe the pain in his knuckles.

Chapter Fourteen

Tears and smiles

When Mary heard that evening about how Mr. Beagley had been treating Lucy and Alfie, she was all for going over to Tresco at once and giving him a piece of her mind, but Alfie told her that it would only make things worse if she did, and Jim agreed. "Let Alfie and Lucy sort it out for themselves, Marymoo," he told her, when they were alone later. "They're looking after themselves pretty well, if you ask me. It ain't right, that's for sure. But it's what we all got to do at school, I reckon, take our punishment, learn to look after ourselves. Not all about reading and writing, is it?"

But Jim thought about that a lot as he lay awake that night, and decided that he had been wrong about it. Mary had been right: that this was not punishment, it was cruelty. Something should be said, and it was up to him to say it, at the first opportunity.

Some days later when he was over on Tresco selling some crabs, he happened to see Mr. Beagley coming along the road on his bicycle. So he stopped him there and then, and told him to his face just what he thought of him, quietly and politely, but leaving Mr. Beagley in no doubt as to how he felt over the matter. "I give you fair warning, Mr. Beagley," he said. "You go easy on our Lucy Lost, and on our Alfie too, or you'll have me to answer to."

"Is that a threat, Mr. Wheatcroft?" Mr. Beagley replied, somewhat shakily—he had clearly been taken aback.

"No, not a threat. It's a promise," said Jim. "More carrot, less stick is my advice, Mr. Beagley, if you understand my meaning, if you know what's good for you, and for the children, come to that."

He never told anyone at home of this meeting, but it had the desired effect. After this meeting Mr. Beagley seemed to find other victims to persecute. He left Lucy Lost more and more to Miss Nightingale's care, and there were no further confrontations with Alfred Wheatcroft.

Miss Nightingale was becoming ever more puzzled at Lucy's inability to speak, or to read and write properly, because she was obviously so intelligent otherwise. She was exceptionally gifted at both playing the piano and drawing too. It was noticeable how well she listened to stories being read aloud, and how considered and thoughtful she was with the other children in the class—all of them being at least five or six years younger than she was. They did not seem to mind at all how silent and strange she was. Somehow they were all drawn to her, taking turns to sit on her lap, wanting always to be near her, and play with her. In time, Lucy became like a silent mother to them, and for Miss Nightingale, she was nothing but a help with the little ones, forever doing up shoelaces, drying tears, wiping noses.

But when it came to speaking, Miss Nightingale was daily disappointed in her progress. Despite all her efforts, nothing she did could induce Lucy to utter a single word. With her writing, though, there were signs of much greater hope and promise. Under Miss Nightingale's gentle guidance, and after slow and tentative beginnings, Lucy was becoming much more confident, able to copy more and more words in her writing book. And when she came to the blackboard now each day, as they all did, each to write up a word for the class, Miss Nightingale was pleased to see she was able sometimes to write out a few longer words too, although she was still very slow and labored in her handwriting. Every day she was forming her letters better— though her spelling was often awry—often joining them up automatically, without ever being shown how to do it, which surprised Miss Nightingale. Writing seemed to be coming to her more naturally every day, almost as if she was relearning it, Miss Nightingale thought, rediscovering something she'd clearly been taught how to do already, but that had been somehow hidden from her.

This was not an illiterate child, not a wild untutored child. And she was very far from being mad or stupid, as Mr. Beagley constantly insisted she must be. If she was backward, as he said— and Miss Nightingale did not believe it for one moment—then there were reasons for it, and she was quite determined to find out what these reasons were.

Lucy's progress with the written word, despite her continuing inability to spell properly, gave Miss Nightingale some encouragement to believe that if she could master the written word, then speech might soon follow. Above all, she felt, she had to get to know this child, to become her friend, to soothe her anxieties, whatever they were. It was fear, she was sure of it, that was at the heart of her troubles. Banish those fears, Miss Nightingale thought, through trust and friendship, and perhaps she might find her voice again and her memory.

So, very much against Mr. Beagley's wishes, she encouraged Lucy to come to the piano and play whenever possible. She was not good at her scales, and like most children Miss Nightingale had taught, showed very little interest in practicing them. But she had a repertoire of pieces that she knew by heart, and that she obviously loved, and she played those always with great flair and commitment. Listening to her play was a sheer joy for Miss Nightingale. She had never known a child to be so deeply lost in her music. When Lucy played, she seemed to be in another world altogether.

Mr. Beagley took every opportunity to remind Miss Nightingale that it was not her job to teach children the piano, that the instrument was there for the playing of hymns in Assembly, but she argued strongly that all children should be encouraged to do what they love to do, that this was how children gained confidence in themselves. Young though she was, Miss Nightingale was not at all afraid of Mr. Beagley and always argued forcibly on the children's behalf, which irritated him greatly. The children, though, liked and trusted her. To all of them as they grew up she had become an elder sister, kindly, strict when she needed to be, but always understanding and patient, and ultimately on their side.

She painted as positive a picture as she could to Mr. Beagley of Lucy's progress, knowing just how unfair and judgmental he could be on her, as he always was on those children who had any kind of learning or behavioral difficulty. For Lucy Lost, she thought, he seemed to reserve a special dislike, a dislike confirmed daily in his attitude toward her, and often echoed in the school logbook, which she insisted on reading from time to time, whether he liked it or not. It was, as she pointed out, not his logbook, but the school's, and she had a right to read it.

FROM MR. BEAGLEY'S SCHOOL LOG, FRIDAY, 15TH OCTOBER 1915

Thirty-three answered the roll. Two absent. Amanda Berry with the measles. Morris Bridgeman with the influenza again. In his case, I rather suspect malingering.

Miss Nightingale claims daily that Lucy Lost is improving, but I see little sign of it. She writes better, I am told, but she still does not speak, and communicates with other children only rarely, and then only in a kind of sign language with Alfred Wheatcroft as a go-between. He is almost always at her side, a partner in iniquity. Miss Nightingale calls her withdrawn, I believe she is mentally disturbed, and that her silence, whether pretended or not, is a sign of an unbalanced mind. A child like this certainly does not belong in a school for normal children, as I have repeatedly told Dr. Crow. It is my firm opinion, and I have told this repeatedly to both the doctor and the vicar, that she should be removed from both the Wheatcroft family and from this school, and be found a place in an establishment suited to the care of the mentally retarded. I have written two letters now to the School Board but have not yet received the courtesy of a reply.

A gull must have flown into the school classroom through the broken window over the weekend. I found the creature dead on the floor when I came into the schoolroom this morning. The inconvenience caused was very considerable. I was forced to delay the opening of school for twenty minutes whilst I cleaned up the mess. Miss Nightingale did not come to work today. It is her nerves, I am told. I was obliged to teach the whole school together. Most unsatisfactory.

Windy day, so the children were inclined to be riotous. I imposed silent lunch and afternoon detention for all.

By autumn, one entire end of the kitchen at Veronica Farm was completely covered with a patchwork of Lucy's drawings. Upstairs in her bedroom you could hardly see any of the walls for her drawings. When the first autumn gales came in—and they were frequent that year—and Alfie and Lucy couldn't go across the channel to school, or go out riding on Peg, she would sit down at the kitchen table and draw, listening all the while to the gramophone. On days like this, Alfie would be out working the farm with his father. There was nothing he liked better than not going to school.

Lucy's drawings were mostly studies of nature from around the island: seals, cormorants, oystercatchers—she drew more oystercatchers than any other bird—but there were gulls and crabs and lobsters, and fish, all kinds of fish, herring, pollock, starfish. Strangely, there were peacocks too, several pictures of peacocks, but all the same, tail feathers fanned out. There were portraits of the family too: Mary baking, Jim mending nets, Alfie shrimping, and a couple of Uncle Billy too, standing on the deck of the *Hispaniola* in his Long John Silver hat, and one of Dr. Crow, puffing his pipe as he sat in Jim's chair by the stove. And there were several of Peg of course. Peg grazing, Peg sleeping, Peg running. Studies of her head, her feet, her ears.

But among the sketches, there were pictures of buildings that neither Alfie nor Mary nor Jim recognized at all: a city with wide streets and grand houses with steps up to the front doors. And there were several of people they did not recognize at all—an old lady and gentleman tending to two horses, another rather grander-looking lady in a great feathery hat, and beside her a soldier in army uniform. There were sketches of a lake with ducks swimming about, and time and again she'd drawn pictures of a giant sitting by this same lake, holding a book in his hands, with ducks gathered around his feet and gazing up at him. It looked as if he was reading them a story.

She drew deftly, and with great skill, the drawings seeming to pour out of her. Once a drawing was finished, she'd move immediately onto the next, almost with no hesitation, as if a new picture came at once into her head and she had to draw it. Time and again they asked about the drawings, about who these people were, where the buildings and streets were. But they were most puzzled by the peacocks. Why so many peacocks? They were all anxious to know more, to unravel the unknown stories behind the pictures, stories that they knew must be there, somewhere deep inside her memory, locked away from her, and from them. They also asked because they felt more and more that she wanted to remember and wanted to tell them, that she longed to remember, longed to speak.

But if they asked too much or too often, or pressed their questioning too hard—and of all of them Mary was the most inclined to do this—they knew she could suddenly become tearful, and run away upstairs to her bedroom, to cry, to be on her own. She cried these days as often as she smiled. Mary and Alfie hated to hear her cry. But Jim would always tell them not to worry about it, that it was a good sign. "Tears and smiles," he said. "All it means is that she's coming out of herself. And that's what we want, don't we?"

———◆———

Lucy and Alfie were out riding around the island on Peg when the doctor next came to visit. It was too rough for fishing, so Jim was home. Mary had spread the drawings out on the kitchen table, and was proudly showing them to the doctor, telling him everything Miss Nightingale had said about how well Lucy was doing at school these days, how her writing was coming on, even her spelling, how well she played the piano, how wonderfully she drew. Jim began to realize after a while that the doctor hadn't said very much since he arrived, and that he wasn't really listening to Mary, which wasn't like him at all.

"Something on your mind, is there, Doctor?" he asked.

The doctor hesitated to reply. "All this is wonderful news," he began. "Wonderful. Wherever I go I hear stories about how the other children have taken to Lucy at school. 'Little Mother' they call her, in her class, d'you know that? But I have some news that is not so wonderful, I'm afraid. It seems that Big Dave Bishop has been telling stories around the islands, about a blanket he says he picked up on St. Helen's, the same day you and Alfie found Lucy Lost over there. He is claiming that this blanket had a name embroidered on it—'Wilhelm,' he says it was— which as everyone knows is the same name as the German Kaiser. So Big Dave Bishop is going about the place telling everyone that Lucy must be German. On Scilly, and all over England just at the moment, this is not a good time to be a German. It is not a good time to be thought to be a German either. I just thought I ought to warn you that I fear there may be trouble ahead."

Chapter Fifteen

ATLANTIC OCEAN, MAY 1915

Torpedo! Torpedo!

To begin with, it looked as if I was going to spend most of the voyage confined to our cabin, because Mama took sick almost before we lost sight of land. After that she was neither well enough nor strong enough to get up. For a day or so I never left her side. She slept for hours on end, and when she was awake she felt so ill that she neither knew, nor cared, where I went or what I did. She lay there, propped up in her peacock dressing gown—wearing it made her feel at home, she said—as pale as her pillows, enduring the misery of seasickness, refusing at first to take any food at all and then only soup.

In the end—and to this day I am ashamed to have to admit it—I tired of sitting there doing very little except watching her. I passed my time waiting for her to wake up. When at last she did, I'd sit her up and arrange her pillows and help her with her soup. She was too weak to do much for herself. Sometimes I'd spend hours on end kneeling on my bed looking out enviously through the porthole at all the other children running about below me on deck, and when there was no one there, at the gray of the sky and the sea beyond, at the wide emptiness of the heaving ocean.

I longed to venture out from time to time, just for a little while, to go up on deck, to run and play. In the end I worked out a plan that would enable me to do it, and salve my conscience at the same time. I'd wait for her to drop off to sleep, then, leaving her a note on her bedside table telling her I'd be back soon, I would slip out to explore the ship, and find friends maybe. The chances were that I'd be back before she ever knew I'd been gone. But I don't think I'd ever have actually done it without the help and encouragement of one who was to become, over the days that followed, such a good friend and companion to me—Brendan Doyle.

Very soon, thanks to him, I got to know the ship, not just as well as but very probably better than any other passenger on board.

He was the cabin steward who brought Mama her soup, who was looking after us on the voyage. I asked him—rather cheekily, now I come to think of it—why he spoke as he did, why his English sounded as it did, more like singing than talking. And he told me that growing up in a little place called Kinsale, in Ireland, might have had something to do with it. How you speak comes with your mother's milk, he told me once. It was,

I thought, a strange thing to say. I didn't know what he was talking about, not then. He lived in Liverpool now, he said, where just about everyone he knew had come over from Ireland too, and spoke as he did. And he told me, that if we were lucky enough, we might just catch a glimpse of Ireland as we passed by on the way to Liverpool in a few days' time.

I liked Brendan at once, because he was kind to me and laughed a lot, and because he did all he could to make Mama comfortable, to try to get her to eat something more substantial than soup—always unsuccessfully, but he never gave up. And he it was who first encouraged me to get out and about a bit more, which chimed perfectly, of course, with the escape plans I was hatching at the time. He said that I was looking just about as peaky as Mama, that it wasn't good for me to be stuck in my cabin all the while, that I should go to the dining room and meet some of the other passengers, that there were children up there I could play with. He would look in on Mama from time to time while I was gone, he said. He would look after her. She'd be fine.

His good advice was all the excuse I needed to leave Mama on her own. So, having let Brendan know, at lunchtime on our second full day at sea, I left a note for Mama by her bed as I had planned, and made my way to the dining room. It was just like I had always imagined the grandest ballroom might be, I remember, a place glittering with lights and chandeliers, where everyone looked very proper and important. As I followed the waiter to my table, I felt everyone staring at me, which I did not like at all. Worse still, I found myself sitting alone, and did not know at all which way I should look. But suddenly I didn't mind one bit anymore, and that was entirely because the music started up. It came from a piano in the center of the dining room, a huge shining grand piano.

I took no notice anymore of the people around me, nor of my sumptuous surroundings, I was simply enthralled by the music. I ate the food that was put in front of me, but paid little attention to it. It was the music that was feeding me. The silver-haired pianist was flashing smiles all around as his fingers danced over the keyboard. And what a piano it was, the most magnificent grand piano I had ever seen. He played, sometimes delicately, sometimes flamboyantly, but always with the greatest ease and with supreme style.

It was at that very first lunch also that I found myself adopted by the family at the table next to mine, who, seeing I was on my own, and taking pity on me, I suppose, invited me to join them. I recognized them at once as the same family who had so nearly missed the boat back in New York. Sad to say I have forgotten their family name, but the two children—Paul, who informed me at once that he was five and that his sister, Celia, was only three—soon became very attached to me, and I to them too. Whenever I ate with them after that—and they insisted I did every time I came to the dining room—the children always made me sit between them. Celia liked me to feed her teddy bear, which I did. She was rather talkative, and told me that it didn't matter her teddy bear had only one eye, that he was quite happy, and you could tell that because he was always smiling.

After I mentioned that I liked playing the piano, they took me over and introduced me to the silver-haired pianist—he was called Maurice, and was French, he said, from Paris.

When I went, as I often did, for walks with the whole family along the promenade deck, I would sometimes find little hands slipping into mine, one on either side. I liked playing at being their older sister, and their parents seemed to like it too. They were endlessly kind, the mother going to visit Mama sometimes in the cabin to see if there was anything she could do for her.

Much as I liked being with them, though, my best times were with Brendan Doyle. Whenever he had time to spare he would take me on a tour around the ship, always somewhere different, always somewhere new. Often we'd go where he told me passengers like me weren't really supposed to go, but that it was all right if I was with him. We went into first class—Mama and I were in second class—and we went down below too into the depths of the ship, where the third-class passengers lived—where everything was very crowded and cramped, where people huddled together dark-eyed and miserable, where children whimpered and cried, and where the smell was overpower-ingly dreadful. But worst of all, and even farther below, were the giant boilers and the engines, where the thunder of the machinery and the pounding of the pistons were deafening, where the stench and heat of the furnaces were so stifling I could hardly breathe. Here, Brendan told me, the men labored long and tirelessly twenty-four hours a day to keep the ship going.

It was down there in the bowels of the ship that I truly felt the power of this great ship, and witnessed for myself how hard it must be for the men working down there. Brendan said there were nearly two hundred men needed to keep the ship going. For me it seemed like a vision of hell itself, and I could not wait to get back up on deck and fill my lungs with fresh sea air again.

I often stood with Brendan on the stern of the ship looking out over the ocean at the ever-widening wake behind us. It was my favorite place, and his too, or so it seemed. To me it was like the pathway back home, back to New York and Pippa and Uncle Mac and Aunty Ducka. Brendan was so proud of the ship. He'd been working on her for seven years, he told me, ever since she was launched. He loved her. The people who worked on her were his family now. He'd never missed a voyage in all that time.

We'd stand there gazing up at the three massive funnels, bright red, black tipped, each one billowing out dark smoke that drifted over our heads, over the wake of the ship and away. "Can you not feel the throbbing heart of her?" Brendan said to me one day as we stood there on deck, marveling at her. "Sometimes I think she's a living breathing creature, a great gentle giant who keeps us safe, and we do the same for her. She's not a ship at all, not to me. She's a friend. The biggest, most beautiful friend anyone could ever have."

And it was true, everything about this ship was awesome. I knew now what drove that mighty ship on through the ocean, what muscle and what work made that smoke, made that wake. "Isn't she just the finest ship you ever saw?" Brendan said. "Isn't she just the best in the entire world?" And she was, she was.

It was here, leaning on the rail at the stern of the ship and looking out to sea, that Brendan and I were standing together on that last morning. We could just make out the coastline of Ireland through the fog.

"In a couple of hours or so I reckon we'll be off Kinsale Head," he said. "If this fog lifts, we should be able to see the town of Kinsale itself clear enough, with a little luck, and maybe a little imagination. I'd like to show it to you, Merry. I told you it was the place where I was born, didn't I? When I was a little fella, I always wanted to go to sea. I'd be sitting there on the harbor wall at Kinsale, swinging me legs, and watching the fishing boats going out and coming in; and the great big ships—with great funnels like ours—steaming by on the horizon. I longed to go wherever they had been, wherever they were going, to see what was beyond. I had to go. There was a whole wide world out there, and I wanted to see it. There was nothing for me at home anyway—too many in the nest, fourteen of us, and never enough to eat. Seven years now, off and on, I've been at sea, and in all that time I've never once been home again. I couldn't wait to get out of the place. But do you know what, Merry? I miss it, miss it bad."

He fell silent for a few moments, and I could see he was feeling sad, which was unlike him. Then out of the sadness came a sudden smile, and a cheery laugh. "I've steamed past the place dozens of times in this ship, Merry, on the way to Liverpool," he went on. "And every time I see it there in the distance, I wonder if there isn't a small boy just like me sitting on the harbor wall, kicking his heels, and watching us going slowly by along the horizon, and thinking how fine and wonderful a thing it would be to go to sea in a great ship like that. I'll go back home one day, Merry, I will, I will. I'll stroll in and say: 'It's me, Ma. It's Brendan.' That'll be a moment. I'll be hugged from here to kingdom come, and Ma will examine me neck and tell me I haven't been washing meself like I should."

His voice was full of laughter now, laughter that was near to tears, I thought. He put his arm around me as we walked away from the ship's rail. "I'm thinking we should be off Kinsale at about two o'clock today," said Brendan, "just after lunch. Tell you what, Merry. We could maybe meet up again then, and I could show you. I shall come and fetch you from the dining hall when the time's right. Would you like that? Mind you, it may be a little later than two o'clock. The captain has had to slow right down in this fog. I reckon we're only doing about fifteen knots at the most. But the fog will very likely have lifted a little by lunchtime, may be gone altogether. Let's hope so. I'll bring my binoculars, Merry, then you'll be able to see Kinsale easy enough." He looked around him, his brow furrowing. "I hate a fog at sea, every sailor does."

I went back down to the cabin after that, and found Mama fast asleep again. I was sitting at the desk, writing her another note to say I was going to the dining room to have lunch, when I happened to notice the newspaper lying there on her bed, on her sheets. She had clearly fallen asleep reading it. It looked to me very much like the same newspaper Uncle Mac had been reading to Mama on the day we sailed. Curious, I picked it up. There was an advertisement in the center of the page, printed in large letters. Someone had underlined it in pencil, and that had to be Uncle Mac, I thought. It took me a long while to read it because many of the words were far too long and complicated for me; some I had to miss out altogether. But at least the print was big, so I could read some of the words, but not enough to make much sense of them.

NOTICE!

Travellers intending to embark on the Atlantic voyage are reminded that a state of war exists between Germany and Great Britain and her allies; that the zone of war includes the waters adjacent to the British Isles; that, in accordance with formal notice given by the Imperial German Government, vessels flying the flag of Great Britain, or any other of her allies, are liable to destruction in those waters and that travellers sailing in the war zone on ships of Great Britain and her allies do so at their own risk.

I had just finished reading this, and was still trying to work out what it meant, when I heard Mama stirring and waking behind me. I put the newspaper down at once, but it was too late. She had seen me. "Give me that newspaper, Merry. Now, this minute." She was angry at me, and I didn't know why. I went over to the bed.

"What does it mean, Mama?" I asked as I handed it to her.

"Nothing." She snatched it from me. "Nothing at all."

"It's what Uncle Mac was showing you, isn't it?" I said.

"It's all nonsense, plain nonsense," she told me dismissively, and dropped the paper into the wastepaper bin. "German propaganda, Merry, that's what it is, and that's where it belongs, in the bin. Let's hear no more about it."

But I knew then that she wasn't telling me the truth. I could tell that she was worried and was trying to disguise it. "What does it all mean?" I asked her. She would not reply. "Does it mean they're going to attack us, Mama? It does, doesn't it? That's what Uncle Mac was trying to tell you, wasn't it? He was trying to warn us. He didn't want us to sail, did he? And it was because of this." I was shouting at her now, and crying too.

"Will you stop it, Merry?" she said. "Just stop it. You're being silly. I have told you, there is nothing to worry about. We will be in Liverpool in only a few hours, take the train to London, and by this time tomorrow we shall be seeing Papa in his hospital. That's why we came, that's why we had to come. And no one's sunk the ship, have they?"

"They still could," I cried. "They still could. Then we'll never see Papa, will we? And it'll be all your fault! I hate it when you don't tell me things, when you talk to me as if I'm a baby. I'm not! I'm not!" I ran from the cabin then in tears. I could hear her sobbing behind me as I left.

I managed to calm myself before I reached the dining hall. The piano was playing and my "family" was waiting for me, beckoning me to join them, as I came in. As we ate our lunch, the two children prattled on, but I wasn't really listening. Celia, as usual, gave me her teddy bear to hold. So I sat it on my lap, but she had to keep reminding me to stroke it and feed it. My mind was elsewhere. All I could think of was how upset Mama must be after what I had said. I had never spoken to her like that before, and was regretting it bitterly.

I was about to leave the table to go down to the cabin to say how sorry I was, when Maurice, the silver-haired French piano player, rose suddenly to his feet from his piano and clapped his hands for silence. *"Mesdames, Messieurs, mes enfants,"* Maurice began, "I am told that we have in our midst today a young lady—she is called Merry, which is a very pretty name—who plays the piano quite beautifully." Paul and Celia's parents were smiling knowingly at me from across the table. They had clearly arranged this. "So, shall we ask Merry to come and play for us?"

Everyone in the dining hall was laughing and clapping. I had no choice. Mortified, but heart pounding with excitement too, I stood up and walked slowly toward the grand piano. Maurice patted the piano stool and stood aside, inviting me to sit down. The dining hall fell silent around me. Everyone was looking at me, waiting for me to begin. I noticed Brendan then, standing by the door, smiling at me, encouraging me. I still couldn't think what to play, nor even how to begin to play. My mind froze. My hands froze. It was then that I thought I felt the gentle touch of a hand on my shoulder. Papa's hand, I was sure of it. He was willing me on, telling me I could do it. And now I could, I could!

I played almost without knowing it, and found I was listening to Papa's favorite piece, my favorite piece, Mozart's "Andante Grazioso." I saw my fingers dancing over the keys. Only then did I know for certain that I must be playing it, it was me making the piano sing. The music took hold of me and I forgot everything else, until it was over, until the applause came long and loud, and Maurice was helping me to my feet, telling me to take my bow. "Three bows, Merry," he said. "Say each time to yourself, as you bow, '*un elephant, deux elephants, trois elephants*'—this is what I always do. This way you take your time. This way you bow low. This way you enjoy the applause." I did as he told me, and he was right—I did enjoy the applause. Bravos rang around the dining hall. Everyone seemed to want to pat me on the back and shake my hand as I passed by. Some I saw had been moved to tears and Celia and Paul were jumping up and down with delight, Celia waving her teddy bear in the air.

Minutes later Brendan was at my table, helping me to my feet and escorting me out of the dining room. "We have to hurry," he whispered. "And that music, girl," he went on, "that music you played in there was supreme, supreme."

Just outside the dining room, we found our way suddenly blocked by a tall man in a tailcoat and monocle who looked down at me sternly from a great height, wagging his finger. "Very fine playing, I'm sure, young lady," he said. "But I would not stay to hear it. Mozart was German, don't you know, so we should not be playing his music. It is enemy music now, until the war is over and won."

"Wasn't that Mozart fella an Austrian?" said Brendan.

"Austrian? German? They are the same," he replied. "Both enemies, and don't you forget it. There are enemy ships, enemy submarines, all around us out there on the ocean, so we should not be playing their music. Plenty of good British music to play! Elgar. Elgar's your man." And with that he strode away back into the hubbub of the dining room.

"Silly old duffer," said Brendan under his breath as we walked up on deck toward the stern of the ship. He looked at his watch. "Just after two o'clock. We should be sighting Kinsale Head any time now. The fog's cleared a bit, so we'll be seeing it well enough, I reckon, if we keep a sharp eye."

We were standing at the ship's rail now, Brendan looking out through his binoculars. "I think the captain's taking us a little closer to shore than he usually does," he went on, "which is good, but I still can't make out Kinsale. Patchy this fog, but it'll clear, Merry, it will. It'll be maybe a few more minutes yet before we can see the town." He turned and looked upward then, as I did too, at the ship's dark smoke billowing up into the wispy white of the fog above us, at the hundreds of escorting gulls wheeling over the ship.

"Will you look at them, Merry? Isn't that a sight? Irish gulls."

He laughed. And then his voice changed, the laughter suddenly gone. "That's strange," he said. "The lifeboats are all out on the starboard side, all ready to launch. What have they done that for? Must be an exercise or something. No one told me. Let's take a look."

As we walked across the deck over to the starboard side of the ship, Brendan began pointing skyward. There was blue sky quite visible now through the fog. He handed me the binoculars. "Gannets!" he cried. "Will you look at that! They're diving. Take a look. See how they slice into the water. D'you see them, Merry? Isn't that the most marvelous thing you ever saw! Can you see? Can you see?" And I did see them, dozens of them, like a shower of white stars falling from the blue of the sky. "After the mackerel, I shouldn't wonder," said Brendan. "They love mackerel, and herring too."

It was a spectacular display. With the binoculars, I could just make out the yellow of their heads as they dived. In they went, one after another, disappearing into the waves, only to rise again miraculously moments later with a fish.

Then without warning, the binoculars were snatched roughly from me. Brendan was looking through them out to sea, but he was no longer interested in the gannets' feeding frenzy. He had seen something else. "Jeez!" he breathed. "Jeez!"

"What?" I said. "What is it?" Then I saw it myself, about five hundred yards away, a trail of bubbles in the sea, and moving rapidly toward us, coming ever closer to the ship. Brendan was shouting up at the crows' nest high above the deck. I couldn't understand at all, not at first, why he had become so suddenly agitated, why he was gesticulating wildly, and screaming at the top of his voice.

"Submarine! Torpedo! Torpedo! Submarine!"

Chapter Sixteen

Live, child, you have to live

An echoing cry went up at once from the crows' nest. Other passengers out walking on the starboard deck were now alerted to the danger, and were running and screaming. And we were running too, Brendan dragging me across the deck, over to the other side of the ship.

It was like a clap of thunder when it struck. The force of it rocked the ship under our feet, throwing us across the deck and sending us crashing into the rails. We were barely on our feet again before another explosion, more muffled this time, a dull boom, shook the ship, but from somewhere deep down below. Under us the deck tilted violently, tipping us both off balance again. But Brendan held on to me and got me to my feet. "It's a torpedo, Merry," he cried. "She's wounded in the heart of her, wounded bad. She's a dead ship. She'll go down."

He took me firmly by the arm and we ran at once back across the deck to the starboard side, toward the nearest lifeboat.

Passengers and crew were pouring up on deck now, consternation and terror on every face. Everywhere about us there was panic. Everyone seemed to be looking for someone else, and pulling on lifejackets as they went. But it seemed no one could be found. There were children crying for their mothers, and mothers searching frantically for their children, screaming for them. I saw not a single reunion in that dreadful fearful melee.

A great fire had taken hold of the ship, flames roaring, clouds of smoke blackening the sky above the ship. It took me some time to gather my thoughts, but when I did, it was crystal clear what I had to do. "Mama!" I shouted to Brendan, pulling away from him and making for the door to the companionway. "I have to find Mama! She's in the cabin."

Brendan grabbed me, held me, and would not let go. "I'll fetch her for you, Merry."

"You promise?" I cried.

"I promise. I'll bring her to you. Now, girl, you're to stay right here by this lifeboat, and wait for me. You're not to move, d'you hear? I'll be back with your mother in just a jiffy, don't you worry. We'll get you both into a lifeboat. There's plenty of them, and we're in sight of land, we'll all be just fine." Then he was gone.

I did as Brendan had told me, and waited, and waited, the ship going down fast all the while. There was chaos and terror all around me as the crew tried to lower the lifeboats. But the ship was already listing at such an angle that many of the life-boats filled with people were left dangling above the sea and unable to be lowered any further. They tilted violently, at every lurch of the ship, throwing passengers screaming into the sea. Some of the boats were lowered in not level at all, but stern- or bow-first, plunging into the water, filling at once and sinking immediately. There were hundreds already struggling in the sea. Many could not swim and were drowning before my eyes. I had to turn away. I could not bear to see any more. But I could not turn away from the screaming, from the wailing of the small children desperate for lost mothers and fathers.

I recognized then one of the older passengers, a kindly looking old lady, not unlike Aunty Ducka back home, who'd sat always on her own in the dining room, and whom I had ad-mired both for her serenity and for the dark green velvet dress she always wore. She had smiled at me that first lunchtime when I came in, when so many others had simply stared. I was grate-ful to her for that, and remembered her now. She sat on a bench, her eyes closed, her lips moving in prayer, her fingers touching the cross she wore around her neck. She opened her eyes then and saw me watching her. She smiled at me, as she had before, and beckoned me over to sit beside her. She did not speak a word, but put her arm around me and held my hand in hers.

There came then a great groan from the depths of the ship, and an explosion of steam like a last breath. Every time the ship lurched and listed again, the old lady held me ever tighter. Then she spoke. "You're young," she said. "You should get in a lifeboat, child, you should save yourself."

"I have to wait for my mama," I told her.

She looked at me long and hard. "If I was your mother, I should not want you to wait for me. I should want you to save yourself. Come along, dear." We stood up then, and with great difficulty, clinging to anything or anyone to save ourselves from falling, made our way through the crowd to the ship's rail, to the nearest lifeboat, which swung there, already overfull. The old lady spoke to a ship's officer who seemed to be in charge. "I want you to take my grandchild," she said. At first he paid her no attention, but she would not be denied. She tapped him repeatedly on the shoulder, till he turned around and had to listen.

"My grandchild must get in that boat," she insisted.

"Sorry. No room, ma'am."

"You have a child at home?" asked the lady.

"Yes, ma'am."

"If this was your child, would you find room for her?"

The officer stared at her, speechless for a moment.

"Then take my grandchild," she said.

He didn't argue anymore. He held out his hand to help me in. The last thing she said to me was: "Live, child, you have to live. Live for your mother, live for me." The lifeboat swayed suddenly away from me as I tried to step across into it. I am not sure in the end whether I leaped in or whether the officer tossed me in, but one way or another I ended up in the bottom of the boat. As the boat was lowered away, I looked everywhere above me for the old lady, or for Brendan, or Mama. There was no face I knew.

There was no face I knew in the boat either. Strange hands were lifting me, helping me to find a place to sit in the boat, which was packed tight from bow to stern. With every sudden lurching of the lifeboat as it was lowered down toward the sea, my heart lurched with it. I cried for Mama, searching for her again and again among the faces of the passengers who crowded the ship's rail looking down at us, a few waving, most crying, but she was not there. She was not there.

All I could think, as the lifeboat struck the water violently, bounced and settled, as the sailors rowed us away, was that I should have gone looking for her myself, that I should never have trusted Brendan, that I should never have got in that life-boat without her. I was crying bitter tears of self-recrimination when I felt a small cold hand come into mine. Celia was there beside me, clutching her teddy bear, and sobbing pitifully.

"Where's Paul?" I cried. "Where's your mother, and your father?"

She shook her head. I looked all around the lifeboat, and back up at the ship, at those faces looking down at us. They were nowhere to be seen. I gathered Celia to me and held her close. She was crying and shaking, but calmer now. She clung to me tightly, burying her head in my shoulder. "We'll be all right, Celia," I told her. "We're not far from land, I know we're not. They'll find us. I'll look after you now. Promise."

I never imagined a ship of that size could go down so quickly. She was gone in minutes. But she did not go down completely. Brendan's beautiful gentle giant was dying. Her stern stayed there above the surface, refusing to sink, the ship's rail where Brendan and I had stood only moments before, it seemed, was still clearly visible.

All around our lifeboat now, in every direction, the sea was dotted with other lifeboats like ours, all distancing themselves as fast as they could from the wreck of the great ship. Many I saw were upturned, with passengers clinging on wherever they could. And everywhere there were people in the sea, struggling to swim toward the lifeboats, or clinging on to them, begging to be helped on board. There were deck chairs floating in the sea, benches, tables, suitcases, and trunks. The ocean was littered with wreckage as far as the eye could see, and among it were hundreds of people, swimming for their lives, many of them losing their lives as I watched.

Already we must have had a dozen or more hanging on to the sides of our boat, clamoring and pleading to be helped aboard. I can hear their voices now, I can see their faces.

"For God's sake, don't leave me here."

"I don't want to die."

"Dear God, save me!"

One young woman grasped at my hand, then slipped away, too weak to cling on any longer. "Tell Mom goodbye," she cried, and disappeared under the water before my eyes. Others clung on where they could, begging us to save them. The sailor on the tiller was shouting at them again and again, telling them to go away, that there were other boats nearby, several only half full, that they weren't far away, that they should swim there, that we would be in danger of sinking if we took on any more. He forbade us absolutely from helping anyone else on board. But despite his orders, and ignoring his curses, when mothers or children swam up to the lifeboat, no one could turn them away. There were some still strong enough, and desperate to live, who managed to haul themselves up into the boat anyway without anyone's help. No one had the heart to prevent them.

Everyone could see the lifeboat was dangerously low in the sea by now, that the water was already washing in over the sides in places, lapping around our feet, deeper all the time. The sailor on the tiller was raging at us. "For Christ's sake, what's the matter with you people? We'll sink if we let anyone else on. D'you see those bodies in the sea? You see them? D'you want to be like them? No one else gets on this lifeboat, you hear me? No one!" But nothing he said made any difference.

The lifeboat was by now completely surrounded. There were hands clinging, it seemed, to every inch of her sides. Faces white with fear were peering in on us, mouthing last appeals for help, last curses, eyes pleading, accusing. The sailor kept trying to tell them. "Can't you understand?" he cried. "You'll sink the boat! You're sinking the boat. You'll drown the lot of us."

One of those still clinging on, and so close to me that I could have reached out and touched him, was an old man. He had not begged to be helped in. He had not said a word, but hung there in silence, shivering, gazing up at me, at Celia. I did not know what to say. I could hardly bear to look at him. Then he spoke: "He's right. We will sink the boat. You are young. I am not. Live, live long and be happy. Bless you." And with that he simply let go and swam away. It was the last I saw of him.

Celia clung to me, ever more desperate now for warmth and comfort, whimpering and crying for her mother. I clung to her, trying to reassure her, and in doing so, to reassure myself all I could. "Look, Celia, d'you see? There are lots of lifeboats everywhere. Your mama will be in one of them, your papa too, and Paul. We'll be fine, we'll all be fine. I'll look after you, and you look after Teddy. Right?"

I talked to her on and on like that. I don't know if it was any comfort to her, but it seemed to work, for a while at least, to take her mind and mine away from everything that had happened, from the dying that was going on all around us, from the horror of all we were witnessing. The ocean itself seemed to be writhing and moaning in despair, crying out in fear, wailing in pity. As the hours passed and the cold took hold of us, I could see that there were fewer and fewer people swimming in the sea, fewer clinging on to the lifeboats, more bodies floating facedown in the water. Lifeboats and wreckage and debris were scattered far and wide. We were more and more alone on the open sea.

I heard now only murmured prayers and the occasional sound of a voice calling out across the water. One voice I remember particularly, calling out from far away across the water, but it was quite clear. It was a man's voice.

"Tell her. Tell my mother. Mrs. Bailey. Twenty-two, Phillimore Gardens, London. Tell her that her son, Harry, died thinking of her. Tell her, please. God save us all." Then silence.

As time passed I tried to force myself not to look at the bodies in the water anymore, fearing if I did that one of them might be Mama. I knew that if she was in the water she must be drowned by now, and I didn't want to see her. I could not help myself, though. I looked. I had to look. How I wish I never had.

I saw her, only because I saw her peacock dressing gown, the colors bright as jewels on the gray of the ocean, peacock blue and gold, the feathers all the colors of the rainbow. She was floating away from me, farther and farther away, facedown in the ocean. There could be no mistake. It was her Chinese dressing gown, the strutting peacock on the back, feathers displayed, the dressing gown she loved, the dressing gown she always wore, that she was wearing in bed the last time I had seen her that morning.

It was her. It was Mama. I felt a strange numbness coming over me. It was as if she had taken the heart and soul of me away with her when she died, and left me with just the shell of myself, an empty shell. There were no tears inside me to shed.

We were all lost.

Chapter Seventeen

No words would come out

It is difficult to remember quite how long we had been in the lifeboat before Celia stopped shivering. At some point I realized she was still in my arms. I thought perhaps she had fallen asleep, or that she might even be dead from the cold. But she was still clutching her teddy bear, still clinging to me. I could feel her breath against my cheek. There was life in her. I talked to her, when I remembered to, tried to shake her awake. To slip into sleep would be to die, and never wake up again. She must not sleep. I must not sleep. When she opened her eyes I could see she did not know who I was anymore. She was calling me Mama, and slipping in and out of consciousness. I hugged her tightly to me, trying to lend her some of the heat that was left in me. I blew on her hands and cheeks, kept talking to her, but she was holding on to me so weakly now, only barely clinging on to life.

Despite my best efforts, I was drifting in and out of sleep. I remember being roused by some kind of a kerfuffle on the other side of the lifeboat somewhere behind me, by the sound of cursing and splashing. I felt the boat rocking violently and looked around me to find out what was going on. The sailor at the rudder was doing all he could to repel a couple of men who were trying to haul themselves up out of the sea into the lifeboat, when he himself was grabbed by the arm and pulled overboard into the water. I saw him surface once and drift away. He was trying to swim, but he couldn't. He could only flail about. The sea stifled his cries and he went down. Then as the men scrambled to climb on, the boat tipped, and the water rushed in and was all around our feet, and quickly up to our knees.

We all knew the boat was going down, that there was nothing we could do about it. As the seawater rose and rose about us, I was trying to shake Celia awake. Just in time she woke enough to do what I was telling her to do, to climb onto my back and hold on. The boat was gone. We were in the sea. The cold of the water took me and chilled me to the bone at once. I swam away as fast as I could from all the screaming and cursing around me, swam clear of all those arms trying to grab me, away from all those piteous cries begging for help from God, from anyone, help that I knew neither God nor I could give.

I still do not know or understand why we try to cling to life when there is no hope left. I was swimming out into an empty ocean, empty of all but debris, the leftovers of a wrecked ship, of wrecked lives, the waves choking me, the cold sapping the last of my strength, and with a semiconscious child trying to hang on around my neck and slipping from me, I felt, with every stroke I took. There was no boat to swim toward, no land in sight, no reason to go on swimming.

I did hold in my head the thought that so long as I swam I would not drown. Above all I did not want to drown. The thought of drowning, of sinking down and down, horrified me, kept my arms moving, my legs swimming. Mama, I knew, I would never see again, but Papa was waiting for me in his hospital bed. I had to try to live to see him again. But any determination in me to survive was weakened all too soon, as my legs were seized by cold and cramp. Every stroke taken was a superhuman effort to keep my chin above water, to stay afloat. And with every stroke I was less and less sure it was worth it.

I was doing nothing but treading water now, my arms working only to hold me up. But Celia was dragging me down. I thought then, and it is a thought so shameful that it stays with me to this day, that I might shake her off my shoulders, be free of her weight, that I could last much longer without her. I could feel her arms around my neck, looser and looser all the time. But she was moaning from time to time. She was still clinging on to her teddy bear. For some reason, I was determined that as long as she was trying to save that little bear, then I would do all I could to save her.

I remember I hummed to her then as I swam. It was as much for me as for her. If I could hear the sound of my voice, then I was still alive. I hummed rather than sang, so that the water did not come into my mouth, hummed all the piano tunes I knew, my Mozart piece again and again, my "Andante Grazioso," Papa's piece. Sometimes I heard Celia humming too in my ear, or was it moaning? Whatever it was, it was a response and it gave me new strength, new hope as we drifted away, out into the empty ocean.

I thought at first it might be an upturned lifeboat I could see. It looked big enough, but it was the wrong shape. Lifeboats were white, and this was not white. Then I thought it looked like a large table of some kind. As I swam closer I could see it was certainly made from wood, a dark wood, a shiny polished wood, but shaped not at all like a table. It was both curved and angular in shape, and was floating in the sea murmuring strangely, singing almost, as if it was something that might have life and breath. A whale perhaps, but I could see already it was too flat to be a whale, too shaped. And whales didn't have edges or curves, not like this. This was man-made, I realized now, and must surely have come off the ship.

I was close enough to touch it, then to lean on it, and hang on long enough to gather the last of what little energy I had left. I hitched Celia up higher onto my shoulders, and hauled myself up out of the sea. I lay there flat on my front, exhausted, with the strength only to breathe. Celia was still on my back, still clinging.

I lifted my head to look about me. And only then did I realize what it was that had saved us. It was the piano, Maurice's grand piano from the dining room of the ship, the piano I had played such a short time before. His piano had become our life raft. I don't know if it was my imagination, but I thought I could almost feel and hear the strings of the piano still alive beneath me. I inched my way with the greatest care toward the center of the piano, for the waves, gentle though they were, were lapping over the wood all around the edges of the piano, and I could see it would be all too easy to slide and slip, and then be swept away and back into the sea. Safer, I thought, once I had reached the middle, I sat up and gathered Celia to me. She was limp in my arms, but still had hold of her teddy bear firmly by the arm. Somehow, we had all saved one another, all three of us, and with the help of a grand piano.

But after a few brief moments of relief, of exhilaration, that we were saved, it came to me soon enough that our refuge was only temporary, nothing but an illusion of safety, that both of us were too cold and too weak to survive for long. Celia was by now hardly conscious of being in this world at all. We were utterly alone on a wide, wide ocean with no land in sight, and little prospect of any help either.

It occurred to me then, that should the waves get up only a

little, and even if we could stay where we were, right in the middle of our piano-raft, in the safest place, we would be quickly overwhelmed by the waves and swept off into the sea. There would be nothing to hold on to, nothing to stop us from sliding off, nor to save us from drowning. The sea was waiting for us, I thought, and would not have to wait long. I looked up. The sky was blue above us, the sea glassy all around us, and there was hardly a breeze on my face. All I had was hope, and precious little of that.

There was nothing for it but to lie down, hold Celia close to me, and wait for rescue, or death. I realized well enough which was likely to come first. I had above all to stay awake, that if I dozed off at all, if I slipped into unconsciousness, my hold on Celia would be loosened, that she and then I could find ourselves all too easily in the sea again. So to keep myself awake I talked, to myself, to Mama, to Papa, to Miss Winters, to Pippa, to Uncle Mac and Aunty Ducka. I talked to Brendan too, but most often to Celia, hoping each time for a response of some kind, any kind. But there was none. There was life in her though, for she still clutched her teddy bear to her, and would not let it go, just as I would not let go of her.

Evening came down, and became night, a long long night of cold and fear. The cold gripped me, froze me. The sea lapped and rocked us gently, and the piano murmured, lulling us. The moon hung above, riding the stars, hiding sometimes behind the clouds, following us, I thought, like a guardian angel. I hummed to it, hummed to Papa as I had promised.

I listened to the moon, listened for him, and heard him, echoing our tune. He was alive, and I was alive. Uncle Mac and Aunty Ducka were alive. Thinking of Aunty Ducka made me smile, when there was so little to smile about. Hadn't I promised her I would keep my feet dry? Another promise broken then.

I heard Papa's voice ticking me off. "Nincompoop, ninny," he was saying. "Who's been a silly nincompoop then?"

Then he was reading to me, my favorite story again, *The Ugly Duckling*. Mama and Papa and Aunty Ducka had read it to me so often that I knew it almost by heart. I drifted off to sleep listening to Papa, listening to Mama, listening to Aunty Ducka, as I so often had at home.

"Night-night, Merry," Mama was saying. "Night-night." She was kissing my forehead, tucking me in.

——◆——

When the moon became the sun, the brightness of it woke me, and only then did I realize I must have been asleep. A bird, a white bird, was perched on the edge of the piano eyeing me with a beady orange eye that blinked. I was so happy to have some company, so glad we were not alone. Another one flew down out of the sun and landed just for a moment beside it, before both lifted off, shrieking. "Gulls," I told Celia. "Look, you see them? They have found us!"

But Celia did not answer. It took me some moments to comprehend that I was not holding Celia anymore. It was her teddy bear I was holding. Celia was not there, nowhere, gone. In the night sometime I must have let her go, or she must have let me go. I hoped it was her who had let me go. I have hoped that ever since. All I knew was that she had rolled away and gone down into the sea with Mama and Brendan and Maurice, with all the others from the ship, down into the sea, where I knew that I too would soon be going. I was sad that I was alone, and suddenly angry, angry with everything and everyone, angry at the world, angry at myself.

Maybe it was anger that gave me strength. I do not know. But suddenly I was up on my feet, and shouting, raging against myself for falling asleep, for letting go of Celia. I wanted it all to be over now, quickly. I would sink the piano myself, drown myself, get it over and done with. I jumped up and down, but it had no effect at all, except, I discovered, that I could make the piano murmur more, make it hum louder under my feet. I leaped up high to land all the more heavily. I danced, I pranced, I trotted and galloped, laughing now through tears of rage, wild with laughter, hysterical with it. Higher, higher I leaped. I stomped, I stamped. But nothing I could do would make the piano sink.

I ran to the edge and stood there looking down into the sea. I told myself out loud that all I had to do was to dive in, to jump in. "It's easy, Merry. Do it. Just do it!" But I couldn't do it. I wasn't frightened, it wasn't that. It was that old lady's voice in my head, the one who had made sure I got into the lifeboat. "Live, child," she had told me. "You have to live." She too was down there at the bottom of the sea, with Mama and the others. They were all telling me to live. Celia was too. I heard her, heard her telling me to look after her teddy bear for her. I heard all of them. I made my way back to the middle of the piano, and sat down cross-legged, holding Celia's teddy bear tightly to me. "We're going to live," I told him. "You and me, we're going to live." The bear was smiling, still smiling. He believed me, and if he believed me, then I would believe me too. I would live.

After that I never lay down, not once. I knew if I did I should be bound to fall asleep again, that I would be bound to roll over the side and into the sea before I could save myself. I would sit where I was, not move, stay awake, and live.

I honestly believe that had it not been for those two inquisitive gulls, I should not have survived. They were not always there on the piano with me, but they returned often enough and stayed long enough to keep my hopes alive. If they had found me, I reasoned, then searchers could too. It was the last reasoning I can remember. I must have been much weakened,

I suppose, by thirst, by hunger and cold. It seemed to me that I was existing now in a kind of limbo, in and out of a world of dreams and reality, unable anymore to distinguish the one from the other, not caring about anything at all, except for Celia's teddy bear and my two birds. Sometimes the birds were gulls, and sometimes they became peacocks, and I'd see Mama lying there facedown in the sea, one of the peacocks on her back, spreading his tail feathers, lifting his head and shrieking. And then it was me shrieking, not the peacock, and the gulls were back there again on the piano and staring at me, silently. I tried to talk to them, to Celia's teddy bear, but no words would come anymore.

In those hours sitting on the piano in the midst of the ocean, I had lost all sense of time, of who I was, where I had come from, or how it was that I found myself sitting cross-legged on a piano in the middle of the ocean, with nothing but a smiling teddy bear and a couple of gulls for company. I was not surprised therefore—for there is nothing much in a dream that is surprising—when the surface of the sea nearby seemed suddenly to bubble and froth, and there rose from the ocean, no more than a stone's throw away, a strange apparition. I could make no sense of what it was.

I thought at first it might be a whale that was coming to investigate me, and I remembered thinking it must be as puzzled as I was to find a piano in the sea. Like most whales, it was shaped like a giant cucumber, growing in length and size with every moment as it broke the surface. Waterfalls poured in sheets down the shining sides of it as it emerged slowly but inexorably from the sea, the waves from the wash of it rocking the piano and tipping it ever more violently. Thinking it would sink now at any moment, I threw myself facedown, clinging on tight to the teddy bear, which had become more important to me than life itself, trying to brace myself with my toes to slow down my inevitable slide into the sea.

The piano, though, righted itself just in time, and I lay there, perilously close now to the edge of it, to the surging ocean that wanted to suck me down and drown me. I looked up then, and realized that this was no whale, but a ship of some kind, of a kind I had never seen before. Whales did not have engines, were not made of steel, did not have numbers on their sides. I could hear the rumble and roaring of engines beneath the sea, and then the rough voices of shouting men. Half a dozen of them were emerging from the vessel now, carrying a small boat between them. They were lowering it into the sea and rowing hard toward me. When they reached the piano, one of them got out of the rowing boat and stepped across gingerly onto the piano. He was on his hands and knees then, and crawling toward me.

Crouching close now, and holding out his hands to me, he said: "*Ist gut. Freund.* Friend. *Kommen sie mit. Komm.*" I shrunk away from him. "*Gnädiges Fräulein.* You come, *ja? Mit mir, mit dem Boot. Kommen sie. Bitte. Komm.*" He was a kind man. I could hear that in his voice, see it in his eyes. He would not harm me. "*Ich heisse* Wilhelm. Your name, young lady, *ihre* name?"

I understood, but I could not answer, because I did not know my name. I tried to speak. I wanted to tell him that I did not know, that I could not remember my name, that I could not remember anything. I tried again and again to speak, to tell him I could not remember. But when I opened my mouth to talk, no words would come out.

Chapter Eighteen

Remember the Lusitania*!*

After Dr. Crow's last visit, the family should have been prepared. They knew there would be trouble. They knew how
some people might be. But nothing he had said, nothing they
might have imagined, could possibly have prepared the family
for the resentment and the anger the news seemed to have
aroused, not just on Bryher, but all around the islands. Lucy Lost
was German. "Wilhelm," the name on the blanket she had been
found with, was all the evidence they needed. Lucy Lost was a
lousy Hun.

The Wheatcroft family of Bryher, hitherto much liked and
respected, had almost overnight become nothing but "Fritz lov-
ers," and some hinted darkly, they could even be spies too.
They found themselves shunned wherever they went. Many of
Jim's fishermen friends, until then his pals of a lifetime, would
look the other way when they saw him coming and leave him
to mend his nets down on the beach by himself. There were

no more jolly quips about mermaids, no more talk about where was good to catch mackerel or pollock that day, no more friendly advice about when or how the weather might change. No words were spoken. None were needed. The averted eyes, the dark accusing looks, the whispered asides were enough.

In church on Sundays, no one would sit down in the same pew with them; and the Reverend Morrison himself, already for some time a fierce opponent of Mary's outspoken pacifism, did what everyone else was doing, and ostracized them completely. His sermons were pointedly more belligerent than ever. He lost no opportunity to remind everyone of the barbaric atrocities committed by the German enemy, the bayoneting of little children in brave little Belgium, and the shameful torpedoing of the *Lusitania,* not a warship, not carrying a single bullet, not a single rifle, but a passenger liner, traveling the ocean in peace. More than a thousand souls had been lost—an event that, he said, "had horrified and outraged, not just ourselves on these islands, but the entire civilized world. Always remember, we are fighting for God and our country, against the forces of evil. Did not the Angel appear to our troops at Mons? Is not God on our side, on the side of freedom and right?"

No one came to the door to buy Mary's eggs anymore. No one came to call at all. And out around the island, everyone she met simply turned their backs on her, and pretended she was not there. Doors remained closed if ever she called on anyone.

No one stopped for a friendly chat, no one so much as greeted her. There was sullen hostility wherever she went.

For Alfie and Lucy at school there was no such reticence. Hailed and celebrated only recently as school heroes, they were now despised, vilified, and mocked at every opportunity. Lucy was utterly bewildered by all this sudden animosity, and shadowed Alfie even more closely than usual on the way to and from school, and whenever she could in the school yard.

Only in the safety of Miss Nightingale's classroom was there at least some sanctuary for her. Miss Nightingale did all she could to protect her and reassure her. To her, all this talk, all this rumormongering, was nothing but vicious, wicked, and cruel. Like all the little children in her class, she did not care, one way or another, whether Lucy was German or not. For Miss Nightingale, Lucy Lost was a sad and deeply troubled child, traumatized even, who, despite her considerable learning difficulties, was clearly a child of great gifts, in her piano playing, in her drawing too, a pupil who needed her help and support, and all the comfort and love she could give her. And for the children in her Infants class, Lucy was still their adored "Little Mother," who played with them and cared for them, and whom everyone wanted for a best friend. In the days and weeks that followed the revelation about her "German" blanket, that classroom proved to be the only haven at school for Lucy Lost.

But for Alfie there was no hiding place. Alfie's class, led by

Zebediah Bishop and his friends, was forever ganging up against him, taunting and insulting him endlessly about his "mad" family, his "loony" Uncle Billy, who thought he was a pirate, and now his "loopy Fritz" sister, who was "so dumb she don't even speak, and don't even know who she is" but who was probably the daughter of the filthy old Kaiser himself. Alfie did try all he could to turn a blind eye, turn a deaf ear, but sooner or later he would find himself drawn into yet another fight. Win or lose, if he was caught fighting, as he very often was, he would be dragged off by Beastly Beagley for punishment. He expected the ruler or the cane, and was always relieved, and a little surprised too, when it didn't happen. Instead, he would spend almost every playtime these days in detention, which meant that Lucy would be left on her own outside in the school yard and unprotected.

But he need not have worried. He'd see her, through the window, surrounded always by a protective gaggle of her little friends. He could hear the cruel jibes and hateful jeering, all directed at her noisily from across the school yard, but it seemed to him that she stayed serenely oblivious to all this hostility. Maybe she could not understand what they were saying, or maybe she was just being brave. To Alfie it didn't matter, he simply admired her more and more.

Once, though, he saw Zeb and his bullyboy cronies circling her like wolves, moving in on her, with menace and malice in their eyes. They frightened off the infants, and chased them away, leaving Lucy to face them alone. Even then, she did not run, did not back away. He was about to dash out to help her, when Miss Nightingale appeared and saved the situation. She came out into the school yard and called Lucy indoors. Soon afterward, he heard Lucy playing the piano—it had to be her because he recognized her favorite piece, the one she played most often on the gramophone back at home. There was defiance in the way she played that music. She was, he was sure of it, letting them all know out there in the school yard that she was not afraid, not allowing Zeb and his crowd to have the last word. The sound of her playing gave him all the strength he knew he would need to face down Zebediah Bishop and his gang when detention was over, or Beastly Beagley or anyone else, come to that.

Miss Nightingale was fast becoming their only friend and ally at school. She was clearly taking every opportunity to call in Lucy from the school yard for as many piano lessons or extra writing lessons as possible. She was protecting her all she could. And after school was over, she made a point of escorting both of them down to the quay on Tresco to catch the school-boat back to Bryher. She guessed, and she was often right, that their tormentors might be lying in wait to ambush them on the way, but that they would never dare do anything with her there. She would stay with the two of them till the school-boat came, then wave them off. But then they were on their own. Every day she'd stand there watching, helpless now to do any more, as the two of them sat side by side in the boat, apart from the others, staring ahead, enduring as best they could all the barbed remarks, the caustic banter, the crude gestures.

But even as she watched, Miss Nightingale could not find it in her heart to condemn Zeb and the others for their cruelty toward Alfie and Lucy Lost. This, she knew, was not their fault. It was plain to Miss Nightingale that Mr. Beagley was the one who was responsible for all this. Day after day, Mr. Beagley was quite deliberately whipping up a storm of war hysteria in the school. At the raising of the flag at the beginning of each day, after the singing of "God Save the King," he would rant and rave about the barbarity of German troops. He'd tell story after story—dreadful stories some of them too—of the summary executions of women and children, of the sinking of our ships, and of the *Lusitania* in particular. He raged against the wickedness of the enemy, and warned against the spies and enemies in our midst, looking hard at Lucy, and at Alfie too, all the time as he did so.

Miss Nightingale could see well enough too that it was Alfie Mr. Beagley was victimizing, as much if not more than Lucy. And she knew why he was doing it too. Mr. Beagley could never abide any defiance to his authority, even if it was only in a look—"dumn insolence," he called it. The children had always to be fearful of him, to cower down before him, to show their obedience to his every whim. Even as a little boy Alfie had never gone along with this. He'd been a thorn in Mr. Beagley's side ever since he arrived in school, and had as a consequence appeared in the punishment list in the school log as much as anyone. From the very first day that he had brought Lucy into school, he had always stood up for her and defended her, facing down Mr. Beagley again and again.

Miss Nightingale relished the moments when Alfie had spoken his mind to Mr. Beagley, but she could see how this had always unnerved and unsettled the man, which of course made him even more vindictive and vicious than usual. He was a tyrant to the children, and to her. She always loved to see such a tyrant tremble. It gave her great delight and satisfaction. In her darkest hours, whenever she thought of leaving the school— and this was often—it was the well-being of the children she kept foremost in her mind, and that changed her mind, and most recently the well-being of Alfie and Lucy Lost. She would stay for them, and protect them all she could.

At home both Mary and Jim were becoming ever more aware of how severely the children were still being treated at school, by the other children, as well as by Mr. Beagley himself. From the way they were themselves being ostracized, it wasn't hard to imagine what the children must be going through every day at school. Alfie did not tell them everything, but they could see the bruises on his face when he came home, and the torn collars. Both of the children were looking more pale and drawn every day.

Jim threatened time and again to go over to the schoolhouse on Tresco and give Mr. Beagley a piece of his mind again. This time he wouldn't pull his punches, he told Mary, this time he would make it stop. But Mary argued that whatever was done should be done peaceably. She decided to appeal directly to the Reverend Morrison, to ask him to intercede on their behalf with Mr. Beagley—after all, he was the Governor at the school, and a man of God. If anyone could and should stop this kind of victimization, it should surely be him. Quite aware of how he regarded her, and what sort of a man he was, she did not hold out much hope. But she had to try.

When she went to see the Reverend Morrison, though, he wouldn't even let her in at the door. Instead he harangued her on the doorstep. "Mr. Beagley runs a fine school, Mrs. Wheatcroft. Before that girl came along there was no trouble. I told you at the time you should never have taken her in, but you wouldn't listen. That is the trouble with you, Mrs. Wheatcroft, you don't listen to your elders and betters. You were always like that over your support for the suffragettes, I seem to remember. You don't seem to care what the good people of these islands think, just as you didn't when you stood up in church that time last summer only days after the war started, and interrupted my

213

sermon, to preach your pacifist views. You were the only one who spoke up against the war in the whole island, and now when you welcome a child of the enemy into your house and people don't like it, you come to me for help. You should learn, Mrs. Wheatcroft, that as the good book says: 'Ye reap what ye sow.'" And with that he slammed the door in her face.

Chapter Nineteen

June 1915

Sure as eggs is eggs

But Mary could not and would not let it rest there. Jim had been right. She was determined now. They would both go over to Tresco, confront Mr. Beagley together, and have it out with him. It was Alfie who, in the end, managed to dissuade them. "If you go and see him, it'll just make things worse for us," he told them. "Beastly will only take it out on us. That's how he is. We got Miss Nightingale on our side. She can look after Lucy."

"And who looks after you?" Mary asked him.

"I do, Mother," he replied. "I look after me, and I look after Lucy. Don't get me wrong, I don't like the way things are. I wouldn't mind if I never set foot in that lousy school again. And Lucy don't like it any more than I do. I don't never know, not really, not for sure, what she's thinking. But I do know she don't like it over there. She don't need no words to tell me that. But we look after one another. Don't you worry none."

There were times, particularly on the way home from school each day, when Lucy seemed sunk in misery. Time and again, Alfie did try to explain to her why it was that everyone had changed so much toward them, that Cousin Dave had told everyone about her blanket, about the German name on it, about the war, about how people hated the Germans, how Martin Dowd and Henry Hibbert, whom everyone on the islands had known, had been killed out in Belgium, and about Jack Brody, who had come home with one leg and half mad, how German submarines were sinking so many ships, like the *Lusitania,* and drowning so many of our sailors.

Lucy seemed to listen to him well enough, but how much, if anything, she was really understanding, he could not tell. He did notice that if he talked too much, for too long, she would simply stop listening. And this made him think that she had perhaps understood quite enough not to want to hear any more about it, that everything he was talking about was troubling her too much, that she wanted not to know, that she wanted him simply not to talk, to shut up. So he did.

All she wanted, it seemed to Alfie, when she got home every day from school, was to have her cake and milk as quickly as possible, and then, whatever the weather, go out at once for a ride on Peg, who was always waiting for them as usual outside the door. Whenever he could, when he wasn't needed out on the boat with Jim or on the farm, he'd go with her. They'd go riding all over the island, galloping along Rushy Bay, trotting up through the heather on Heathy Hill, walking the coastal path around Hell Bay. They would clamber in among the cairns on Shipman's Head. Peg was sure-footed, and seemed to relish a good clamber, the steeper and rockier the better. If the tide was low enough, they'd go splashing through the shallows all the way across to Tresco and then to Samson Island, and up over the sand dunes onto the path through the bracken up to the deserted cottages by the well. Here they'd sit down out of the wind, and have a rest and a drink, before mounting up again for the ride back home, before the tide came in and cut them off.

The two of them rode as one now, taking turns up front, the one clinging on to the other, loving every moment of it, never wanting it to end, never wanting to go home. They'd go anywhere where there was no one about, where there would be no one to glare at them or shout at them. Only riding round the island on Peg, and on their own, could they seem to be able to forget entirely about school and Beastly Beagley, the cruel looks, the harsh words and the stinging fists—all of it. They'd come trotting home along Green Bay, scattering the oyster-catchers and gulls and turnstones as they came, their spirits lifted and renewed. As they came past the *Hispaniola* they would sometimes see Uncle Billy working away on deck. They would keep their distance. They knew better than to interrupt him.

But if he wasn't on board, they would ride round and round the boat to see what progress had been made. Day by day, the lugger was looking nearer to completion. The bowsprit was in place, all the masts now. "I never thought Uncle Billy could do that," Alfie told her one day as they rode around it once more. "No one did."

One evening, late, after just such a ride, they jumped down and left Peg as usual to have a drink in her favorite puddle by the gate. They were walking up through the field toward the farmhouse, when they saw Mary on her knees, washing down the front door, scrubbing at it hard. She heard them coming and stood up. Alfie had never seen her look so upset. Then, as they came closer, they saw what it was that she had been trying to scrub off. Painted across the door in great white letters were the words: "Remember the *Lusitania*."

Lucy walked up to the door and stood there, staring at it, her head on one side. Then she reached out her hand. She seemed to be tracing the letters one by one with her finger. "Don't do that," Mary snapped, pulling her hand away, and wiping her fingers roughly on her apron. "You'll get paint all over yourself. It says *Lusitania*, Lucy." She read it out slowly for her then, syllable by syllable. "Lu . . sit . . . an . . ia."

Mary was looking closely at Lucy then, frowning at her, lifting her chin, to look deep into her eyes. "You've heard of it? You have, haven't you, Lucy? Look at me, Lucy. When I said it, you recognized that name, didn't you? I saw you did." There was real anger in her voice now. She took Lucy by the shoulders and swung her around to face her. "Lucy, you have to speak to me. You can, I know you can. You have to tell us. It was a ship, a very big ship, and they sank her. The Germans sank her. She was torpedoed, a few months ago now. It was a terrible, cruel thing to do. A thousand people died. Have you heard about it? Did they tell you?" She was shouting at her now, shaking her. "Who told you, Lucy? Did they tell you in Germany? Are you German, Lucy? Are you? Why don't you speak to us? Why?"

Alfie stepped between them, rounding on his mother, as angry now as she was. "Because she can't, Mother! She can't speak to you, nor to any of us. You know she can't. You're frightening her, Mother, can't you see? Don't shout at her. Everyone shouts at us all day. Don't you start."

Mary dissolved suddenly into tears. "For God's sake, just ask her, please, Alfie. Ask her if she's German. Surely she knows that much. Ask her. We've been looking after her all this time, we got a right to know, haven't we?"

"But I thought you said it didn't matter, Mother," Alfie said. "Whether she's German or not, she's one of us now. That's what you said. Family, you said, remember?"

"And so she is," Mary cried. "It don't matter to me, Alfie, not one jot. Course it don't. But look at the door! It matters to them, don't it? Think who done this, our friends, our neighbors. They hate us now."

"You think I don't know that, Mother?" Alfie said. "You think Lucy don't know? It's not her fault. None of this is her fault." Mary looked at Lucy then, saw the hurt and bewilderment in her eyes, and realized what she had said, what she had done.

"Oh, Lucy," she cried, "how could I say such things to you? How could I? I didn't mean it, not like that. I'm sorry, so sorry." She opened her arms to her. Lucy hesitated only for a moment, and then ran to her. They held one another, Mary rocking her gently to her and sobbing. "Forgive me, Lucy. Forgive me." Lucy reached up slowly, and touched her face.

That was when Alfie noticed the broken glass on the ground all around their feet. He looked up. Two windowpanes had been shattered.

"Lucy's bedroom," he said. "They done that?"

"The stone landed on her bed, and some of the glass too," Mary told him. "She could have been hurt, badly hurt. How could they? How could they do such a thing? When I brought Uncle Billy home a few years back, some of them didn't like it, and some of them still don't like having him about even now, I know that. But they leave him be. They never did anything like this, not like this."

"We'll mend it, Mother," Alfie said. "We'll put it right."

Mary was trying hard to put a brave face on it. But this latest incident had angered her, and hurt her, so much that she could not lift her spirits, not even for the children. Lucy went inside, put on a record, and went upstairs to be alone, leaving Alfie and his mother sitting at the kitchen table, both of them deep in thought.

"Which is she, Alfie?" Mary asked after a while, leaning forward across the table, her voice low. "Honestly. What d'you think? German? English?" Alfie didn't have time to answer. "If she turns out to be German," Mary went on, "like they're saying she is—and like they all hope she is too—they'll take her away from us. You know that, don't you, Alfie? Seems to me that's what they always wanted to do, one way or another—to take her away from us. First the vicar says that all she's good for is the madhouse in Bodmin. And there's plenty who've been saying the same. Then Mr. Beagley says she'll be taken away if I don't send her to school. So we send her to school, and when we do, they treat her like this. Now she's German—well, according to them she is. And now they're saying she should be sent off to some prison camp for enemy aliens, or some such place, and all because of a German name on her blanket. They won't do it. They can't, because they won't never be able to prove it, not after what I done."

"What d'you mean, Mother?" Alfie asked.

"I done it a long time ago, just in case," she said, leaning closer, her voice a conspiratorial whisper now. "I always thought this might happen. Cousin Dave is a blabbermouth, known for it. I never thought he could keep his mouth shut for long, that sooner or later he'd talk. Then they'd be bound to want to see the blanket, wouldn't they? So I cut the name tape off. It was falling off anyway, only held on by a stitch or two. None of you have noticed, have you? And nor has Lucy. And just to be sure, I checked that teddy bear of hers at the same time. Lucky I did. Found a label on it. Steiff or something, it said. Bit of a foreign-looking sort of a word too, I thought. Not hardly English, is it? So I cut that off as well.

"Good thing I did. While you was at school today, they came round, Reverend Morrison, Cousin Dave, a dozen or more of them, a whole delegation from all over, wanting to see the blanket. So I showed them, didn't I? The blanket and the teddy bear. You should've seen Cousin Dave's face, Alfie," she went on, with a laugh. "I'm telling you, it was a picture, a real picture!"

"So it's all right then," Alfie said. "They can't think she's German anymore, can they?"

"But that's the thing," Mary told him. "They do. People believe what they want to believe, Alfie. They got it in their heads she's a Fritzy now, and that's that. Mr. Beagley tells everyone she don't speak 'cos she speaks German. She does it deliberate, he says, to hide it, so's we can't tell she's German, 'cos she don't want us to know it. And that's what worries me, Alfie, worries me sick. I mean, what if he's right? I want her to speak, course I do, but I don't want her to speak German."

"She's English, Mother," Alfie said. "She's got to be. She listens, she understands, not everything maybe, but enough. She nods sometimes, smiles. Don't you worry none, Mother, Lucy's English, sure as eggs is eggs."

"I been thinking about that too," she said. "She understands, all right—I seen it in her face. But maybe that's because she's learnt it a little, English, I mean. She could have picked it up, since she's been here. You talk to her all the time, don't you? And she listens to you, and she listens to us. So that's maybe how she can understand a little English. But she don't speak it, do she?" At that moment Lucy came down to put on a new record, and came to sit on Mary's lap. Both of them felt they couldn't talk about it anymore, not with her there.

That evening a storm blew in. No boats went out the next day, nor the next, no fishing boats, and no school-boat, which came as a blessed relief for Alfie and Lucy. The wind howled about the chimneys, rain lashed against the windows, lanes became rivers, birds were buffeted about the skies. In Green Bay, all the boats, the *Hispaniola* among them, rolled and tossed and reared on their moorings. On Sunday morning, they woke to blue skies and still trees and a calm sea. Mary went off to church, alone, determined not to expose the children to any further hostility, but equally determined not to be intimidated herself. Nothing and no one was going to keep her from going to church. She would face them down. When she came back, she stood in the doorway, in tears, unable at first to speak at all.

"What is it, Marymoo?" Jim asked her.

"It's Jack Brody," she said, "he's dead."

<hr />

Everyone on the island was there in church four days later for the funeral. The Wheatcrofts sat alone, as usual, in their pew, until Dr. Crow joined them, for which they were all grateful. When Mary went up to Mrs. Brody after the burial to express her sadness, Mrs. Brody turned her back on her and walked away. Dr. Crow accompanied them back home afterward, and sat with them for a while listening to the gramophone, to Lucy's favorite piece, which she put on and played over and over again. They all sat in silence and let the music fill them.

<hr />

From Dr. Crow's journal, 17th October 1915

I would never have believed that a people usually so kind and generous-hearted, so courteous and considerate, could become in so short a time so vindictive and spiteful, so wicked and vengeful. It seems people are as fickle as the weather. Just as the world about us can be balmy and calm and peaceful one day, and the next, completely transformed by tumultuous seas and roaring winds and angry clouds, so I have learned, a people can turn and change, all kindness and gentleness banished by malice and bigotry.

We all have, I am bound to acknowledge, a darker side. There is a Dr. Jekyll and Mr. Hyde in all of us. But I have never before witnessed such a transformation in almost an entire community. I am known, along with a few on these islands, Mrs. Wheatcroft for one, as someone who has spoken out against this war. In recent months I have had to endure some criticism, some adverse comments, and even the occasional insulting remark, but all this has been as nothing compared with the indignities and unpleasantness visited upon the Wheatcroft family over these last days and weeks.

Like so many others from all over the islands I went over to Bryher today for the funeral of poor Jack Brody. I knew, as indeed did everyone there, his mother included, that death could not have come too soon for poor Jack. For him it was nothing but a blessed release. But at the funeral service, this was no consolation to anyone.

His mother had found him in the morning in bed, his face turned to the wall. He had just had enough, she told me when I came to see her on Monday last to discover the cause of death. I believe she was right. Upon examination I think it likely Jack died of heart failure. That is what I wrote on the certificate, but it would be nearer the truth to say that he died from sadness. I wonder how many there have been, or will be, like Jack

Brody in this war, young, brave, with so much to live for, but left so wounded and scarred in body and soul that all will to live is destroyed.

I sat beside the Wheatcroft family in church today, because I could see that no one else would. I knew why well enough—everyone knows by now about the blanket Big Dave Bishop had found on St. Helen's. As with most funerals I have attended of young people, the grieving was particularly painful for everyone to bear. But coming, as it did, hard upon the news of yet more merchantmen sunk off Scilly in the Western Approaches, with the endless appalling losses reported from every front, feelings were running high.

The vicar in his sermon caught the mood perfectly when he declared, in his customary sanctimonious tones, that the suffering and the death of Jack Brody, the cowardly and barbaric execution of Nurse Edith Cavell in Belgium, and the sinking of the Lusitania with such great loss of life which had so shocked the entire world, could leave none of us in any doubt, "any doubt," he repeated, looking right at us in our pew, "that this war is a Godly war, a righteous struggle for good against evil, that we all have to do our part and fight the good fight."

Reverend Morrison would not acknowledge me, nor even look me in the eye after the funeral service—punishment no doubt for my known views on the war, as well as for my evident solidarity for the Wheatcroft family.

I did not stay for the gathering in the hall afterwards, but instead walked back to Veronica Farm with the Wheatcrofts, to whom, it seemed, no one wished to speak with either. I had heard talk in recent days of the goings-on at Mr. Beagley's school, ever since Big Dave Bishop's story had got about, how cruelly Lucy and Alfie had been treated by the children and Mr. Beagley alike. Knowing Mr. Beagley, I was not at all surprised at this news.

I had met up with Jim Wheatcroft by chance, a few days before, whilst on my rounds on Tresco. He had brought in his catch to sell, and was sitting on the quayside, looking not at all his usual cheerful self. He told me about how, on account of the blanket, no one came to buy his fish these days, that most people—some of them family—would not even speak to him anymore. Wherever he went they shunned him. They were treating Mary the same, and the children too. He wasn't just disgruntled, he was angry, angrier than I ever thought he could be. He told me he would never speak to Cousin Dave again, he said. He did say also, that when it came down to it, all of it was because of the war, that I had been right about it, and so had Mary, that it was poisoning people through and through, all over the islands. Then, thanking me for my friendship to them and for my efforts on Lucy Lost's behalf, he had wished me well and left me.

So it was not entirely for medical reasons that I went back with the family to Veronica Farm this afternoon. I went with them as much as their friend now as their doctor. They remain first and foremost my patients of course. But even so, I did go out of kinship also, sensing how beleaguered and isolated the Wheatcroft family must be feeling. I was not wrong. Indeed, I found them to be hardly the same people I once knew. Mrs. Wheatcroft, usually the mainstay of the family, was quite distraught, and seemed to have lost her spirits entirely. Lucy Lost had withdrawn into herself again, which considering everything that had been happening at school, I should have expected, I suppose. It seems—and I have learnt this from Miss Nightingale—that she is to be found often on her own at school and crying quietly. So much of the progress I had previously seen in Lucy has clearly been lost.

We sat for a while listening to Lucy's favorite record on the gramophone, none of us speaking, all of us lost in thought. When Lucy went upstairs, Mrs. Wheatcroft took the record off and sat down at the kitchen table, disconsolate, head in her hands. Still no one spoke. I did so, only to break the silence. I expressed my condolences as best I could for the hard times they were enduring. "I'll do whatever I can to help," I told them, and I meant it. But it sounded rather formal and hollow. "Lucy doesn't seem so well," I went on. "Are they still persecuting her at school?" No one answered me. "I shall speak to Mr. Beagley if you wish me to."

"That's kind, Doctor," Mary said, her voice no more than a whisper. "Kind."

Jim sat slumped by the stove in his chair, with Alfie nearby hunched in the inglenook, poking at the fire and looking as dejected as his father. Even so, they were, I felt, grateful that I had come back with them to the house, and were trying their best to make me feel welcome. But try as they did, I could see their hearts were not in it. It was just that neither they nor I could find anything to say, and so, for some time, we said very little. I lit up my pipe. I've always found that smoking my pipe helps me through difficult moments. It keeps the hands busy, the mind elsewhere, temporarily at least.

"Did you see, Doctor, as you come in," Jim said, speaking suddenly out of the silence, "did you see their paint smudges all over the door? You know what they painted on it, on our door, do you? 'Remember the Lusitania.' They did that. They wrote that. It's like they think Lucy herself fired the torpedo. And all because of a lousy blanket. I'm telling you, Doctor, sometimes I think this isn't a place I want to live anymore."

A while later Lucy came downstairs into the kitchen clutching her blanket and holding her bear. She went and sat on Mary's lap, and laid her head on her shoulder. Her presence seemed somehow to lift the gloom. I had noticed before that Lucy could have that effect on them, but it was more apparent now than ever. We talked then, and had tea together. That was when they began to talk about it, and once they began, it all came out. They seemed to want to tell me everything. There was a name on the blanket, as Big Dave Bishop said there was, and it was "Wilhelm." And one of the words Lucy had spoken, Alfie told me, was "Wilhelm." They didn't know what to make of it, but Alfie said he was sure she was English.

Mary told me that she knew what people would think if it was found out, which was why she had long since cut off the name tape, and cut off a German-looking label she had found on the teddy bear too, but how that had made no difference when she had showed both the blanket and the bear to the vicar and everyone else when they came to the house. The island, she said, had made up its mind that Lucy was German, and that's what they would go on thinking, until and unless Lucy spoke English. And now they had daubed white paint on her front door and thrown a stone through Lucy's window.

I was enraged at their treatment, but also touched that they had taken me into their confidence, and entrusted me with their story. I wanted to help them if I could. "It is clear to me that Lucy will not talk," I told them, thinking aloud, "unless she first remembers. I feel sure it is her inability to remember, or her unwillingness to remember, that is preventing her from speaking. Whether she speaks in German or in English, it is no matter. That is what we have to remember. All that matters is that she finds herself again, finds out who she is."

"True enough, Doctor, that's true enough," Mary said, her eyes brightening. "But we know who she is, don't we? She's Lucy. So, I'm thinking now that I don't much mind anymore whether she speaks or not. English, German, or Chinese. Who cares? We love her as she is. If she never speaks, never remembers, we'll all love her just the same. We won't ever let anyone take her away, and we don't care what language she speaks. She's family. She stays with us."

Mary kissed Lucy on the top of her head. "Come on, Lucy," she went on, getting up out of the chair. "We've got things to do. Let's leave the men to it, shall we? Up we get. Boots on. We'll feed the hens, see if there are any eggs. And then we'll go down and see Uncle Billy. Give him a couple of eggs. He likes his eggs. Have you seen how that Hispaniola of his is coming on, Doctor? Beautiful, isn't it? She's brought him back to life. They've brought each other back to life. And d'you know what Uncle Billy told me about Lucy yesterday? He said: 'That girl's not a stranger anymore.' He's taken quite a shine to her, like we all have, come to that."

After they had gone out, Jim, Alfie, and I sat in silence for a while, and then I had a sudden thought, the kind of thought that comes to you sometimes in a flash out of nowhere, and you wonder why you never thought of it before. "Maybe," I said, "maybe you should retrace her steps, try somehow to rejoin her to her memory, take Lucy back to where she came from, to where you found her, to St. Helen's, to the Pest House, wasn't it? You never know, something there might awaken her memory."

Jim looked doubtful for a while, but then he was leaning forward in his chair. I could see he was thinking it through. "Why not?" he said, nodding. "Worth a try, I'd say. And the doctor was right enough about the music, weren't he, Alfie? That got her out of bed, didn't it? Got her interested, got her outside, got her to school, got her riding that horse. But she didn't do any of it with me, Doctor. She done all that with Alfie, most of it anyway. If she talks again, then it'll be to Alfie, you can be sure of that. You do it, Alfie, you take her over there to St. Helen's, like the doctor says. Could work. And we haven't got a better idea, have we? You'll give it a go, won't you, Alfie? She'll come in the boat with you now, won't she?"

"She'll come," Alfie said, and the more he thought about it, the more he liked the idea—it would be a day off school too. "She'll be frightened. She still don't like boats much, don't like water, but maybe if we do a bit of fishing. I'll make it a fishing trip. Tomorrow, I'll take her over tomorrow, shall I? If the weather's right. There's a bit of a sea running at the moment, but maybe it'll blow through by morning."

I left the family an hour or so later in much better heart than I had found them, after another cup of tea and some of Mrs. Wheatcroft's cake, to which she knows I am rather partial. It was as good as ever. As I walked

away from the house, Mrs. Wheatcroft and Lucy Lost were busying them-
selves scrubbing down the front door, observed by that horse who was
grazing in the field nearby. Father and son were mending the broken bed-
room window. It occurs to me that I have examined no one, offered no
medicine, or medical advice, and yet I feel that I have perhaps done the
best day of doctoring I ever did.

What will come of all this trouble and strife, and what will become of
Lucy Lost in the end, Heaven only knows. But the Wheatcrofts are good
and fine people, people that I have come to like and respect. As for Lucy
Lost, to me she is like a young swallow fallen from the sky. That family
has picked her up and cared for her. It is surely up to them and to me, to
all of us on these islands, to keep her from harm, to do all we can to help
her fly again.

One thing I know for sure: Lucy Lost will only ever fly once she re-
members who she is, from whence and from whom she came, and to
where and to whom she must one day return. I am hoping most fervently
that a visit to St. Helen's might possibly stir a memory, might just give her
the help she needs. But I have to say, it is only the faintest of hopes.

Chapter Twenty

The Pest House

All night long Mary lay awake beside Jim, worrying whether it was such a good idea to take Lucy back to St. Helen's, whether it might awaken something in her memories that would disturb her, that would remind her only of something she wanted to forget. The more she worried about it, the more she was convinced she shouldn't go. In the end she nudged Jim awake. She had to talk to him. "She shouldn't go," she told him, "Lucy and Alfie, they shouldn't go over to St. Helen's today. I don't like it. I got a bad feeling about it."

"Don't you worry yourself none, Marymoo," he said, still half asleep, "that old *Penguin* of mine might toss you about, might give you a rough old ride, but she'll get you there. She won't never sink, not that boat. I should know, Marymoo, I been out in her often enough. Lucy will be all right, and Alfie knows what he's doing. I taught him all I know, didn't I? It'll be fine, you'll see. Now let's get some sleep, shall us?"

But Mary kept on, revisiting again all the anxieties of her long night awake. "It's not the boat, Jimbo. It's her, it's Lucy. What happens if she remembers, like the doctor says she might, and then she don't like what she remembers? What if remembering is worse than not remembering? And anyway, the doctor could be wrong, couldn't he? Who's to say that just 'cos she remembers things, that she'll suddenly be able to speak, to tell us who she is? I want to know who she is, you know I do. So do we all, but she may not be ready to remember. Maybe it's best if she remembers in her own good time, talks in her own good time. Maybe we're trying to make things happen too quick."

She was silent then for some minutes. Jim thought she might have talked herself out, done all her worrying and gone to sleep. But she started up again.

"Things in the brain, Jim, you can't make them happen if they don't want to happen. Like with Uncle Billy. In that hospital they tried to make him something he wasn't, tried to make him behave different, like he was someone else. That nurse he had was the only one in the place who understood him and was kind to him. She'd read to him, spend time with him. She was the one who brought him in that *Treasure Island* book, read it to him, listened to him read. She knew who Uncle Billy was, half out of his head maybe, a dreamer, but himself, and that you couldn't and shouldn't change him. She just helped him, did what she could, saw Billy was happiest when he was living in his dreams, and let him be.

"It's the same with Lucy. I've been thinking, that maybe we should just leave her be. I've been trying too hard to make her remember, and I shouldn't have. If she don't remember who she is, nor anything about herself, and stays silent and locked away inside herself, then maybe that's how she wants it to be, maybe she can live with that. And if it's all right with her, then who are we to try to change it, Jimbo?"

Jim didn't answer, because he knew it wasn't really a question.

"And then I been thinking something else too, Jimbo," she went on. "Let's suppose the doctor is right, and Lucy comes back from St. Helen's and somehow she's remembered who she is, and where she came from, all of it. And just imagine how it would be if she opens her mouth, and talks, and she tells us the whole story of her life, and it's all in German, every last word. What're we going to do then?"

Jim propped himself up on his elbow and looked down at her. "You know your trouble, Marymoo?" he said. "You do too much thinking, and most of it in the middle of the night. You can't think straight in the middle of the night. You only think the worst. That's when the brain should be resting, sleeping, not thinking. If you're right, Marymoo—and you usually think you are—then there is a God in his heaven, which as you know

I have my doubts about. Then that God of yours will look after Lucy, won't he, even if it turns out she speaks German? God helps those who help themselves, don't he? That's all we're trying to do, help Lucy help herself. Isn't that what the good book says? Isn't that what you believe?"

Mary didn't reply for a while. "It's what I try to believe, Jim," she said. She turned away from him then, and added, "But sometimes I find it hard to believe. Believing's not easy, y'know."

"It'll all seem better in the morning, Marymoo," Jim said, lying down and turning over.

———•◦•———

It did seem better too. The next morning as they all walked down to the boat in Green Bay, Jim was full of last-minute advice for Alfie.

"You'll have high tide all the way, Alfie. Southwesterly breeze. The waves will still be coming in after the storm, so it'll be choppy in the middle of the channel. Keep her under the lee of Pentle Bay till you come toward Cromwell's Castle, then make for St. Helen's. Take your marker from the high rock in the middle of the island, you can't miss it. That'll see you through. But look out for Foreman's Rock. Got a mind of his own that rock, moves around all the time. Treacherous beggar, so you look out, Alfie. Eyes peeled like I taught you. And when you get to St. Helen's, come in slow. There's rocks hidden away in the weed, nasty rocks, sharp rocks. Look for the weed. Where there's weed, there's rocks. So you take care now. You bring my *Penguin* back safe and sound, and Lucy too."

Mary was helping Lucy into the boat, settling her down, wrapping her in her blanket, and making sure the lunch basket she had prepared and the fishing gear were safely stowed under her seat and in the dry. They saw Uncle Billy was out on deck, looking at birds through his telescope. They shouted and waved, and he took off his pirate's hat and bowed low.

"You know what Uncle Billy told me," Alfie said. "He told me that once the *Hispaniola* is finished—and by the look of her it won't be long now, will it?—he said he's going to sail her away for a year and a day to the land where the bong tree grows, or something. That's from one of they poems he reads us, isn't it, Mother? Uncle Billy, he likes his books, don't he? Knows so many poems and songs and stories, keeps them all in his head. How does he do that?"

"'Cos he's clever," Mary said. "That's how. Clever with his hands, clever in his head. Once he reads something, once you tell him something, Uncle Billy never forgets. That's how come he's like he is, Alfie. Trouble is, there's a few things he'd like to forget, and can't."

Jim took Alfie to one side. "Never mind about your Uncle Billy, Alfie," he said. "You just keep your mind on where you're going, on what you're doing. Remember what I told you: in the corner of the Pest House, left-hand corner as you look at the fireplace, that's where we found her, hiding in amongst the bracken she was, remember? That's where she must've spent most of her time over there. It's the only shelter on the island. That's the most likely place, I reckon. So, take her there first, right?"

"But what'll she be looking for, Father?" Alfie asked.

"She won't know till she finds it," Jim told him. "And make sure you have a good look around the whole island while you're there. Take her everywhere. She must have been marooned there on her own for weeks, months even, judging by the state of her when we found her. Dr. Crow thought so too. So like as not, she'll know every inch of the place. Keep close to her, Alfie, keep your eye on her, so's you can see if she recognizes anything."

It was early. There was no one else about on Green Bay, except Uncle Billy, which was how they wanted it. Jim and Mary pushed the boat out and stood watching on the shore as the sail went up, saw the wind flap it and crack it and catch it, and then the boat was dancing away from them out into Tresco Channel, Lucy wrapped in her gray blanket, her bear hugged to her, clutched tight. She looked pale and cold, and a little bewildered, nervous but not frightened, excited rather.

"It's up to Alfie now," Jim said. "Let's hope he'll bring back a fish or two, if nothing else. He's got a good nose for mackerel, my boy."

"He's my boy too, y'know," Mary said.

"Our boy, then," Jim laughed, "and our girl, eh, Marymoo?"

"Our girl," she agreed.

They watched them sail away up the channel, out around Puffin Rock, and stood there watching till they were clear of it, and tacking in a fair breeze past Samson. "Let's hope," Mary breathed as they turned away. "Let's pray."

Hooded under her blanket, Lucy looked nervously about her as the boat dipped and rode in the swell. Every time the spray came over the side, or the boat leaned suddenly in the wind, she gave half a cry or a sharp intake of breath. She was holding on tight, wherever she could, her knuckles white. "Better'n school, Lucy?" Alfie laughed. She managed a smile then, and it wasn't long after that she was sitting there without holding on anymore at all, hugging her knees, and looking all about her, growing more confident and happy by the moment, and happier still when she saw the arctic terns come swooping down, diving into the water all around them.

Alfie decided this was the moment to get fishing. There would be rougher water ahead, so any kind of distraction was going to be helpful. But he needed her to take his place at the tiller so he could have his hands free to bait the line. When he helped her up onto her feet to come and sit beside him, she did it quite willingly, with little hesitation. She was only at the tiller for a few minutes, but she took to it as if she had been doing it all her life. It was the same when she was fishing. Once she had the line in her hand she seemed to know instinctively what to do, and to forget altogether that she was out in the sea in a boat. Alfie was amazed at her.

Lucy clearly loved the wait and expectation of fishing. Her concentration, Alfie saw, was complete. She caught three mackerel quite quickly. Whenever she caught a fish, she was beside herself with excitement, but then, once caught, hated to see them wriggling on the hook, and would make Alfie take them off and throw them back in the sea at once. She was so intent on the fishing by now, that she did not seem to notice at all the rearing and plunging of the boat as they came out of the protection of the channel and into the swell of the open sea. Alfie saw her eyes widen once with fear as the spray came over the side and hit his face. But he whooped and laughed and wiped it away, and her fear too was soon laughed away and forgotten, and she was back to her fishing.

As they sailed along Pentle Bay, they had to tack all the way. So it took time. Lucy caught no more fish, but she was still intent on her line, looking up only when she was distracted by the birds. Alfie could see how she loved to see the cormorants standing like sentinels on the rocks, wings outstretched to dry, the herons and egrets stockstill in the shallows. Alfie told her the names of all the birds they were seeing, where they nested, what fish they liked. They saw seals too, not close, but each sighting, however far away, of a shining whiskery head bobbing up and turning to gaze at them was greeted by Lucy with squeals of joy.

It was Alfie who spotted the school of porpoises dipping and diving through the sea off St. Martin's, the curves of their backs glinting in the morning sun. "Must be twenty or thirty of them at least!" Alfie cried. "Never seen so many in all my life. Isn't that something, Lucy? Isn't that something?"

Lucy was up on her feet in the boat and clapping her hands in wild delight, laughing out loud as he had never heard her before, a joyful, ringing laugh, ringing out like bells, Alfie thought, laughter so close to words, so near to talking.

Suddenly, ahead of the school of porpoises, way out in front, Alfie noticed there was a much larger one who was not swimming as the others were, but was more stately, it seemed, and when he rose each time to the surface, he blew. It was some moments before Alfie realized it couldn't be a porpoise at all, that it had to be a whale, a pilot whale! Alfie had seen them before often enough, but never close to porpoises like this.

"Whale!" he yelled. "It's a whale, Lucy. Look!" Lucy had seen it too by now. But the sighting didn't excite her, as Alfie had expected. Instead it was troubling her, Alfie could see that.

The laughter was gone. She simply stared at it, more in fear than wonder, he thought. "He won't hurt us," he told her. "Gentle as lambs they are, Lucy. Beautiful, isn't he?"

Both whale and porpoises disappeared shortly after. They looked for them and looked for them, but they didn't come back. Alfie felt strangely alone on the ocean without them, sad they were gone. Lucy seemed to feel much the same way. She didn't want to fish anymore, but instead sat there huddled under her blanket, clutching her teddy bear, gazing out to sea, alone in her thoughts.

So far as he could, Alfie kept close to the shore all the way, where the sea was calmer, before having to steer into the faster rougher water around Foreman's Rock. St. Helen's was now in sight. For some time now, Alfie had been looking out for some sign that Lucy might be beginning to recognize where she was going. There had been none. And there was still none now, as they came sailing in over the sandbar toward the island, the Pest House quite visible, and behind it, dominating the whole island, and rising sheer from the bracken, the great rock of St. Helen's. Alfie pulled down the sail, took up the oars, and rowed in through the weed, through the shallows.

There was little wind now though, and less and less as they neared the island. There was a gull on every rock, it seemed, eyeing them with deep suspicion, menace in every eye. It was as if they hadn't moved, Alfie thought, since the last time he was here. Alfie leaped out into the shallows. He picked up Lucy, carried her to the water's edge, and set her down. Pulling her blanket around her shoulders, she looked about her only briefly. Then, teddy bear in hand, she bent down at once and began looking for shells. There was still no sign that she had recognized anything at all.

By the time Alfie had finished hauling up the boat and throwing out the anchor, Lucy was walking away from him, up over the sand toward the Pest House. He had expected her to wait for him, to want to stay close to him as she usually did. He called after her, but she walked on, over the pebbles, up toward the top of the beach, and then over the dunes beyond. She waited for him there, and as he came up to her, much to his surprise, she reached out and took his hand in hers. She was holding his hand tight, quite unable to take her eyes off the Pest House.

She led him there now, along the sandy path toward the door. From the chimney top a gull looked down on them. Lucy noticed it and clapped her hands at him, shooing him away. When he flew off shrieking, she turned and smiled at Alfie, pleased with herself, he thought. Then he thought something else too. She had frightened off the gull, not just for fun—Lucy didn't do things like that. She had done it because this was her home, not the gull's. This was her place, and she knew it.

Still holding Alfie by the hand, she stepped into the Pest

House. She made straight for the fireplace, taking him with her. She knew exactly where she was going. She reached in under the lintel of the chimney, feeling for something, and finding it. When she turned around, she was holding a flask, a water flask. She handed Alfie her teddy bear to hold. Then she unscrewed the flask, put it to her mouth, and drank.

"*Wasser,*" she said, offering it to him with a smile. "*Gut.*"

Chapter Twenty-one

Whale-ship

"Wasser. Gut." Thinking of those words now, all these years later, and of my miraculous rescue, it is as impossible to believe as it was then. It seemed as if I must be in a dream, because I could make no sense of anything, and dreams, as we all know, don't make sense. I did not remember, and had no idea, how it was I had come to be there on the piano in the middle of the ocean, clutching a teddy bear. I only knew I was hearing words and seeing things that I did not understand. I did not comprehend then that the language I was hearing was German, nor that the giant black whale-ship that had surfaced from the sea nearby was in fact a submarine. The truth was that German was not a language I knew at all, and I had no idea then what a submarine looked like.

To me they were all part of a strange blurred vision, a dream I was living through. I imagined that this dream might be the beginning of dying, that when I came out of my dream, I would be dead. I did not mind anymore about dying. Perhaps I was too cold, too tired, too sad. I simply accepted that whatever was going to happen would happen. There was inside me a great emptiness. There was no pain, no fear. I was void of all feeling, except cold.

So I did not resist or struggle as my rescuer carried me down into the waiting life raft. I felt no relief at the time, no joy at my rescue, no sense of what was happening to me, when other hands were reaching for me and grabbing me. As they rowed me across the sea toward the whale-ship I looked up and saw what looked like an iron-clad turret, tall and high above the middle of the ship, and men clustered there, leaning over and shouting down at us across the water.

There were three sailors in the life raft, all of them bearded—I do remember noticing that. I was sitting in the boat beside the one who had climbed up onto the piano and rescued me. He had his arm around me and was holding on to me tight, talking to me all the time. I knew from the gentleness in his voice that these must be words of comfort, but could not understand a word he was saying.

The two other sailors rowed hard through the sea, every stroke deep and long, and cheered on all the way by the sailors watching us from the whale-ship, which seemed to grow, in both length and height, before my eyes as we came closer to it. It occurred to me then that I was right, that I was dying inside my dream, that this journey across the water was indeed part of dying. Some old familiar story echoed in my head, that to be rowed across the water was how it happened, the journey from one life to another, from one world to the next.

Then we were alongside the whale-ship and strong hands were helping me, hauling me up a ladder, and at last into the turret. Every face I looked up into was pale and bearded, with sunken eyes, all ghostly in appearance, yet these men were neither sad nor frightening nor ghoulish as ghosts should be. Most of the faces were smiling and laughing as they peered down at me. They gripped me with cold hard hands, dirty hands too, I saw, but real hands, alive hands, not the hands of ghosts. And they smelt alive too, of damp and smoke and oil, but of people too. They smelt of live people. They wore long leather coats that were slippery and wet to the touch.

It was only when I found myself standing there up on the turret surrounded by these men, who all looked upon me in utter amazement, that I truly began to realize I must be still in the land of the living, that these were certainly not ghosts at all, and that I was neither dead nor dying. It came to me then that when I woke up from this dream I might well be alive as they were. But alive or dead, I did not much mind. I was beyond caring.

I found myself being manhandled down a ladder into the half-dark belly of the whale-ship. Then my sailor, my rescuer, hand on my shoulder, was ushering me down a long passage-way—it was like a tunnel, dimly lit, lined with pipes and tubes and wires—and on both sides of me were men lying there gazing at me from their bunks and hammocks. Everywhere there was the stench of wet clothes and unwashed feet, and toilets. The fumes of oil and smoke were heavy in the air. They called out to me. From their tone, from their eyes, I felt they were greeting me. Some of them, as I passed by, were making jokes and laughing. But I knew they were not making fun of me, because they were not laughing at me, rather laughing because I was there, a stranger in their ship, and they were pleased to see me. They seemed fascinated by me, intrigued. I didn't like to be stared at, of course, but I sensed that it was only out of curiosity, that there was no hint of malice behind their eyes.

Then ahead of me, from far away, from somewhere at the darker end of this gloomy tunnel, I heard the sound of music playing. It was a song I didn't know, but it didn't matter. It was music, and as I walked, it was playing louder all the time. The gramophone, I discovered, was hidden away in a corner up against the steel hull of the whale-ship. It was steel everywhere I looked, above my head, under my feet, behind the web of pipes and tubes. Some of the men were singing along with the song on the gramophone or humming or whistling it. It came to me then as I made my way past them that these men were singing it for me, that it was their way of welcoming me into their boat. I didn't mind the stench so much after that, nor the staring eyes.

My sailor stopped me, pulled aside a curtain, and hands on my shoulders, guided me into a small cabin, no more than a cupboard space, with a narrow bed and a few shelves. There was hardly room to turn around. He handed me a blanket and a long shirt and indicated to me that I should get out of my wet clothes then went out, drawing the curtain behind him. I wondered why I was suddenly unsteady on my feet. Then I knew we were moving, the whole ship thundering and rattling around me. Beyond the curtain, the music played on and the sailors sang on.

I got out of my wet clothes and into the shirt, which was so long and so large that it hung around me like a tent. It was then that I realized to my horror that I was no longer holding my teddy bear in my hand, that I must have let it go, left it on the piano, dropped it in the sea, or left it in the life raft that had brought me to this whale-ship. Somewhere, somehow, I had lost it. I would never see it again. I had never in all my life felt more devastated and lonely as I did then, as I did in that moment. I lay down on the bed, pulled the blanket around me, and turned my face into the pillow, and wished I was dead. I slept then, for how long I did not know.

I woke and turned over. There was a man in a peaked cap and leather coat sitting beside the bed on a camp chair. He was reading a book. I sat up. He saw I was awake and closed the book. I felt drops of water falling on my head, dripping onto my face as I looked up. He smiled, reached forward, and wiped my forehead and my cheeks with his handkerchief. He was gentle about it, and smiling too.

"Do not worry," he said. "There is not a hole in the boat. It is what you call in English 'condensation,' I think. We are under the water now, so there is not much air, and what we have is wet, damp, and full of moisture—little drops of water, you understand. We have forty-five men down here, all breathing this air, and people are warm. We make heat. There are engines too, which make a lot of heat. This is why it rains a little inside the boat. So, as you see, condensation." He handed me from the table a plate of bread and sausage. "Here," he said. "Some food. I am sorry. It is not much, and not very good either. I should rather say, it is horrible. But it is all we have, and I am sure you are hungry. I think when you are hungry, it does not matter what the food tastes like."

The bread, I noticed then, was covered in a strange white furry fluff. "It is bread, I promise you," he went on, pushing back his cap, "and quite good, but we call it 'rabbit.' I think you can see why we call it this. It is like fur on a white rabbit. It grows on bread down here in these damp conditions. It is fungi, like mushrooms. It will not harm you. Later we have hot soup, good soup to warm you."

He spoke with a strong accent, but very slowly and correctly. "You are from the *Lusitania,* I think. Is this so?"

I said nothing, not only because I could not understand what he was talking about but because I knew by now that my voice would not work, that however hard I tried I would not be able to make the words to speak a reply.

"Most unfortunate," he went on, "such loss of life is most regrettable, and the *Lusitania* was a fine ship. I wish to say that it was not my U-boat that sunk your ship, but it might have been. I would have done the same. My father always said to me: 'Never apologize, never explain.' He was only half right, I think. I will not apologize, but I will explain. This is war. The *Lusitania* was supposed to be a passenger ship, only for the transport of passengers. But she was carrying arms and ammunition and soldiers from America to England, which is of course quite against the rules of war. Even in war there must be rules."

The ship creaked and groaned around us. "That is the pressure of water on the hull. It happens when we are deep under the sea. Do not worry. She may leak and she may drip, but she is well made. She is tired, though. We are all tired. Even the food is tired. You know how long it is since we left home? Twelve weeks and four days. No baths, no shaves. There is no water to spare for such things. But it is lucky for you, I think, that Seemann Wilhelm Kreuz was not tired this morning when he was up on watch. I thought he had gone mad, lost all his senses—this happens sometimes in U-boats, when we are on long voyages at sea.

"He comes to me in my cabin—this is my cabin, that is my bed you are lying on. So, I am still asleep and he comes this morning and wakes me up. 'Herr Kapitän,' he says to me. 'There is a piano floating on the sea off the starboard bow. And there is sitting on it, Herr Kapitän, a small girl.' Of course I do not believe him. Who would? But then I go up into the conning tower and I look. And there you are." He laughed then, and shook his head. "I could not believe my eyes!"

The sausage, like the bread, did not look in the least tempting. But he was right. I was so hungry by now that I would have eaten anything. It was unlike any other sausage I had ever tasted, greasy, and full of gristle. But I did not mind one bit. I could not look at the bread as I bit into it. I ate it all the same, all of it.

"So, *gnädiges Fräulein,* our rabbit is good, *ja?*" he said. "Seemann Kreuz says he does not know who you are, your name. Do you have a name? No? Very well. So I will tell you my name first. I am Kapitän Klausen of the Imperial German Navy. Now it is your turn? No? You are perhaps a little shy, *ja?* English? American, perhaps? I hope you are one or the other, because English is the only other language I speak. I have English cousins. I spent holidays with them in the New Forest. We rode horses. And I can play cricket! There are not many Germans who can play cricket. I would say that if there were, then maybe the Germans and the English could have a cricket match, instead of a war. We should all like that, I think." He smiled at that, but was quickly serious again, reflective, sad even.

"Most children are not as quiet as you," he went on. "I know this. Sometimes I wish they were. My daughters, they talk all the time. They chatter like sparrows. Lotte and Christina—they are twins, but not identical. They are younger than you, seven years now. It is, I think, maybe because of them that you are here now on this U-boat. But it is because of my uncle too. You should know about my uncle. He was a sailor—we have had many sailors in our family. Many years ago, his ship, the *Schiller*, she was called, went onto the rocks on the Isles of Scilly, which is off the west coast of England. Many were drowned. My uncle was rescued from the ship by a lifeboat. He was saved by Englishmen, islanders from Scilly, who rowed out to the wreck in a little boat. Those people saved more than thirty German passengers and sailors, and buried the rest with respect. It is because of this act of courage and kindness that the order was given at the beginning of this war that no German warships will ever attack any boats of any kind around the Isles of Scilly. It is because of this, and because these people saved the life of my uncle, that I agreed to stop the ship and pick you up. It is also because Seemann Wilhelm Kreuz and my crew also insisted we must.

"But, little girl, whatever your name is, you are quite a problem for me, for all of us. When I saw you on the piano, in spite of all I have told you, I did not wish to stop. It is dangerous to stop, and it is also against the rules of the Imperial German Navy for a submarine to pick up survivors and take them on board. And as you know from school, I hope, rules are important and must be obeyed. But Seemann Wilhelm Kreuz, like me, has children at home—he has a boy—and he argued most respectfully but insistently that once having seen you, we could not leave you alone on the ocean to die. The other sailors on watch agreed with him. I have to explain that on a boat like this, all of us so close together and far from home are in constant danger. We work together. We live together, we may very well die together. We are like a family. A good father listens to his family. And a good Kapitän does the same.

"So I asked every man on the boat. Should we stop to pick you up? Should we not? Every one of them was in agreement to bring you on board. And when I thought about it, thought of Lotte and Christina, and my uncle, and of the *Schiller,* I was in agreement too. Many of them, most of them, of course have children of their own, and some of the young sailors on board are so young they are almost children themselves. What is it that we should do with you now? That is the question. A submarine on war patrol is no place for a child. I cannot take you back to Germany, where they might well court-martial me for bringing you aboard. And so, since you are very likely English or American, I have decided to set a course for the nearest landfall in England. And do you know where this is? It is the Isles of Scilly. We are just a few hours away, and will be there by nighttime. If the weather is good, if the night is dark enough and it is safe to do so, we shall surface, and find somewhere to put you ashore. We know from the *Schiller* that they are good and kind people there. You will be among friends, and safe, and we shall go home to our families. And so, all will be well."

He stood up to go, and straightened his cap. He was much taller than I had thought. "As you see, my cabin is not very comfortable. But it is the best room on the boat. I must ask you not to leave the cabin. I have given Seemann Wilhelm Kreuz the responsibility of looking after you during the rest of your stay with us."

He looked down on me, long and hard. "I think you are angry with me, or perhaps you are sad—this is why you do not speak. My little Christina, she is the same sometimes. You are angry perhaps because I am German, I am the enemy, and I sink ships. Sadly, this is true. This is what I am. This is what I do. We may be at war, but I am a sailor, we are all sailors. We love ships. To sink a ship, to watch it go down, is a terrible thing. War makes men do terrible things. You have a right to be angry, a right to be sad." He turned up his collar and was pulling aside the curtain to leave, when he remembered something. He reached deep into his coat pocket, pulled out my teddy bear, and handed it to me. "Seemann Kreuz found this. He says it is yours. It is not likely, I think, to belong to anyone else."

I was overjoyed. I tried to thank him, tried to speak, but no words would come out.

He left me then, but I was no longer alone. I had my teddy bear. I looked into his smiling face. I loved this bear, but I had no idea why. It is hard to explain how it is not to have memories. But I shall try. You are lost in a world you do not understand, a world in which everything and everyone is bewildering, a world with which you have little connection, to which you do not belong. It is as if you are locked in a darkened room with doors all around instead of walls, where every door you try to open is locked fast against you. There is no way out. Some light does creep in under the doorways, so you know there is light out there, that it is the light of memory. You have memory. You have a glimpse of it under the doors, but you can't open the doors, you can't reach it. You know you must be someone, come from somewhere, but that you will only remember when the doors open, when the light floods in.

As it was, I had no idea at the time what a submarine or a U-boat was, nor even what a German was, nor even that there was a war. So nothing the captain of the whale-ship told me had made any sense at all. All I knew was that this tall man with a silvery beard had given me back the teddy bear that I loved. It was soggy, soaked through, but I had it back. He had been kind to me, and I liked him.

I should have stayed where I was in his cabin, as he had told me, and had it not been for the gramophone, I would have done so. The music was familiar, but I didn't know why. It was piano music. No one was singing anymore now. As I stepped out through the curtain and wandered down the passageway I could see on either side of me that the men were mostly asleep on their bunks and in their hammocks, their blankets pulled up over their faces. A few were still awake and watching me as I passed by. One of them sat up on his elbows and called to me. "Allo! Allo! What is your name? I speak English, *Fräulein*. Little girl, I have chocolate. You like chocolate?" He was reaching out to me, and offering me a piece of chocolate from the flat of his hand. "Is good, *sehr gut, mein Kind.*" I took it and ate it. It was good too. "You like our boat?" he went on, laughing. "*Sehr komfortabel, ja?*" I walked past him.

There was an open door ahead of me and I wanted to see what was inside. I was about to step through, when I felt a hand on my shoulder holding me back. I turned to see who it was. It was my rescuer, Wilhelm Kreuz. He was shaking his head and frowning at me. He wasn't angry, just telling me I should not go any further. "Torpedo room," he said, and I could tell he was not pleased with me at all. "*Nein.* You must not go in there. *Verboten. Verstehen?*" He took me by the hand and took me back down the passageway toward the cabin, much to everyone's amusement. But I could tell Wilhelm wasn't amused one bit by all the whistling and catcalling that followed us down the boat. He made me sit on the bed and he closed the curtain. Then he crouched down beside me and gave me a ticking off.

"Here," he said, wagging his finger in my face. "*Du musst hier bleiben.* Here. Understand? *Verstehen?* Stay here." Then he sat back on the chair looking about him and wondering, I could tell, what he was going to do with me. Suddenly he knew.

"Chess," he said. "We play. I teach you." The chessboard he took down from the shelf above was broken in two, and when he emptied all the pieces out and set them up, there were two pieces of chalk for two missing white pawns—they wouldn't stand up for long because of the vibration of the boat. So sitting at the little folding table in the cabin, watched by my teddy bear, who sat by the chessboard on the table, Wilhelm Kreuz and I played chess, for hours. He didn't need to teach me. Somehow I knew. I had no idea how. He played well. But I played better.

I thought about that afterward, that maybe Wilhelm was just being kind and letting me win. I shall never know. I only knew that whilst I was playing, nothing else seemed to matter except what was happening on the chessboard, my next move, his next move. I have wondered too how it was, that when so much else was forgotten, I knew so well how to play chess with Wilhelm, how to beat him. I was able to play instinctively, knew how every piece moved, how to think ahead, set traps, avoid traps, guess what his next move would be. I could play chess, and that had to be from memory. So I was remembering something, understanding something. I was aware of it even then too, that I did have some powers of recall, some understanding, but it was patchy and fleeting. Nothing seemed to be joined up. Nothing seemed to make much sense to me, except chess.

Hours must have passed playing chess that day with Wilhelm. He did not try to talk. Speaking English was not easy for him, I could tell. His face was set with concentration, frozen in a frown, except when he thought he had made a clever move. Then, he would smile at me with satisfaction, in triumph even, and sit back, folding his arms and chuckling to himself.

My next move would often take the smile off his face, and then he would cast his eyes to heaven, shake his head, and slap his own wrist in frustration. He was always very polite and shook hands at the end of each game, and applauded my victories. And he was funny too. When he lost he would sometimes wag his finger at my teddy bear, pretending to tell him off. I didn't understand exactly what he was saying of course, but I think I caught the gist of it. I thought he might have been telling the teddy bear not to help me, to keep out of it, that it wasn't fair to have to play against two of us. Then he would turn the teddy bear round, so that he couldn't watch the next game. And after I had set up the pieces again, I would turn the teddy bear round again, and he would chuckle. I liked his chuckle. It was not put on, as laughter so often can be, but came naturally to him, easily, as easily as his smile.

It was in the middle of a game, some time later, that someone called for Wilhelm from outside the curtain. It was the captain's voice. Wilhelm got up, shrugged on his coat and cap, showed me the watch on his wrist, and circled his finger round three times. He would be gone for three hours. He laid me down, gave me my teddy bear to hold, put the blanket over me, and showed me that I must pull the blanket up over my face so that the drips gathering above me did not fall on my face while I was asleep. Then he saluted me, and left me. The whaleship might have been damp and dripping, the oily sweaty stench of it might have been stifling, but it was warm, and I had my teddy bear, and there was music playing. The churn and rumble of the engines was regular, rhythmic, and I was soon asleep.

Chapter Twenty-two

SCILLY ISLES, MAY 1915

Auf Wiedersehen

I woke not knowing where I was at all, only that it was dark all around me, pitch-black, not a chink of light. I could hear the churning of engines, and whispering voices nearby, muffled and urgent. My ears were popping, and I had the strongest feeling that my stomach was sinking, and yet in spite of that, I was somehow floating upward, rising feetfirst and steeply, and then rocking so violently that I had to hold on to the sides of my bunk to steady myself. I was still struggling to remember where I was. It was the stench of the fumes that finally reminded me.

I heard the sound of the curtain being pulled aside, and a sudden light filled the cabin. With the light came a voice, then a face. It was Wilhelm. He handed me some clothes, my clothes. "Here. For you," he whispered, "you dress now. *Schnell. Schnell.* The *Kapitän* says we must go." He went out then, drawing the curtain behind him. My clothes smelt of oil now, like everything else, but also as if they had been singed. I could feel they were still damp, but at least they were warm. It took a while for me to put them on, because the constant movement of the boat kept throwing me off balance. Dressing and holding on to something at the same time was not easy. But once back in my own clothes, I felt more like myself again.

By the time Wilhelm came back some moments later I was sitting there on the bed, teddy bear in hand, ready to go and waiting, but where I was going and what I was waiting for, I had no idea. Wilhelm wrapped a blanket around my shoulders. *"Meine mutti,"* he said, "she makes this for me. It is for you to have now. Warm, you must be warm." He was smiling then as he tapped my teddy bear on his head. *"Und* you have also your little friend. *Das ist gut.* To have a friend is always good."

He helped me to my feet then, took me by the hand, and led me out of the cabin and down the passageway, past the bunks and the hammocks, past all the faces gazing at me. Some of the sailors lifted their hands in silent farewell. Some nodded and smiled as I passed, and said, *"Auf Wiedersehen."*

One or two said, "Goodbye, little girl."

I was climbing a ladder then, Wilhelm helping me up, and suddenly I was out in the cold fresh air, the night all about me and the surging sea and the stars. Some distance away I saw land, the shape of what looked like an island lying low and dark in the sea. A life raft was waiting in the sea below, two sailors at the oars, one of them holding on to the ladder. It would be a very long way down that ladder.

"Seemann Kreuz will help you. You will not fall." I recognized at once the voice of the tall dark figure who stood before me now. It was the captain. I could see the shape of his peaked cap against the sky.

"I hope that you have enjoyed your stay in our boat, that you found my bed comfortable," he said. "I wish we could bring you in closer to the shore, but it is not deep enough in these waters. There are rocks everywhere in this place, like teeth waiting to bite us. So Seemann Kreuz and two of my sailors will row you to the nearest island. On my map it is called St. Helen's. It is small, not many houses, not many people. There, I hope, you will soon find someone to look after you, and food and shelter. But we shall not put you ashore with nothing. We should like you to have a small gift so you will remember us. Seemann Kreuz will give you some water, and some sausage and some 'rabbit' also—you remember our rabbit bread? It is a specialty of our boat, you could say a delicacy!"

He laughed as he shook my hand. "Off you go, *gnädiges Fräulein*. I am happy we found you on your piano. All my men are happy too. And we do not often have much to be happy about when we are at sea. You must go now." He saluted me then. *"Auf Wiedersehen,* little silent girl. Remember us and we shall remember you."

I turned and looked down the ladder at the heaving sea below, the life raft rising and falling against the side of the boat. My legs would not move. I could not do it. I could not climb down that ladder, not in a million years. Wilhelm must have known it, because it was his idea to crouch down and give me a piggyback. I went down the ladder, eyes closed, clinging on around his neck. Then we were sitting in the life raft and being rowed away, leaving the submarine quickly behind us, until soon it seemed no more than a distant shadow resting on the ocean.

No one spoke in the life raft. My eyes were becoming more accustomed to the darkness now. There were a few stars out. As we neared the shore, the two sailors dipped their oars ever more carefully, pulling on them slowly, so we were only gliding through the water now. At the tiller, Wilhelm was leaning forward, searching the shoreline for the best place to bring the boat in. We came around the head of the island, where waves were rolling in, where cliffs reared high and rocks tumbled into the sea in piles, and came at last, to my great relief, into much calmer waters. We saw a broad strand of sand bright under the stars. Here they rowed in and beached the boat.

Wilhelm leaped out into the shallows, and was pointing up now toward the dunes. I saw then what he had already noticed, a house, with dark windows, and a single chimney, and a gull perched on top. I knew gulls liked to warm themselves on chimney tops. So there would be a fire, and I would soon be sitting close to it, warm and safe. Wilhelm lifted me out of the life raft and set me down on the sand beside him. He crouched in front of me, putting his hands on my shoulders. "Here is England. You go to the house, *ja*? They will look after you now."

He handed me then a tin flask, and a small paper bag. I could feel the sausage inside, and the bread. "*Wasser,*" he said, tapping the flask. "*Wasser. Ist gut.* Food also. For you, and for your little bear, if he is hungry." The sailors were calling to him from the boat, urgently. "*Ich kann nicht bleiben, mein liebling,*" he went on. "*Wir müssen nun gehen.*" He reached out, touched my cheek. "*Entschuldigung,*" he said. "I go now. I am sorry. For the *Lusitania,* I am sorry."

Then he turned, pushed the boat out, and was gone. I watched them rowing away and stayed there until I could see them no more. I was sad to be alone again, and fearful too, as I looked about me. This was a strange and dismal place. The island seemed to me to glower like a dark frown, and the sea growled and hissed at me. This was not a place I wanted to be. But there would be a fire in the house at the top of the dunes, and people to welcome me in, and hot food, and a bed. I began at once to walk up over the steeply shelving sand. The gulls, perched on the rocks everywhere I looked, were eyeing me as I passed. I hoped whoever lived there in the house would be more friendly than they were.

I should have been longing to meet these people, to hear English voices again. But I knew there would be questions, lots of questions about who I was, where I had come from, how I had arrived here, none of which I could answer. What little I did remember, and this was very little, my tongue could not speak. I did not know why that should be either. So how could I explain myself, explain any of it?

As I came up the track toward it, the house loomed larger than I had imagined it to be, a sturdy stone-built place, severe in its aspect, with close-cropped grass all around. The gull on the chimney did not move even as I approached the front door, but sat there as still as the house. I think I realized already from this stillness that it was empty, that no one lived in the place, even before I discovered that there was no front door, no glass in any of the windows. I stepped over the threshold into a house that was almost entirely open to the night sky. There was an open fireplace set into the end wall, stone seats on either side, but I could see no other sign that the house had ever been lived in, no furniture, no nothing. The place was a deserted ruin, where only bracken lived now, and brambles and ivy that climbed its way up the walls and out through the windows. Above me the gull shrieked suddenly, as if to tell me, "My place! My house! Go away!"

Then, squawking at me angrily, it lifted off and flew up into the night.

It came on to rain then, a blustering downpour that drove me to seek shelter at once. The open fireplace was all there was. Here, under the only part of the roof still intact, I would at least be dry and out of the wind. I made my way through the undergrowth, and crawled into the back of the fireplace. I sat on the stone seat and huddled there in the corner under my blanket. I would wait there till first light, I thought, until I could see properly where I was going, then go and find another house, one still lived in, where there would surely be the friendly faces and the welcoming warmth I had been hoping for and expecting.

Cold, and colder with every hour that passed, I could not sleep. That night was the longest of my life. I thought it would never end. As soon as the stars left the sky, at the first hint of gray light that night before dawn, I was up and out of that gaping house, relieved to leave its emptiness behind me. I took all I had in this world with me, my blanket, my teddy bear, the water flask, and the bag of food they had given me, and set off, with hope in my heart, around the island, in search of other houses, in search of anyone who would take me in and help me. I had no idea how big the island might be, nor how many houses and people I would find.

It did not take me long to discover, with a sinking heart, that there was no other house at all on the island. I did find in among the bracken the remains of what might have once been a house or a chapel perhaps, for there was a gravestone there with a name carved on it, so weathered that I could not decipher it. But besides those remains, and besides that ruin where I had spent the night, there was no other human habitation to be found. There were, I could see, lots of other islands all around, dozens of them, scattered over the sea, as if some giant in a rage had cast fistfuls of giant boulders into the ocean. And I could see also there were houses on many of these islands, but all of them were far away, too far for me to swim to. I could see boats too, several of them, fishing boats, rowing boats, some drawn up on the beaches, some moored offshore, some of them out at sea. There were boats out there, people out there, houses out there, if only I could reach them.

What was certain was that my island was completely deserted, except for the gulls that watched me wherever I went, that wheeled above me, mewing and screeching, making it quite clear to me that they resented my intrusion into their world. The little piping birds that scavenged the foreshore and the seaweed and the rock pools seemed to accept me, but they hardly noticed I was there. They ignored me. They were pretty, but they were little consolation to me. I was overwhelmed now by such misery as I had never known before, by a sense of complete hopelessness and isolation. I didn't have any idea what to do, except to get up and explore my island more thoroughly.

I had discovered already that the island was not just small, but tiny. I walked all around it in no time at all, and was very soon back to my ruined house again, which was just as well, because another squall was blowing up, whipping the sea into a frenzy of waves, and blowing the gulls and crows about the sky like leaves. I reached my house just as the rain came down, and crawled again into the shelter of my fireplace. Hunger was gnawing at me now, and I was weak from emptiness. I had to eat. But I knew now I had to make my food last, that I might find very little else to eat in this place. So I ate just enough to keep me going, and no more. Between them, the sausage and bread and water warmed me through and gave me new strength to try to work things out in my mind.

My only hope, I decided, lay in reaching one of those other islands, that was obvious to me now. But they were unreachable. I had no boat. I could not even try to swim that far. I may have been able to see them, but they could just as well have been a hundred miles away. Even if there were people living on them, they couldn't see me. I could not shout or scream. I had no voice. I couldn't light a fire. I had no matches. I had only one choice, it seemed to me.

There was a huge rock behind my house, a rock that dominated the whole island. It was without question, the highest and most visible point on the island. I would climb up there—although I could see that might be far from easy—reach the top, and once there, look out for a passing boat. Then I would wave, stand there and wave, until someone saw me. Sooner or later, someone out there, on one of those islands, or out in a boat, would have to see me, and come to my rescue. I made up my mind there and then to climb that rock.

I left everything behind on the stone seat in the fireplace—I knew I would need both hands free for the climb—and set off toward the foot of the rock. Standing there looking up, I saw it was an even more daunting prospect than I had imagined, higher, steeper, and terrifying. But I had to do it. I had no choice. I started to climb, trying not to look down, concentrating only on reaching the top. It was treacherous in places, where the rock was slippery from the rain. My legs trembled with the effort of it, and with fear too. Whenever my fingers or my foot slipped, my heart would race. I could feel the pounding of it in my ears sometimes. I kept telling myself that every small step upward was bringing me closer, that I could do it, I would do it. By the time I reached the top, I had no breath left, no strength in my arms or legs. I wanted to stand up and punch the air in triumph, but all I could do was sit there, heaving and breathless, trying to recover.

I looked around me. There were islands everywhere, near and far, like large and small dumplings, scattered all over the sea. Now in sudden bright sunlight, the sea was turning from turquoise to green before my eyes. On some islands, the bigger ones, I could see the lines of cottages, farms and churches too.

And there were people. I could see them quite plainly now, tiny figures in the distance, making their way along the seashore, standing on quays, working in the fields. And there were boats coming in, going out. My exhaustion suddenly forgotten, I was on my feet at once and waving wildly with both arms. Forgetting myself, I tried to shout. But the best I could manage was a hoarse whisper, more like a gasp, and even that was hurting my throat so much that I had to stop.

How long I must have stood there waving I do not know. Wherever I looked, there were fishing boats out and about all around the islands. It was the boats that kept me waving. But I could see in the end that none were coming anywhere near my island, that I was too far away from them to be noticed, however hard I waved. But I waved all the same—what else could I do? I waved until my shoulders were on fire with pain, till I could scarcely lift my arms at all. I stood there and waited, hoping and praying that one of the fishing boats might turn and sail in my direction. When at last one of them did, I found the strength to wave yet again. But even as I was doing it, I knew it was futile. The gulls seemed to know it too. They wheeled above me, cackling at me, mocking me. Then they began diving on me, trying to drive me off the rock. But I would not go.

All day long I stayed there, hoping against hope that my luck would change, that someone would come near enough to see me. I was sitting, hugging my knees against the cold, too tired to wave anymore, too tired even to stand. An evening wind had got up and I was now chilled to the bone and shivering uncontrollably. But I still stayed, still hoped. Only when darkness came down, did I accept defeat, and begin the long climb down. By then, my legs were stiff and I could no longer feel my fingers or my feet. I am sure that was why I fell. I must have lost my grip and slipped. I don't know. I do not even remember the fall, only that I woke up on the ground with bracken all around me, my head and my ankle throbbing, and above me, the gulls circling, cackling, mocking me again. I felt my forehead. It was sticky with blood.

Chapter Twenty-three

From another world

I limped my way back to the ruined house, longing now for a drink, longing for my sausage and bread. I saw what had happened the moment I stepped through the doorway. Littered everywhere, in among the bracken and the brambles, were the remains of the brown paper bag. There wasn't a trace of bread or sausage to be seen anywhere. My teddy bear lay facedown on the ground in a puddle.

I knew at once who the culprit was. There, on the chimney above, he sat. If gulls had lips, he'd have been licking them. He looked so pleased with himself. I picked up a stone then and hurled it at him. It clattered against the chimney, but near enough to frighten him away. He flew off squawking. It was a sort of revenge, a little triumph, but it gave me no lasting satisfaction. When you are hungry, I discovered, truly hungry, there is no satisfaction in anything but food. And if you have no food, but instead only water to drink, you drink all you can, because you need to fill your stomach with something, and something is always better than nothing. I drank all the water left in my water flask, to the last dribble, down to the last drop, gulped the lot down. The flask was empty before I ever thought of saving any for later.

I lay curled up under my blanket on my stone seat in the fireplace, not frightened at all of the gathering darkness, not worried about how I was going to survive now on this deserted island without food or water, not concerned anymore about whether or not I might be rescued—I was too angry with myself to think of any of this. I could not get it out of my head how stupid I had been not to have hidden my food away from the gulls. Why had I not thought of that? And now, to make matters worse, I had drunk the last of my water. So now I had no food, no water. What a fool I had been. Nincompoop! Ninny! Those words kept coming into my head again and again.

Cold crept through my blanket that night and seeped into my whole being. I could not sleep for coughing and shivering. Then, as if by a miracle, the dark clouds scudding across the night sky seemed to part, to be drawn aside like curtains, and there, bright and full and lovely, was the moon. At the sight of it, I began to hum softly. I had no idea why. I only knew that hearing the sound of my voice, knowing that I had a voice again, even if I could only hum, lifted my spirits. So, as I watched the moon above, I went on humming. I may not have been able to make words, but I could make a tune. I hummed myself to sleep that night.

I woke, and there was a glimmer of dawn in the sky above. I was cold and cramped and thirsty. I got to my feet, forgetting altogether my twisted ankle. I felt a sharp stab of pain. It gave beneath me and I fell. I tried to stand again, tried to walk, leaning heavily against the wall, testing to see what weight, if any, I could put on my ankle. There was no strength left in it, and the pain was agonizing if I tried to walk on it at all. I knew now that unless and until it healed, I could never climb that rock again to wave to passing boats. But rescue seemed so much less important to me now. I had no water, no food. I had to find both. I was already more thirsty than hungry. For some reason, I had it in my head that food you can do without for a long while, but water will keep you alive for weeks.

I was beginning to try to think things through, to work out what I had to do to survive, and how to do it. First of all I knew I needed a stick to lean on, or some kind of crutch. I could not walk without one. I had seen no trees on the island. But washed up on the shore, I thought, you could find driftwood. The sandy beach where I had landed might be a likely enough place to find some. It wasn't too far. So, with the greatest of difficulty, I limped and crawled my way back along the track, slid down the dunes on my backside, and was back on the beach. There was no driftwood to be seen, nothing but a line of shells and seaweed left by the tide. I staggered down to the water's edge. A crab scuttled away from me into the shallows. I thought of pouncing on it at once, of catching it and killing it and eating it, but I could not bring myself to do it. It gave me heart, though, as I watched it disappear. I could have eaten it. I would not starve in this place.

I stood there on the sand and looked around me. This was my world now, and it was a lovely world too, a sun-dancing sea under blue blue skies, the islands all around green and gray and yellow, the hilltops purple under the morning sun, and everywhere the piping of birds filling the air. It was truly a paradise, I thought. And there was water everywhere, but seawater, not drinking water. I could die of thirst in this paradise, and within sight of help too. I made my way slowly back up the beach, and had to crawl up the sand dunes on my hands and knees toward the track. Had I not been on my hands and knees, I should never have seen, lying there in among the reeds, a curl of old rope, bleached by the sun, with a pulley attached, and beside it the remains of a wooden door. Beyond it, there was driftwood, and lots of it, some half buried under the sand. This had not been washed up, I thought. It was too far from the beach, a long way from the tide mark on the sand, too high up on the dunes. And there was a huge pile of it. This had been gathered here deliberately—for what I did not know, but what I did know

now was that someone had done this, which meant someone had come here. People come here! They came to do this. They could come again. Suddenly I was fired with new hope. And a moment later, it got even better. I pulled the pile of driftwood apart until I found what I was looking for, a piece of wood sturdy enough for a crutch, and about the right length too.

Happier altogether now, I hobbled back toward the ruined house. I must have had water on my mind again because a sudden thought came to me as I reached the doorway. People hadn't only been visitors here. They had lived here once, in this house. You can't live without water. No one can. You wouldn't build a house on an island if there was no water. So there had to be a well somewhere, and I would find it. I would search every inch of this island until I found it—it was only a small island, it couldn't take long to find it. Then I could take my flask and fill it up at the well as often as I needed to. I could live for at least three weeks like that. And if necessary, if I really had to, I could catch a crab and eat it. And there were limpets on the rocks too—I had seen them. I could eat those maybe. And sooner or later, some fisherman would come by in his boat close enough to the island—perhaps the same person who had gathered that pile of driftwood on the dunes—and I would be found and rescued.

All I had to do was find that well, and then wait there on

the dunes every day for a boat to come by, and all the while my ankle would be healing, and then I could climb back up the rock again and wave.

Filled with all these high and heady hopes, I began my search there and then for the well that I knew had to be there. I thought it best to start near the house. Logically, I thought, a well was more likely to be close to the house than far away on the other side of the island. I thought too, a well would be easy enough to find. I was wrong. The bracken and the brambles that seemed to cover most of the island were head high. I could find no path through them. I had to beat my way through the undergrowth, swiping and swinging with my crutches as I went. There were places where the bracken grew too high and too thick to venture, where brambles tore at my legs and whipped me across my face and my neck. It was a jungle.

All that day and the next I kept up my search, and I was not going entirely hungry either, because I was finding enough tiny unripe blackberries to sustain me, to keep the hunger at bay. But my longing for water was fast becoming a craving. I was reduced to going on all fours and sipping from puddles whenever I found one. There were not many, and the water was foul. I was still searching for a well, but with less purpose now, less determination and less hope. My heart was not in it. I hadn't the strength to slash my way through the jungle of bracken and brambles anymore, to go searching in thickets where I hadn't been before. I was wandering about more aimlessly all the time, the growing hopelessness of my situation reducing me often to tears. At nights, the cuts and scratches I had all over me now would not let me sleep, and the pain in my ankle was constant. I lay curled up under my blanket, holding my teddy bear close to me, and trying to rock myself to sleep. But nothing could banish the hunger cramps that tormented me.

I didn't hum my tune to the moon anymore, because there was no moon, and if ever I tried to hum now, it gave way to whimpering, and to sobbing even. I tried so hard not to sob, not because I was trying to be brave—my sense of despair had brought me way beyond that by now—but because I knew that if I gave way to the sobbing I would soon find myself wracked by fits of coughing that would not leave me, that shook my whole body.

How many days passed, and how many nights, I do not know. But one night as I was lying there trying to rock myself into sleep and out of my coughing, trying to forget my sting-ing legs, my throbbing ankle, a great storm blew in, the wind howling round in the chimney, flashes of lightning turning night to day above me. Until now, I had been dry enough in the fireplace, but now rain and wind blew in and drove me into the corner under the stone seat, where there was at least still some shelter to be found. I sat huddled there, my knees drawn up under my blanket, my teddy bear clutched tight, and tried all I could to stop myself from coughing my heart out. My chest ached with it, my throat was sore from it. Exhausted, in the end I must have fallen asleep.

When I woke it was to the sound of running water. I saw it then, when the lightning flashed. Water was pouring down the chimney into the fireplace below, like a waterfall. I knew what I must do at once. I took my flask down from the ledge where I kept it, unscrewed the top, and held it under the flow till it was full. I drank till I could drink no more, and then filled it once again. This time I promised myself I would eke it out, make it last, be sensible. And so I did, so I was. But after that torrential thunderstorm, there was no more rain for a while, and very soon the flask was empty again, and all the puddles had dried up in the sun. My ankle was all the colors of the sunset. I looked at it often. I was quite proud of it, and it was less swollen now. I could use it more, but it was still weak.

The night of the thunderstorm was the last night I can really remember. All I know is that I drifted through the days after that, too weak to climb the rock, or to look anymore for a well, contented enough to sit for hours on end in the dunes on the lookout for passing fishing boats. They did pass by, but always far away. I did manage to catch some little crabs in the shallows, and I did knock limpets off the rocks and scoop out the flesh inside. I came across birds' eggs sometimes and feasted myself on them. They were the best meals I had. I was often sick afterward. I recall hours spent curled up in my fireplace, clutching my stomach and groaning in agony. It did rain again, never enough to fill my water flask, but somehow I must have managed to collect enough to keep myself going. I tried always to leave some water in the flask till it rained again, never to drink it all.

In the end I had neither the strength nor the will to leave my fireplace anymore. I was giving up. I knew I was, and I didn't care. All hope of survival, all hope of rescue was gone. There were times when I felt I was drowning in great waves of sadness. It wasn't that I had nothing to live for, but rather that I realized now that I would not live. I often thought as I lay there that it would have been better to have slipped off my piano into the sea. It would have been quicker. This way was slow and painful and sad. There were moments when the sun shone warm above, and seemed somehow to shiver all the cold and sadness out of me for a while. Then I was glad to be alive again, and could almost believe that where there is life, there is hope. I must have clung to these last vestiges of hope, must have kept drinking water, which is why I was still alive that day when I heard a voice calling from far away, when I heard footsteps coming toward the house, and saw a boy crouching there in the bracken, holding out his hand to me. When he spoke, his words seemed to be coming from another world.

Chapter Twenty-four

Horrible Hun!

It soon became obvious to Alfie that Lucy knew the whole island like the back of her hand. He trailed around after her as she raced along the tracks, as she leaped through the heather. As he followed, all he could think about were those words Lucy had spoken: "wasser" and "gut." They didn't sound at all English to Alfie. "Gut" sounded like "good," but it wasn't, and "wasser" like "water," but it wasn't. Alfie knew what this must mean, that everyone had been right. Lucy was German. There could be no doubts about it now, however much he did not want to believe it. Every word he had ever heard her say could have been German, probably was German, certainly was German. The more he thought about it, the more it had to be so.

Like a wild goat she scrambled over the rocks and skipped through the shallows. Everywhere she went, Alfie followed—and keeping up with her was not at all easy. He had never known her to be so agile, so fleet of foot. Breathless with excitement, she seemed to be making new discoveries all the time, like a hound at the scent, seeking and then finding. And many of these discoveries prompted some kind of dramatic reenactment in mime and movement, all of them quite incomprehensible and mystifying to Alfie.

But she was—Alfie could see it—trying harder than ever before, mouthing words that would not speak themselves properly, and talking all the while with her hands as best she could. All her guttural utturings, and the clicking of her tongue, reminded Alfie of old Ma Stebbings down at Atlantic Cottage on Popplestones Bay, who had been born deaf, he'd been told, and with a cleft palate. Not a word she said did anyone understand. She too let her hands and her eyes do her speaking for her, but even so, Alfie could never make much sense of what she was trying to tell him. The trouble was that old Ma Stebbings was liable to get angry with you for not understanding, and then you'd have to walk away, and she'd get angrier still.

It was different with Lucy. She didn't get angry, she just kept on trying to explain herself; and besides, with Lucy he really wanted to know what she was trying to say, wanted to encourage her to keep trying.

It was hard, though, and confusing, because the stories she was trying to tell him, so far as he could make out, were stories that seemed to have little connection with one another, like scattered pieces of a jigsaw puzzle. One moment she was pointing out to sea, toward White Island, then sat herself down cross-legged on the sand and began drawing something in it that looked like a cucumber. Then she was picking up a limpet shell and pretending to eat it.

Up on her feet again, and taking his hand, she raced back to the Pest House, pointed out to him the long-since-discarded shells littered everywhere, then collapsed on the ground in the fireplace, clutching her stomach and groaning, clearly pretending to be in pain. A moment later, spotting a gull sitting on the chimney, she was on her feet and gesticulating angrily at him and hurling stones. Discovering an old stick—driftwood, it looked like—in among the bracken in the Pest House, she limped about like Uncle Billy did when he was being Long John Silver—what Uncle Billy had to do with all this, Alfie had no idea—and then she was off again, out of the Pest House and running down the track, only to throw herself down suddenly on all fours and act as if she was a dog drinking out of a puddle, all of this accompanied by much waving of hands, and an outpouring of attempted words that sounded more like gargling to Alfie than anything else.

Alfie could understand something of what each mime meant, but they were all acted out so fast, one after another, that together they made very little sense at all. He asked her often to slow down, to show him again, but by then she was always off again and running.

They ended up at midday on top of the great rock behind the Pest House. He wanted to sit her down, have the bread and cheese they'd brought in the boat with them. He thought this might be the moment to try to get her to talk. But neither talk nor food seemed to interest her. All she would do was wave and jump up and down at the sight of every passing fishing boat. And when she tired of that, she lay back on the rock, looking up at the sky. Pointing up at the half moon still up there, she began humming her tune. She patted the rock beside her, inviting Alfie to come and join her. They hummed together then. After a while, they were silent, listening to the sea, to the wind, to the oystercatchers, watching the gulls wheeling and crying above them.

"They don't like us much, do they?" Alfie said. "I think they want us to go. About time we did, I suppose."

Lucy didn't need his help climbing down any more than she had on the way up. When she reached the bottom, and she was there long before he was, she fell over clutching her ankle and grimacing in pain. Alfie thought for a moment this was for real—the acting was that convincing. But then he saw the smile in her eyes. He remembered then the swollen ankle she had had when they brought her home. "Your ankle, it happened here then, didn't it?" he asked.

She nodded. That was the moment Alfie finally found he could begin to work out her story, put two and two together.

"So you rowed here, right?" he said. "And you lived in the Pest House—there's nowhere else, is there? And you ate limpets, and you were up on the giant rock waving so someone would come and find you. And no one did, did they? Not till we came along, and you were half dead by then. But what's the cucumber you drew in the sand got to do with anything? And I still don't know where you came from, do I? We got to know everything, Lucy, don't you see? We got to. You got to tell us. And where's the rowing boat? You couldn't have come on your own. Who brought you? And that water flask, who gave you that?"

She was looking at him as he was speaking, and thinking hard. He could see she was. She wanted to answer him. She was going to tell him. Before he knew it, she was up on her feet and running again, leaping over the heather, and racing down the track toward the beach.

Alfie thought he must have upset Lucy with all his questions. He ran after her, calling her back. By the time he found her again she was on her knees in the sand, a cuttlefish shell in her hand, and drawing feverishly. She didn't look up even when he was standing right over her. She just kept drawing. It looked like a cucumber again, a giant cucumber. Then he thought again. There was something coming out of the top of it. A spout! It was a whale! It had to be a whale! At once the Jonah story came back to him, one of those silly stories going around just after Lucy had first been found, that she'd been carried in on the back of a whale.

But beside the whale she was drawing a boat, a rowing boat, and now there were three men sitting in it, one of them holding up something in his hand, the flask, the water flask. The drawing done in the sand, Lucy sat back on her heels, and, taking a deep breath or two, spoke very deliberately and clearly. Pointing down at the man in the boat, the one with the flask, she said: "Wilhelm. *Wasser. Gut.*"

Words again. The same words. But German words. Alfie was already thinking that he would keep it a secret, and just hope that she never uttered another word when they got back. To speak would only be to betray herself.

She bent forward suddenly and drew another figure in the boat, a figure holding something, a teddy bear, with a smile on his face, *her* teddy bear. Laughing, she sat back again, pointing to herself.

"Ninny," she cried. "Nincompoop! Ninny! Nincompoop!"

Lucy giggled out the words time and again. Alfie could see she was simply loving the sound of herself, reveling in this sudden ability to speak, as surprised by it as he was. Alfie was loving the sound of the words too, but for another reason altogether. They were English words. English! English! *Nincompoop!* Father would call him that sometimes, Mother too. How could she possibly know such a word unless she was English?

In his relief, he was laughing with her, then dancing and prancing with her, all over her drawing in the sand, both of them echoing those words, those wonderful, beautiful words, over and over, louder and louder, until every gull on the island seemed to be airborne and shrieking in alarm. Or was that laughter too?

Alfie wanted only to get back home fast now, as fast as possible. He could not wait to break the good news. He would take the quicker way home. He sailed away from the beach at St. Helen's and out toward the lighthouse on White Island. He knew that, whatever the weather, around White Island the waves would always be heaving in from the open ocean, but it was safe enough on a day like this. Wind and tide and current would be with them. And anyway, he thought, it would be exciting. And so it was, the little boat keeling over as she flew along, up and down the waves, each of them a mountain to climb, both Alfie and Lucy laughing and screaming in wild exhilaration born of shared fear and shared delight. They rode the waves, rising, plunging, surfing, every time they crested a wave shrieking out in unison: "Nincompoop! Ninny! Nincompoop!"

Soaked through by now, and breathless with it all, they came out of the wind and waves, and into the quieter, more sheltered waters of the Tresco Channel. Alfie was quite sure now that their day on St. Helen's had achieved more than Dr. Crow or

any of them could have hoped for. Lucy had most certainly remembered, how much Alfie did not know. But she had remembered. And she had talked—admittedly, mostly just the
same two words again and again—but those words were English. There had been, without question, some reawakening of
her memory and some rediscovery of her voice. This had to be
just the beginning, Alfie thought. Surely, after this, the words
would flow more easily and all her memories would in time
come flooding back. Very soon now they would know who
Lucy was and all about her.

It was low tide by the time they sailed into Green Bay. No
one seemed to be about except for Uncle Billy. The *Hispaniola*
was high and dry on the sand. He was down on the beach,
working on the rudder. Then he was walking round the boat.
He appeared to be checking it all over, examining the hull, pat-
ting it affectionately. He must have seen them coming in through
the shallows, but he did not acknowledge them. He was busy,
they knew that, and therefore best left alone, so they did not
bother him.

Alfie had thrown out the anchor and was taking down the
sail when he looked up and saw Zebediah Bishop and his gang
coming along the beach. And then they were charging across
the sand toward them, the whole pack of them, shouting as they
came, as if they were baying for blood. Alfie steeled himself for
what was to come. They could have made a run for it, but there

was nowhere to run to, nowhere to hide. Home was too far away across the field. They'd never get there. Lucy was holding the water flask almost as if she was going to use it as a weapon.

"S'all right," Alfie told her, trying to sound as if he believed it. "They're just having a bit of fun. They don't want a fight." They were only yards away now. *Tough it out,* Alfie was telling himself. *Whatever you do, just tough it out, don't show them you're frightened.*

"What do you want, Zeb?" he asked.

"Weren't at school, was you?" Zeb replied. Then at once he turned his attention to Lucy. "Where you been off to then? Back to Fritziland, is it?" he scoffed. "Have a nice time, did you? Been bayoneting little children, have you?"

He made a lunge for the water flask then and snatched it from her. "What's this then?" He unscrewed the top, drank from it, then spat it out, wiping his mouth with the back of his hand. "Hun water," he said. "Horrible Hun water, horrible just like you." Then he was looking at the flask more closely, examining it. "Well, well," he said, "would you believe it! S'got writing here. You know what it says? I'll read it for you, shall I? It says, in big letters, Berlin. Berlin? Look at this, lads," he went on, holding it up, showing it to them, his voice becoming ever more threatening and triumphant. "Now, we done our capitals at school, and we all know Berlin ain't in England. That's 'cos it's in Germany, isn't it?"

As the crowd closed in around him, Alfie put up his fists. "Don't you come no closer, Zeb," he said, "or I'll give you a bleeding nose. I will." He could feel Lucy hiding behind him now, clinging to his coat, hanging on to him, her forehead pressed into his back. There was yelling all around them. Alfie stood his ground. Suddenly, Lucy sprang out from behind him and leaped on Zeb, taking him and everyone else completely by surprise. But the surprise was quickly over. Alfie was knocked over from behind to the ground. Then the punching and kicking began. As he curled himself into a ball, he saw Lucy sitting astride Zeb and pummeling him, but then the others pulled her off and began kicking her too as she tried to crawl over toward him. Alfie looked up into the faces above him, all laughing and howling and chanting, "Horrible Hun! Horrible Hun! Horrible Hun!"

Chapter Twenty-five

Ugly Duckling

Quite suddenly, the kicking stopped, the chanting stopped. When Alfie looked up, they were scattering in all directions. Only then did he see and understand why. Uncle Billy had Zeb by the collar, lifting him off his feet for a moment or two, then dropping him to the ground like a sack of potatoes. Whimpering through his choking, Zeb staggered away up the beach. Uncle Billy picked up the water flask where Zeb had dropped it and gave it to Lucy. He helped them both to their feet and brushed them down. Then he said, punching the air: "Yo ho ho!"

"Yo ho ho!" they echoed back. Then all three of them were chanting it again and again, Lucy too, all of them punching the air together. "Come. Look," Uncle Billy said, taking each of them by the hand. "My *Hispaniola,* she is finished." Hand in hand, they walked across Green Bay toward the cutter. They stood there looking up at it, admiring it. The boat gleamed from bow to stern, the sails flapping and slapping in the breeze, the Jolly Roger flying from the masthead. She was magnificent.

"Tomorrow," Uncle Billy was saying, "I sail for Treasure Island. There are seven seas out there, and I shall sail them all, till I find Treasure Island." And without another word, he left them, walking up the beach to the boathouse.

That was when Peg came wandering along the beach to find them. So they had a ride home, but not straight home. Peg wouldn't go straight home. They had to go where she wanted to take them, all around the island, under Samson Hill, past Rushy Bay and Popplestones and Hell Bay, and all the way, neither spoke a word, until they were upon the moor above the Shipman's Head. There Peg decided to stop and graze. They dismounted and sat on the soft thrift, gazing out over the ocean, both lost in thought.

After a while Alfie spoke. "Father says that's America over there, over two thousand miles away across the Atlantic. I'm going there one day. They got all sorts over there. Mountains, deserts, buildings as tall as the sky, cowboys and Indians, hundreds of cars. I've seen pictures in magazines. Uncle Billy showed me. He's been there. He's been everywhere. He won't go to Treasure Island, though. That's just him talking as he does. He's always saying that, how he's going off around the world again one day. But he won't. You been to America, have you, Lucy?" He didn't expect her to answer, and she didn't.

"Lucy," he went on, "you said 'yo ho ho.' You said 'nincompoop.' You said 'ninny.' You said 'Wilhelm,' and those other German words. You said 'piano.' You can say others. You can talk, you know you can. You got to tell me. I got to know. As soon as everyone hears about your water flask—and they will, believe me, they soon will—they'll think what they want to think. And I got to be able to stand there and say for certain that you're English. Trouble is, I don't know what to believe anymore. One minute you say German words, and the next you say English words. But then—I been thinking—you could have heard Father calling me nincompoop, or Mother maybe, couldn't you? And you were just copying. What are you, Lucy? Who are you?" He picked up the water flask, and was looking at it. "It says '*Berlin,*' Lucy."

She said nothing, but sat stone-faced, her chin on her knees, looking at Peg grazing in among the heather. She seemed not to have been listening to him at all, to have gone back into her shell.

Back home, she stayed that way all evening, refusing her food, not bothering to put on a record even, wandering restlessly about the kitchen, looking for some time at each of the drawings on the walls, lost in them, it seemed, and not interested at all in anything or anyone else.

Of course, Jim and Mary wanted to know everything that had happened to them that day on St. Helen's and questioned

Alfie closely, about the actual words Lucy had spoken, and about the fight on Green Bay, and how Uncle Billy had come to their rescue. But it was the water flask that most concerned them. "Trouble is," his father said, "Zebediah was right. It's writ here. 'Kaisers Fabrik. Berlin.' You can't argue with that, can you, Marymoo, not even if you want to. It's German. Either she found it washed up on the island, or someone gave it to her. And I know which they'll be thinking when Lucy and Alfie go to school tomorrow, and they won't have no Uncle Billy to look after them, will they?"

"They won't be going," Mary said firmly. "I'm not sending them off to that school, not tomorrow, not ever, if it comes to that. You stay home, Alfie. We all stay home together, look after one another, eh?" She reached out then and caught Lucy by the arm as she passed by. "Lucy dear," she said. "Come and sit down, won't you? You must be tired out. Would you like a story? Shall I take you upstairs now, and read you a story?"

Lucy shook her head.

"Alfie then? You'd read to her, wouldn't you, Alfie?" She shook her head again, then left the room, but she was down again in a few moments, with a book in her hand. She took it over to Jim and gave it to him.

"I don't read very good, Lucy," he said. "I mean, I can read, course I can. But I didn't do much of that schooling lark." She pressed the book into his hands, insisting, and then got up onto his lap. Leaning her head back against him, she closed her eyes and waited.

Jim had no choice. He opened the book. "The Ugly Duckling," Jim began.

"That's her favorite, that is," Alfie said. "I've read that one to her plenty of times."

Jim read hesitantly, stumbling over the words sometimes, and often stopping to apologize when he did. But that didn't seem to bother Lucy. She may have had her eyes closed, but Alfie was watching her, and he was quite sure she was listening to every word. After a while, she opened her eyes. She was staring hard at one of the pictures on the wall, and frowning.

With Jim still reading, she got off his lap and walked across the kitchen to the gramophone. Alfie thought she was going to put a record on, but she didn't. She simply stood there, gazing up at the picture. It was one of several she had drawn of the giant sitting down by a lake, reading a book to the ducks gathered around his feet. Then, very deliberately, she went and fetched her pencil box from the kitchen dresser, took out a pencil, and wrote something on the bottom of the picture. She put her pencil back and went upstairs, leaving Jim still reading the story. He stopped then.

"I told you I don't read books like I should," he said.

"What's she writ there? What's it say?" Mary asked. Alfie went to look.

"'*Papa*,'" Alfie read. "It says 'Papa.'" They all gathered round the picture to look. "It's the story, Mother," Alfie said. "That Ugly Duckling story. It must be. That man, he's her father, and he's reading a story to the ducks, isn't he? Stands to reason. And that's why she asks for that story again and again. It reminds her of him. That's him, got to be. That's her father."

"But he's a giant," Jim said. "Look at him. He's as big as the trees about him, almost. And look at the size of his feet. He's got clown's feet."

"Big or small, don't matter," Alfie said. "All that matters is that she remembers him. She remembers her father."

———◦•◦•◦———

Later that evening, way past the time they were usually in bed, the three of them were still sitting around the kitchen table, trying to piece together all the clues they could glean from the drawing of Lucy's father. In particular they were trying to work out where the lake might be, with the tall trees behind and the buildings in the distance. And why was this giant of a man wearing such old-fashioned clothes? As Jim pointed out, the coat he was wearing was a lot like Uncle Billy's Long John Silver coat. "Come to think of it, maybe it is Uncle Billy. He's got a long neck like Uncle Billy, hasn't he? And a nose like a crow, which Uncle Billy has too."

When Mary objected to this, Jim went on. "I don't mean

nothing by it, Marymoo," he said. "But he has, you know he has. Maybe it's him, maybe it's a picture of Uncle Billy. She likes Uncle Billy. Maybe Uncle Billy tells her stories. He likes stories, likes his books, you know he does."

"Then why's she gone and writ Papa underneath, Father?" said Alfie. No one could answer. Talk turned then to Uncle Billy and the *Hispaniola,* and what a wonderful boat she was, now that she was finished.

"Best idea you ever had, Marymoo," Jim said. "Once a shipbuilder always a shipbuilder, that's what you said. Over five years ago, when you first brought him home from the asylum, and you set him to work on that old hulk of a lugger in Green Bay, I thought you was mad. But you said, give him something to do. Man's got to keep busy, you said. You told me he could do it, and you told him he could do it too, and now he has."

"He's showed them all right, has my brother," said Mary, fierce with pride. "But you found him all that washed-up timber, Jimbo. You gave him your tools, all he needed. But the rest he done all on his own. They'll think twice before they call him Silly Billy now. Silly Billies don't build boats that beautiful."

"He's off tomorrow, sailing away to Treasure Island," said Alfie. "That's what he told us. And I had the feeling he meant it too."

"He's said that from the day he started," said Jim, with a

laugh, "when it were nothing but a rotting hulk on the beach. Him and his Treasure Island! Him and his yo ho ho! He means it all right, but he won't do it. Dream talk, that's all it is."

"Just so long as he's happy," Mary said. "After all he's been through, he deserves to be happy. So far as I'm concerned he can be who he likes in his mind, go where he wants to. We all got to dream, Jimbo, haven't we?"

The wind got up that night and blew itself into a gale that shook the whole house so that it creaked and rattled and growled all night long. When they woke, they heard the gramophone playing downstairs, playing Lucy's tune again. Lucy had not done that before, she had never put the music on before breakfast. Alfie thought that was strange. When he came down, he found the kitchen door was wide open and no one was about. When they looked, Lucy wasn't in her room either, nor was she outside feeding the hens. Lucy was nowhere to be found.

Alfie was the first to notice it. There was writing now on every one of her sketches all around the kitchen. Some had "Mama" written in large letters across them. All the drawings of the giant reading to the ducks by the pond now had "Papa" written underneath. Above the drawing of the big ship with the four funnels she had written her own name, for some reason, but she had spelled "Lusy" with an *s*, instead of a *c*. The one of the log cabin in the forest, with the porch all around, now had "Barewood" written across the top in capital letters.

And on every one of the several horse drawings—a horse running, a horse lying down, a horse standing in a stable, a horse rolling—she had written either "Bess" or "Bunty"; except for the last one, which she had put up on the wall only a few days before, the one that was of a horse face looking through the window, ears pricked. It was "Peg," and she was recognizably different from the others. There were other names too, under the pencil portraits she had done: "Aunty Ducka," "Uncle Mac," "Miss Winters," and of a young girl about her age, "Pippa"— there were several drawings of Pippa.

They were still looking at the names and the drawings when Lucy came running into the house, breathless, wildly gesticulating at them, trying to tell them something, stamping her foot in frustration that they didn't immediately understand her. She was beckoning them to follow her, then running out again, across the field down toward Green Bay. One look was enough. The *Hispaniola* was gone. Other boats in the bay, including Jim's, were scarcely moving on their anchors. The storm had taken the wind with it and left behind only a breeze, and a gently breathing sea. There was no *Hispaniola* out in Tresco Channel, and no sail farther out to sea.

"Must've been blowed off her anchor in the night," said Jim. "Uncle Billy will be home in the boathouse, don't you worry none, Marymoo."

But Mary was already running up the beach calling for Uncle

Billy. He wasn't in the boathouse. They went up and down Green Bay, searching for him, shouting for him.

"Do you think he's really gone and done it, Mother?" Alfie said. "Sailed off to Treasure Island, like he said he would."

"He wouldn't have," said Mary, becoming more distraught with every moment. "He's not mad. He's not!"

"He'll be here somewhere," Jim told her. "We'll find him soon enough. Don't you worry."

"You're right, Jimbo." Mary was struggling to hold back her tears. "He's still on the island, I know he is. We got to find him."

"He'll be out looking for her, for the *Hispaniola*," said Jim. "That's what he'll be doing, he'll be up on the hills, on the cliffs, looking out to sea. That's where he'll be. That's where we'll find him." He sent Alfie and Lucy out to search the other side of the island. Peg had followed them down to the beach by now. So they mounted up and went looking. All that morning they searched, from Samson Hill to Heathy Hill, from Popplestones and Stinking Porth to Hell Bay. There was no sign of Uncle Billy, and no sign of the *Hispaniola*.

By that afternoon every boat on the island was out looking for Uncle Billy and the *Hispaniola*. Soon, all over Scilly, wherever they had heard of the disappearance of Uncle Billy, the islanders got in their boats and went out searching. Every fishing boat was out at sea, every gig, the lifeboat too. None of the rumors and tittle-tattle about Silly Billy, nor the stories about Lucy Lost being a German, mattered anymore now. One of their own was lost at sea, a boat was missing, a boat that everyone knew, mad as he might be, Silly Billy had built with his own hands. By nightfall no one had found any trace of either man or boat.

The next morning, Sunday morning, gifts of bread and jam were left in the porch at Veronica Farm, and prayers were said in churches all over the islands for Uncle Billy. In Bryher church, the Wheatcroft family were no longer left in their pew alone. Heartwarming though this newfound kindness was, nothing could bring any comfort to Mary. She was in despair. Time and again, Jim tried to remind her that Uncle Billy didn't just build boats, that he'd been at sea for most of his life, sailed the world, that if anyone could handle the cutter it was Uncle Billy.

"You build a boat, you know how to handle it, Marymoo," he told her. "The skills of a sailor once learnt are never forgotten. You'll see, Marymoo. We'll look out at sea, this morning, tomorrow morning, whenever, and he'll come sailing in on the *Hispaniola,* just as cool as a cucumber." But no words could soothe Mary's grief, and grief it was, for with every day that passed, and still no sign of Billy, she was beginning to believe the worst, that Billy was gone for good, dead and drowned out there somewhere, and never coming back.

In the days that followed Uncle Billy's disappearance, Lucy hardly left her side. This silent child who could offer no words of consolation was the only one who seemed to understand her loss, the only one who could be any comfort to her at all. Mary knew, as everyone else on the islands did, that when they went out looking now every morning, searching the shoreline, the rocks and the cliffs, it was wreckage they were expecting to find, or a body.

Chapter Twenty-six

I am not Lucy Lost

It was at dawn four days after the disappearance of the *Hispaniola* that her sail was sighted off St. Mary's. As she came close into the harbor, the few islanders who were up and about saw that there was more than one man on board. Word spread fast.

———◆———

From Dr. Crow's journal, 23rd October 1915

I write my journal, in part, as a record of a doctor's life in these remote and largely unknown islands, but also so that I myself might later be reminded of times past, when memory dims. If there is one day that will linger long in my mind, and in the collective memory of these islands, it will be today. There never was in my life a more momentous day.

Roused early by the sound of the church bell ringing, and by a great kerfuffle and hullabaloo in the street below, I leaned out of my window and saw the town was full of people, and all of them hurrying by in a great state of excitement, every one of them it seemed on their way toward the quay. I called down, inquiring of them what might be the cause of all this commotion.

"It's the Hispaniola," came one reply.

"It's that old Silly Billy from Bryher," came another. "He's come back, and he isn't alone either!"

I dressed as fast as I could and went out into the street to join the throng. I was, as I soon discovered looking around me, rather more properly dressed than some. There were those who, in their haste, had thrown on little more than a dressing gown over their nightclothes, and some were still in slippers. Several of the children, I noticed, were running along barefoot in their pajamas. We were all carried along in the rush of the crowd. It seemed to me that everyone on the island must be there, all of them eager to reach the quay and have a first sighting of the Hispaniola.

By the time I came round the corner, and saw her, she was already tying up. There was much jostling in the crush of the crowd. Like everyone else I wanted to have a closer look, but could not find a way through the press of the crowd, until, that is, I heard someone calling for me.

"Is the doctor here?" came the cry. "Someone send for the doctor!"

I imagined at once that Uncle Billy must have fallen ill, or been injured in some accident or other, which would explain why he had been gone so long. The crowd made way for me as I came through, but this was no longer an excited crowd. A hush had descended on the quayside now, which brought to mind another silent crowd in another place, on the beach at Porthcressa some months before, when I had been called out to attend to two poor sailors washed up drowned on the sands. So already I was fearing the worst. But then I realized that this was altogether a different kind of silence, a silence born of hostility. I was soon to understand why.

Looking down from the quay onto the deck of the Hispaniola, I could see there were three men on deck. One lay prone and still, another crouched over him, while Uncle Billy busied himself about the boat, hauling down the sails and stowing them away, paying no attention whatever to the crowd gathering to watch on the quay above him, one or two of whom were now shouting at him as I climbed down the ladder onto the deck.

"What'd you bring them back for, Billy?"

"They're not our boys!"

"They're Fritzis, they're Huns."

"Look at their uniforms, not like ours."

"Dirty beggars!"

Then it was me they were shouting at: "You don't want to bother with them, Doctor!" "Not after what they done."

I stood there on the deck, looking up at the sea of faces above me. That long look—and it might have been more glare than a look—I am pleased to say, was enough in the end to silence those few malign voices. No more was said. But perhaps that was also because many had now noticed what I had already seen at first glance, that the sailor lying stretched out on the deck was dead. Perhaps some had also seen that, whoever he was, wherever he came from, he was young, hardly more than a boy; his beard, unlike that of the other sailor, still sparse and downy with youth. Kneeling beside him now, I felt his wrist and his neck for any sign of a pulse, just to be sure. But I had no need to. There is a stillness in death, a pallor, that is quite unmistakable. I knew from the eyes of the other sailor as he looked at me that he did not have to be told.

"Sein name... His name was Gunter, Gunter Stein. Aus Tübingen. I also live there. The same town. He was the youngest on the boat. Nineteen years old. Sein bruder, Klaus, was also killed in Belgien, in the army. His mother now, she has no sons."

His English was good, hesitant and interspersed with German, much of which I could not understand. He submitted only reluctantly to my examination. It was evident, even at a cursory glance, that he was bewildered and disorientated, and fearful too of the crowd of onlookers, who were quieter now, but nonetheless still hostile toward him. He was also clearly dehydrated, and weak, unsteady on his feet as he stood up. His face was blistered, and raw in places, from exposure to wind and sun.

Uncle Billy, being an intensely shy and private person, as I knew from past experience, would not allow himself to be examined, especially in front of all these people. So I did not examine him, but rather studied him closely as I asked him questions. He too, quite evidently, had been suffering from exposure and exhaustion, but his gaze and his bearing seemed strong. He answered me, as I had expected, never looking at me, and in short, sharp sentences, his voice and his face deadpan as usual. But even so I managed to glean from him something of what had happened out there at sea. As far as I could discover, the Hispaniola had been several miles south of Scilly, becalmed and drifting with the current. Uncle Billy had woken one morning to hear a voice calling him.

"I thought it were a voice in my head," he told me. "But it weren't." He saw a life raft nearby, with two sailors on board, and he picked them up. He seemed neither to know nor care who they were, nor where they came from. He had some water left to give them, but very little, and soon there was none. All his food was gone. "One of they sailors died," he said. "And I were sad about that. He were only a boy, like Alfie." He told me that he didn't want to talk about it anymore because it made him sad, and that he needed to go home right away, that he wanted to see Mary and Jim and Alfie.

"Maybe it would be better," I suggested, "if I send word to Bryher and they came over to see you here, on St. Mary's. Meanwhile you can come back to my house and rest. You need rest and food, Billy. They'll be here soon enough. You shouldn't be going out on that boat again, not now."

"I don't like strange houses," he said. "And I don't like strange people. I ain't coming."

"I'm not a stranger, Billy," I told him.

"They are, up there," he replied, turning away from me, and from them. They were intimidating even for me, and none of them were strangers to me. They were all my patients. But I knew how Billy hated to be stared at. There were hundreds of faces staring down at us now from the quay, and not a smile to be seen among them. I knew how obstinate Uncle Billy could be, that there was no possible way I could persuade him to come with me back to my house through that crowd unless people moved away. So I decided to take matters in hand, to address the crowd, speaking to them with as much authority as I could muster.

I knew I could not do this all on my own. I needed an ally, someone up there on the quayside, someone upon whom I could rely. Searching the faces I found the person I was looking for: Mr. Griggs, harbormaster, coxswain of the St. Mary's gig, town councillor, church warden, a man I knew was much respected and admired.

"Mr. Griggs," I said, raising my voice so that all could hear, "I'd be obliged if you would first of all send for the undertaker to take this poor lad away. I shall ask you also to send word to the Wheatcroft family on Bryher that the Hispaniola is back, and Uncle Billy too, both unharmed. Meanwhile, because these two men are in need of medical attention, I should like to take them back home to my house, where they can be properly cared for." My audience, I saw, was listening, and I was much encouraged by this.

"You'll agree with me, Mr. Griggs," I went on, "when I say to everyone here that this is not a spectacle, that we should not stand and gawp, but we should rather remember that a young man has died, a young sailor from Germany, who is called Gunter. He was some mother's son, like poor Jack Brody was, and Henry Hibbert and Martin Dowd. They fought for our country, as did this young man for his. So we should show proper respect for him, no matter where he comes from, the same respect shown by you and your forebears to those Germans saved, all those years ago, from the wreck of the Schiller, as well as to those who perished, and who lie buried in our churchyard, German and English side by side."

When I had finished, I was waiting for cries of protest, or at least a voice or two raised against me, but none came. Instead Mr. Griggs spoke up. "What the doctor says is only right and proper. Let's show the proper respect."

Almost at once came a murmur of assent from the crowd, which began to disperse, or at least to move back from the edge of the quay. Mr. Griggs saw to everything after that. Within minutes the undertaker's two-wheel handcart had been fetched, and Gunter Stein's body was borne away covered in a blanket, the islanders looking on, bareheaded and eyes lowered as the cart passed them by. Many were crossing themselves. No one spoke. It was quiet and calm, and the onlookers that were left stood back. Uncle Billy came with me—unwillingly, but he came.

It was a strange procession, the Reverend Morrison leading the way, then the undertaker and his cart, the pace measured and solemn, with the three of us following close behind, the German sailor on one side of me, and Uncle Billy on the other, touching my elbow from time to time, for reassurance, I think. And behind us came Mr. Griggs and dozens of islanders. People were lining the street as we made our way toward the undertaker's. All that could be heard was the shuffle of footsteps and the rumble of cartwheels over cobblestones. As we passed the post office, there were a few who turned their backs as we passed by, and there was, I could feel, some silent hostility in the crowd as they scrutinized the German sailor at my side. But there was also a certain respect, and great curiosity too, many of the children pushing through, pressing forward, necks straining to get a better look.

It was at this point that I began to notice that the German sailor walking beside me was himself as curious as many of the onlookers, almost as if he were searching among the crowd, and among the children in particular, for faces he knew. He never spoke a word, not until the undertaker turned his cart off the High Street and into the alleyway beside his workshop. "Mein Freund, Gunter," he said. "They will bury him in the church?"

"Yes," I told him.

"Gut. That is gut. Gunter will be happy to be there with all who drowned from the Schiller."

"You know about the Schiller?" I asked him.

"Of course. Many in Germany know about this, everyone on my boat. Mein Kapitän, he told us. His uncle was saved from this ship. Many others also, he said. And the dead were buried here in your church. It is because of the kindness shown to us by the people here, that it is forbidden to attack any ship close to these islands. And now I too am saved by a sailor from Scilly, Gunter also. It was too late for him. But he will be among his friends. One day I shall tell his mother, and she will be happy."

Even as he was talking, as we passed on down the street toward my house, he was still searching the crowd, but for what, for whom, I had no idea. "Ich kann das Mädchen nicht sehen," he said, speaking to himself, then turning to me. "I cannot see the girl. She is not here."

"What girl?" I asked. "You know someone who lives here?"

"Ja, I think so. I hope so," he replied. But he said nothing more.

Mrs. Cartright met us at the door. She did not look pleased with me. "Three for breakfast, Doctor? Do I look to you as if I lay eggs myself?" Her indignation was jocular, but meant nonetheless. "Some warning would be appreciated in future, Doctor," she said, standing back and allowing us in. "And wipe your feet, if you please." And when I asked for two hot baths to be drawn for our guests, and a suit each of dry clothes from my wardrobe, she gave me that look of hers, as only Mrs. Cartright can. I waited for the sarcastic quip that I knew would inevitably follow. "And is there anything else I can do for you, Doctor?" she said. "I have, as you know, nothing else to do." Then with an imperious swish of her skirts she flounced away down the passageway into the kitchen.

An hour or so later, after bathing and changing, after I had treated both of them for sunburn and blisters—camomile lotion is still best for this, I find—the three of us were sitting at the table, eating a most excellent breakfast, Mrs. Cartright bustling about as she does when she wishes it to be known how inconvenient and troublesome I have been. With her there, I felt I could not yet continue the conversation that the German sailor had begun in the street, much as I wanted to. I was intrigued by how much he knew of the wreck of the Schiller, which was certainly among the most famous wrecks on Scilly, but also, apparently, in Germany too. I could see that both my guests were far too busy eating to talk. I decided to be patient. There would be a time for questions and for talk later.

I could hear the crowd gathered outside the house. I could see them through the curtain. Every time I looked, there were more of them. On more than one occasion, Mrs. Cartright went outside to remonstrate with them. Some left, but despite her most vociferous protestations, most lingered on, waiting, but for what I could not imagine. There was some excitement at the arrival of Major Martin, commanding officer of the garrison. Mrs. Cartright answered the knock at the door.

"Major Martin, how nice. And have you come for breakfast too?" I heard her ask, her tone rather chilly. She showed him in. I knew of course that he had come for the German sailor, and that indeed was what he immediately confirmed. Major Martin can be a pompous fellow, but he is essentially well-meaning. With the German sailor he was courteous, if a little haughty, I felt. I have tended his soldiers often enough up at the garrison, so we know one another quite well. I told him that I should like to keep the German sailor here for a few hours more, to keep an eye on him further. Major Martin then asked me what his name was, and I had to confess I did not know, that I had quite forgotten to ask. So the major asked him directly, formally, speaking unnecessarily loudly, I felt, as some people do with foreigners.

"Seemann Wilhelm Kreuz," the sailor replied.

"Your ship?"

"U-boat nineteen."

"It was sunk?"

"Yes."

The major seemed satisfied. "I shall leave him in your custody then for a short while longer, Doctor, as you suggest. He is of course a prisoner of war, so I shall have a guard posted outside the door until the prisoner is fit to leave." He asked me then if there was anything else he could do. I did say that the crowd outside was disturbing us, and unsettling Uncle Billy.

It was true that all through breakfast, as the crowd grew in number outside, and ever louder, Uncle Billy was becoming more and more agitated.
It was hard enough, I could see, for him to be in a strange house, and
Mrs. Cartright's somewhat brusque behavior was clearly unnerving him.
His eyes were darting continually this way and that. He kept telling me
he wanted to see his sister, and I was at pains to reassure him that she
would be with us soon. He was more at ease after Major Martin's inter-
vention, when the crowd quietened down, and was visibly more relaxed
when Mrs. Cartright had finally cleared away the breakfast and left us
alone.

This was the moment I felt I could ask Wilhelm Kreuz the question
that had been on my mind all through breakfast. Instead, he spoke first,
rather stiffly and slowly, choosing his words with care.

"I wish to thank you so much for your hospitality, Herr Doctor," he
began. "My Kapitän was right. The people here are kind." He paused before he went on. "I have to say something, and to ask you something also.
I was here once before, Herr Doctor, a few months ago. And I brought
someone with me, ein junge Mädchen, a little girl. This is all I know of
her, because this is all she told us. It is difficult to believe, but we found
the girl on a piano in the middle of the sea. It was after the sinking of the
Lusitania. You will know of this, I think. She had with her a small bear, a
toy, you understand. We had to save her. She was a child. At home I am a
teacher in school. Ich bin auch ein Vater. I am a father too. I could not
leave a child there. All the men on the boat agreed. Unser Kapitän, he
agreed also. But we could not take her home with us. It is verboten in the

Kriegsmarine, you understand, to do this, to rescue survivors from the sea. So, when he looked at the map, he decided the closest place, the safest place, to put the little girl ashore was on the islands of Scilly. Here. He told us then of his uncle, and how the people of the Scilly islands came out in a boat and saved him from the wreck of the Schiller many years before. They would also be kind to this little girl, he said. So in the nighttime, we came here and put her on the shore. She is eleven or twelve years old. And she plays chess very well. Is she here? Do you know her? Is she well? Kannst du mich verstehen?"

I scarcely knew what to say, so fast were my thoughts racing, my heart beating.

Uncle Billy spoke up then. I had not thought until that moment that he had been listening at all. "I know Lucy," he said. "She is my friend. She is Alfie's friend. I like her."

"Ah, so her name is Lucy," said Wilhelm.

"Did you give her a blanket?" I asked him. It was all too incredible. I needed to be quite sure.

"Yes, to keep her warm," he replied. "My mother, she made it for me."

There was something else I had to know. "Was it your submarine that sank the Lusitania?" I asked him.

"No," he told me. He could not look at me for the tears in his eyes. "It was not us. But it could have been. We sank many ships, Herr Doctor, English, French. It is a terrible thing for a sailor to sink a ship, to watch it go beneath the waves, to see men die. You can hear them shout, hear them scream. For a sailor to kill a sailor is like killing a brother. There were

315

many brothers on the Lusitania, and mothers and fathers, and little children like Lucy. We could save only this one. So we did."

There was a knock on the front door. "It is like living in a marketplace," Mrs. Cartright grumbled as she stomped down the passageway to answer it. "Doctor," she called out. "You have visitors from Bryher. Shall I let them in?"

"If you please, Mrs. Cartright," I replied.

I shall not even try to describe here the untrammeled joy of the reunion I witnessed in my dining room this morning. The look on Uncle Billy's face when he saw his sister was something to behold.

"Yo ho ho!" he cried.

And "Yo ho ho!" they replied.

I found myself moved to tears as the Wheatcroft family greeted one another, all of them unable, it seemed to me, to make up their minds whether to laugh or cry. In those moments, for Mary and Jim and Alfie, all that mattered was Uncle Billy, so they hardly noticed me or Wilhelm Kreuz at my side. Lucy did, though. Lucy stood there staring at Wilhelm Kreuz, unable to take her eyes off him. After a while I cleared my throat, to remind them that we were there, and I introduced him.

"This," I began, "is Wilhelm Kreuz. He is a sailor in the German navy. Uncle Billy saved him from drowning, rescued him." They looked bemused. Mrs. Cartright was in tears.

I invited them all to sit down, before I went on. "I think I should perhaps explain something about this man, something rather remarkable. Some months ago, Wilhelm Kreuz and his shipmates saved the life of the girl we know as Lucy Lost. Lucy Lost, it seems, was a passenger on the Lusitania. Some time after she was sunk, Wilhelm tells me, they came across Lucy Lost lying on the ship's piano in the middle of the ocean. They picked her up, rescued her, and brought her to a friendly shore, to Scilly, to St. Helen's. Isn't that right, Lucy? They saved your life. This man saved your life. And now Uncle Billy has saved his life, picking him up out of the sea, and bringing him to Scilly. As my dear mother used to say: what comes around, goes around."

I never in all my life enjoyed telling a story more. After I had finished, no one in the room spoke. But all of us were looking to Lucy for some sign of recognition. There was none, not at first, not for some time. The clock was ticking away on the mantelpiece, and as it struck the hour I witnessed a sudden transformation come over her face. Where there had been bewilderment in her eyes, there was in a single moment the sudden light of understanding, and a smile of recognition on her face. She got up and walked across the room, taking the blanket from around her shoulders, and then offering it to the German soldier. Standing before him, she looked up into his face, her eyes never leaving his. "Thank you, Wilhelm," she said, "for your blanket, and for saving me too. I couldn't thank you before. I wanted to, but I couldn't talk. And now I can." She spoke without hesitation, without struggle, the words simply flowing from her.

Then she turned and spoke to us all. "I am not Lucy Lost," she said. "I am Merry MacIntyre."

She told us of the sinking of the Lusitania, how her mother and Brendan and so many others had been drowned, little Celia too, and how

Wilhelm and his whale-boat had come up out of the sea to save her. Perhaps because it was all so freshly remembered, that she told it just as if she was seeing and living it all over again, told it all so vividly, that I felt I was living it with her. I think we all did.

They have all gone now, Wilhelm Kreuz under escort to the garrison, and from there no doubt to a prisoner-of-war camp on the mainland. Anyone who knows what he did for Lucy—or, as I should now say, for Merry—will, I trust, remember him as a good German, a kind German, one, I am sure, of many. Even in the midst of this terrible conflict, we should all do so well to remember that, and remember him.

Mrs. Cartright, who was as enraptured as the rest of us by Merry's story, has left me one of her "nice fish pies" for supper, as she always does on a Friday. She knows perfectly well I do not care for it. But she says it is good for me, and I must eat it. So I have, washing it down with a glass of beer. I am now sitting by the fire as I write this, gazing into the flames, smoking my pipe, and thinking that with such people in the world as the Wheatcroft family, and Merry MacIntyre and Wilhelm Kreuz—and Mrs. Cartright despite her fish pie—all will be well in the world after this present conflict is over. Please, God, if you are up there, may it all be over quickly.

Chapter Twenty-seven

The end of it all, and new beginnings

So it was that sitting there around the table, in my dining room, we drank tea and listened as Lucy's story unfolded. She told us at last who she was, that her name was Merry MacIntyre, told us about her family and friends and school in New York, about her soldier father, now lying wounded in a hospital near London in England. She remembered the name of it, she said, Bearwood Hospital, because they had a cottage of the same name back home in America, in Maine.

My grandma, Merry MacIntyre, takes up the story again where Dr. Crow's journal left it. What follows is in her voice, as she told it, word for word. I recorded her some thirty years ago in New York. Grandpa was there, but he always said it was more Grandma's story than his, really, and that anyway she was better at telling it. Her memory of childhood was razor sharp, but she could not remember where she'd put her glasses down ten minutes before, nor where she kept the sugar in the kitchen cupboard. She was ninety-four. They died shortly after, within weeks of each other. It was the last time I saw either of them.

— • ◆ • —

Recording of Merry MacIntyre, 21st September 1997

I have often wondered since why it should have been at that moment in Dr. Crow's house on St. Mary's that I discovered myself again, my lost voice, and my lost memory. When I think back— and at my age I think back a great deal—I realize it was by no means instantaneous. For many weeks and months before, I was a nobody in a strange and incomprehensible world. I had had fleeting flashing glimpses of some previous life—a muddled, confused vision of my past. I could speak, but only in my dreams. In my dreams I knew who I was, who everyone was, all the people and places in my life: Mama and Papa, Uncle Mac and Aunty Ducka, Pippa, Miss Winters and everyone at school, the statue in Central Park, Bearwood Cottage, Brendan, the Lusitania, the submarine, Wilhelm—they were all as clear as bells, inside my dreams.

How this happens I do not know, but even as I was dreaming, I was conscious I was dreaming, that what I was dreaming was real and true, and I would always promise myself that when I woke up, I would remember everything, remember who I was, remember how to speak. But later, when I woke, I never did and I

320

never could. It was as if I was lost in a fog, and the fog was inside my head and would never lift. Does that make sense? It doesn't to me.

I do know now that without Alfie, in particular, and Mary and Jim, without Uncle Billy and Dr. Crow I should still be lost in that fog. I should never have discovered that I had a life before I came to Scilly, that I was Merry MacIntyre, and not Lucy Lost. And I know also that without Wilhelm Kreuz, I should never have survived at all.

As I was telling them my story that day in Dr. Crow's house, I could almost feel my missing memories unlocking as I was speaking. A whole world was opening up for me, my world, the world I belonged to, the world that made some sense to me at last. And when at last I heard my own voice, I felt like singing. The fog had lifted. I was floating on air through it, out into the light.

After I had finished telling them everything, there was only one question. It was Mary who asked it, or Mother Mary, as I later came to call her. "But I don't understand," she said, "when I first saw you, lying there half dead on the beach, the day Alfie and Jimbo brought you back from St. Helen's, you spoke. You spoke just one word. 'Lucy.' You said your name was Lucy."

"Lusy was the ship," I told her, "the nickname of the ship, the Lusitania. You remember my friend Brendan? He always called the ship the Lusy. Everyone who worked on the ship—stewards, sailors, stokers—they all called her the Lusy. 'The Lucky Lusy,' they called her, Brendan told me. 'The Lovely Lusy.' Perhaps I was just trying to tell you the name of the ship."

Mrs. Cartright, who was very tearful, I remember, told me I was a very brave little girl, and gave me a huge slice of her lemon drizzle cake with my tea, for being so brave—much bigger than Alfie's, which pleased me a lot, but not him. Everyone got a slice of it, Wilhelm too, because he was, as Mrs. Cartright said—and in front of him too—"a nice Fritzy, not like all they other horrible Huns."

When the soldiers came to take Wilhelm away shortly afterward, he stood up straight and bowed his head to me, and called me 'gnädiges Fräulein,' and said he hoped we would meet again one day, that he would never forget me. I did not know what to say. I think I was too overcome to speak. Then he was gone. I never saw him again. I don't know if he ever forgot me, but I have most certainly never forgotten him.

We all sailed home to Bryher that afternoon on the Hispaniola. Dr. Crow saw us off on the quayside. He would, he said, be contacting the Bearwood Hospital near London—he was sure he could find someone who knew where it was—to get news to Papa that I was alive and well. This he did, but it took some time, and sadly the news did not reach the hospital until it was too late.

He had recovered well, faster than expected, and already been sent back to the trenches. It could not have been easy to track him down, but Dr. Crow persisted, and at last found out where he was, with his regiment near Ypres in Belgium. Dr. Crow told me nothing of any of his searches at the time, only that everything was being done to find Papa. I tried not to think of Papa too much, but in the months that followed I could think of little else. I feared for him, pined for him, longed for the sound of his voice, to see him coming toward me, arms outstretched, to have him catch me up and whirl me round. I knew how sad he must be to have been told he had lost both Mama and me on the Lusitania. I sang to the moon whenever I could, hummed to it, listened to it, told him I was alive.

I thank God I did not know much then of the dangers he was in, nor of the horrors of that dreadful war. They kept such things from me. Mother Mary prayed with me every night for him. I believed her completely when she said that God would look after Papa and bring him back to me. I was surrounded by my new family, cocooned in their love and care. They reassured me, calmed my fears, helped me through those darkest hours, when I remembered Mama and the peacock dressing gown in the sea. When I cried, as I often did, I never had to cry alone. There were always comforting arms around me, comforting words, comforting smiles.

Beyond the farmhouse as well, beyond my Scillonian family, I could feel the warmth of the whole community, and at school too—Mr. Beagley excepted. He alone remained as he always had been. Beastly. But everyone else, now that they knew my story, was doing their very best to make me feel one of them again. In every look there was regret for past suspicion and wrongs and hurt. With every kind deed a friendship was made or renewed. All the harsh words were soon forgotten. With Alfie at my side I became absorbed as never before in the life of the family, the island, and the school. Their sadnesses and disappointments and tragedies were mine too—and there were many of them during those long dark days of war. But their joys were my joys. I belonged there. I was an islander, a Scillonian.

There was a rhythm to my life on Bryher, the boat to school with Mr. Jenkins rowing us across, playing the piano at school—which Miss Nightingale insisted I did for every morning Assembly now—riding Peg around the island with Alfie after school, going out fishing sometimes on Penguin at weekends, drawing in the boathouse with Uncle Billy, making bread with Mother Mary, and sometimes there were trips out to the Eastern Isles in the Hispaniola to see the seals, all of us on board, the Jolly Roger flying, all of us singing out loud Uncle Billy's Yo Ho Ho song as we sailed along. And of course, there was always church on Sundays. Mother Mary leading us there, singing the hymns louder, more fervently than anyone else, and of course we were never again left alone in our pew. But happy as I was in my island life, every night I grieved for Mama, and worried over Papa away at the war. I sang to the moon. I listened to the moon. Some nights I heard Papa singing, I know I did. But sometimes I did not, and then I cried myself to sleep because I thought he must be dead.

I remember it was after school, and I was riding around the island with Alfie. He was for some reason badgering me to get home as fast as we could, but would not tell me why. I wanted to take my time. He knew I liked to stay out riding on Peg as long as possible. But Alfie was up front. He had the reins, and he was trotting and cantering home as fast as Peg could go. I couldn't stop him. So in the end I gave up grumbling and enjoyed it. As we came along Green Bay she almost broke into a gallop.

When we reached the farm, we did not stop as I had expected, but rode on past Veronica Farm down the track toward the quay. I asked Alfie where we were going, but he wouldn't reply. The boat from St. Mary's was in. Dr. Crow was there, Mary and Jim, and Uncle Billy, and dozens of islanders too, all in a huddle on the quayside. There was a man in uniform, I saw, in among them. I thought at first it must be the officer from the garrison I had met at Dr. Crow's house, the one who had taken Wilhelm away that day. But then I saw that the soldier had a moustache and was taller, considerably taller, was walking toward us as a giraffe walks, with a long and loping stride, with sloping shoulders and a long neck. It was a walk I knew, a moustache I knew, shoulders I knew, a neck I knew. But only when he took his cap off was I quite sure that it was Papa. I ran to him. He caught me up in his arms and whirled me round. We clung to each other then on the quayside until the tears stopped. It was a long time, a long hug.

Chapter Twenty-eight

Those we remember

That night outside the house, Peg wandered up to introduce herself to Papa, and the three of us stood there listening to the fall of
the sea on the shore. Two of us at least were looking at the moon,
a full moon, a bright moon, our moon. We hummed our tune
together, but we no longer had to listen to the moon. We were
together again.

That, in a way, I suppose, was the end of it all, but of course it
wasn't. There never is an end, because there are always new beginnings. Papa could stay for only a couple of days. Soldiers don't
really have holidays, he explained, not in a war, just a few days'
leave, if you were lucky, to see family and friends. We spoke of
Mama, of course, and of the sinking of the Lusitania. But not
much, and I never told him about her peacock dressing gown.
That would have been too hard for him to bear, I thought. We
cried together a great deal when we were alone, because our
thoughts often turned to Mama.

But when we were with my Scillonian family, we talked more of what was to happen to me now. Papa was quite determined that I should not go back across the Atlantic to New York. "Not with those U-boats prowling the seas," he said. There was a distant aunt of his who lived in Bath, on the mainland of England, who had agreed to look after me until the war was over. She lived in a handsome stone house, he told me, with trees all around, and with a good school nearby, of which she happened to be the headmistress. But I was every bit as determined not to go there, as he had been not to let me sail back to New York. We had quite an argument—perhaps the first argument I ever had with Papa.

Mother Mary was the one who intervened on my behalf, and passionately too. She said it would not be right to send me to live with a complete stranger, that I was one of the family now and should stay with them for as long as I liked, at least until the war was over, and that whatever happened I would always have a home with them. She turned to Jim and Alfie then for support. I remember well what Jim said: "Course she should stay. We quite like her, don't we, Alfie?"

Alfie didn't say anything, but just smiled.

So it was arranged. Father went back to the war, and I stayed on Bryher for the next three years, and did most of my growing up there. All this time I was falling in love with Alfie, I think, but without knowing it, until, that is, I saw him in his uniform and he was sailing off to the war in the winter of 1917. We wrote letters to one another every day for a year, until the war was over, until he came home. I've kept all his letters, every one of them. I did a lot of writing, writing often to Papa as well, and to Aunty Ducka and Uncle Mac and Pippa, but my spelling never improved. Still hasn't, to this day. I love to draw, though, and I play the piano every morning. The "Andante Grazioso" is still the piece of music I love to play most of all.

Quite soon after the war was over, Alfie came home. So he was there already by the time Papa arrived to take me back to New York. I told him I was staying, because I wanted to be with Alfie, to marry him and spend my life with him. Papa was sad, I could see that, but he did not object. He gave me away at our wedding in Bryher church, with everyone on the island there, Peg too, waiting outside in the graveyard, and grazing away. Someone had plaited flowers in her mane and tail. She didn't seem to mind. Alfie and I rode her home to Veronica Farm afterward. That night a gale blew in, and Papa had to stay on with us longer than he intended, so that he got to know my Scillonian family, my other family, and was soon at his ease with them. When he finally left, he made me promise I would come to New York, to see him, and Uncle Mac and Aunty Ducka. It was a parting that all children in the end have to make, and was hard to bear. But I had Alfie with me.

Five years later, Alfie and I went over to New York. I will not pretend I was not nervous on the Mauretania, the liner that took us across the Atlantic. Alfie and I dropped flowers in the sea for

Mama, and for Brendan and little Celia, as we passed by the coast of Ireland off Old Kinsale Head. I am glad we went when we did, because Uncle Mac and Aunty Ducka were old now and frail. And Papa, I discovered, had never really recovered from the war, either in mind or body. So many of them never did. It was plain that all of them wanted me to stay, needed us to stay. So, after much soul-searching, we did.

Alfie found work on the same great ships that had brought us over, and in time became ship's captain. Three times, over the years, I joined him on board his ship with our children, and we sailed for England and made the journey over to the Scilly Isles to see grandparents there, and family and friends, to bring our children to meet them. We wanted them to tread the fine white sand on Rushy Bay, and walk the wild cliffs around Hell Bay. Here we would sit on the soft thrift and tell them about Mother Mary, and Jim, and Uncle Billy, and Peg, and Dr. Crow as well, all of them gone by the time of our last visit, but all still remembered. Thank God for memory, I say—which I know all too well these days we should never take for granted. And thank God too for our children and for our grandchildren. For without them, who would ever tell the story?

And if our story lives on, mine and Alfie's, so do we.

So do those we remember.

To End

My own life has in many ways mirrored Grandma's and Grandpa's. I was brought up in the family house in New York, spent my summers in Bearwood Cottage in Maine, learned how to sail there, rode in Central Park, fed the ducks on the lake, listened to my father reading me *The Ugly Duckling,* and bit by bit picked up the family story as it was told to me. Which is why when I was older I decided to come over to England and go to the Scilly Isles to find out all I could about the place my grandfather came from, and that both of them had talked about so much. And once here, I found I could not leave, that this place is where I belong. Veronica Farm is my home now, has been for many long years. I have my family here all around me, grandchildren of my own living on the island. I am a fisherman, a farmer—I grow daffodils, thousands of them every year—and I'm a bit of a writer too.

As I write this, I am alone at the kitchen table in Veronica Farmhouse. But I'm not quite alone. I am being watched from the kitchen dresser, by a certain raggedy-looking one-eyed teddy bear. All the while, as I've been writing this, I've been reading bits of it out loud to him to see if he's happy with it. I've just read this last chapter to him. He's still smiling. So that's good. It's important he likes it.

READ ON FOR
SOME BACKGROUND TO
LISTEN *to the* MOON

The S.S. *Lusitania*

The sinking in May 1915 of the *Lusitania,* known familiarly as "the *Lusy,*" shocked the world. She was at one time the biggest, most luxurious ship in the world and had held the Blue Ribbon for the fastest crossing on the Atlantic. She could cruise at twenty-five knots. A passenger ship, she was making the crossing from New York to Liverpool when she was sunk.

The *Lusitania* was torpedoed on May 7 by a German submarine—a U-20—twelve miles off the Old Head of Kinsale on the south coast of Ireland. She went down in only eighteen minutes (the *Titanic,* in comparison, took over three hours to sink), so the loss of life was large. 1,198 passengers drowned, 128 of them men, women, and children from the U.S. At the time, it was the greatest single loss of civilian life in warfare, and the first such loss of any kind suffered by the United States of America.

In theory, submarine attacks were limited by international agreement to military and merchant vessels. As a passenger ship carrying civilians, the *Lusitania* should therefore have been

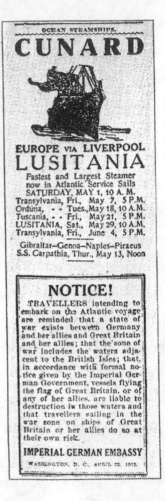

exempt from such aggression. As a result, and although at the time America was still a neutral power, the incident caused huge diplomatic friction between the U.S. and Germany, and many believe it played a role in America's eventual entry to the war.

Seeing the ship explode and sink, the people of Kinsale put to sea in boats to rescue survivors and bring back the dead. It was some hours after the ship sank that they came across a grand piano from the dining room floating on the ocean. There are reports that a girl was lying on it, although it is not at all clear whether she was alive or dead.

A great and continuing controversy surrounds the sinking of the *Lusitania*. The German Embassy placed notices in American newspapers weeks prior to the sailing, stating that vessels flying the British flag in waters surrounding Britain were liable to be targeted. Ironically, these ran prominently alongside advertisements to sail on the *Lusitania*. Passengers were greatly worried by this, but nonetheless, the ship was almost full when she sailed.

After the ship was torpedoed and in the face of international outrage, Germany maintained that the *Lusitania* had been carrying munitions destined for the European front and was therefore a ship of war. A German company even brought out a medal to celebrate the sinking of this, the biggest British ship—and in response, the British too brought out a medal to commemorate the dead and to condemn the sinking as an atrocity and an example of German barbarism. Sentiment against Germany and Germans rose among the Allies, and stiffened their determination to win the war. Perhaps more importantly, Americans were enraged, and anti-German attitudes rose significantly, all of which made it more likely that sooner or later, they'd enter the war on the Allied side.

The U.S. did join the Allies in the struggle against Germany and her comrades in 1917. The controversy regarding the *Lusitania*'s cargo continues to this day. Britain and the ship's owners have always maintained that the ship was carrying only non-explosive ammunition, a kind allowed by the rules of war. However, some have argued that the ship was secretly carrying larger munitions and explosives, and that this may have contributed to the second explosion that caused her to sink so quickly.

Divers visiting the wreck have failed so far to find conclusive evidence. But as recently as May 2014, the British government released secret files from the 1980s warning that "something startling" might be found on the wreck and that divers breaching its structure faced "danger to life and limb."

Due to these perils, and the great sensitivity surrounding the question on all sides, the full truth of what the *Lusitania* was or wasn't carrying may never be known.

The U-boat Campaign in World War I

The Royal Navy had a surface fleet far superior to that of the Imperial German Navy, and blockaded Germany successfully for much of the war. In response, the Germans launched a U-boat campaign to prevent supplies from coming into British ports. They wanted to starve the Allies into defeat, a campaign that was hugely effective and very nearly succeeded. Allied losses were appalling. Five thousand Allied ships were sunk and thirteen million tons of shipping destroyed. Though losses were heavy on the German side, also—178 U-boats were lost and 5,000 men killed. But there were in this dreadful war of attrition remarkable acts of kindness. One U-boat captain surfaced to warn British sailors on board their merchantman (a non-naval vessel) that he was about to torpedo their ship and that they should take to their lifeboats, which indeed they did, and lives were saved. There was also an instance of a U-boat commander coming to the rescue of Allied men in their lifeboats and towing them closer to shore.

The Scilly Isles lie some twenty-five miles out in the Atlantic, off Land's End in Cornwall. An archipelago of five inhabited islands—Bryher, St. Agnes, Tresco, St. Mary's (the largest island), and St. Martin's—it also comprises several uninhabited islands and some more recently deserted, among them St. Helen's.

The isles are the first landfall for ships coming across to Britain from southern Ireland and the United States. There are about 2,000 inhabitants who have traditionally been great seamen and fishermen who farm early potatoes and narcissi to eke out a livelihood on these windswept islands. Nowadays, tourism plays a greater part in their economy and their lives. There is, it is said, a greater concentration of wrecks in the waters around Scilly than anywhere else in England, so treacherous are the rocks and currents, so exposed are these islands to violent storms.

St. Helen's lies between St. Martin's and Tresco, and was lived on by monks who dug a well and built a chapel centuries ago. Since then, it has been used as a quarantine island, and a

Pest House was built there to house the sick and dying who could not be brought ashore for fear of infection. The ruins of the Pest House are still there to this day. The island is visited only rarely by passing yachts and researching writers!

The S.S. *Schiller*

Among the hundreds of wrecks lying on the ocean floor around Scilly, one of the most famous is that of the German ocean liner S.S. *Schiller*. She went down on May 7, 1875— exactly forty years to the day before the *Lusitania*. There was heavy loss of life. Three hundred thirty-five died, almost all Germans, despite the best efforts of the Scillonians to rescue them.

They did, however, manage to save over thirty passengers. When the story of this rescue, and of the respect and dignity shown to their dead by the people of Scilly, reached Germany, there was widespread admiration and gratitude among the German public. So much so that even forty years later, during World War I, the order went out to the Imperial German Navy that no Allied ships sailing close to the coast of the Scilly Isles were to be attacked. None were.

Thank you for reading this Feiwel and Friends book.
The Friends who made

LISTEN *to the* MOON

possible are:

Jean Feiwel, PUBLISHER

Liz Szabla, EDITOR IN CHIEF

Rich Deas, SENIOR CREATIVE DIRECTOR

Holly West, ASSOCIATE EDITOR

Dave Barrett, EXECUTIVE MANAGING EDITOR

Nicole Liebowitz Moulaison, SENIOR PRODUCTION MANAGER

Anna Roberto, ASSOCIATE EDITOR

Christine Barcellona, ASSOCIATE EDITOR

Emily Settle, ADMINISTRATIVE ASSISTANT

Anna Poon, EDITORIAL ASSISTANT

———◆◆◆———

Follow us on Facebook or visit us online at mackids.com.
OUR BOOKS ARE FRIENDS FOR LIFE.